VICTIM AND SUSPECTS

From Heather's remarks last night, it didn't shock Sarah that Heather not only ignored Sam's request, but was fidgeting with her cell phone. Sarah rechecked the mental note she'd made to find out what it was that Heather had against Alan. Barbie and Rose also were obviously not complying. Sarah added them to her mental checklist.

Running the list through her mind, Sarah tried to think if anyone besides Heather had expressed negative feelings for Alan or if she had seen any of them interact with him in a way that might provide a motivation for murder.

Rose had experienced that séance-like episode where she kept repeating "evil" and almost fainted, but Sarah wasn't sure if her reference was to Alan as a person or to the murder itself. Barbie hadn't said anything negative about Alan, but she definitely wasn't thrilled when he stopped her from following Starr into the big dining room on the day intros were taped. It might have thwarted Barbie at that moment, but not being able to fix her daughter's makeup didn't seem like enough of a reason to murder someone.

In some ways, Jane had the best motive for having killed him because he reneged on part of what she viewed their deal to be. Still, Sarah couldn't believe it. Jane was a schemer, and a lot of other things, but from the few times Jane's façade had cracked in front of Sarah, she didn't think Jane had the coldhearted ability to murder anyone. The killer had to be someone else. But who?

Books by Debra H. Goldstein

ONE TASTE TOO MANY

TWO BITES TOO MANY

THREE TREATS TOO MANY

FOUR CUTS TOO MANY

FIVE BELLES TOO MANY

Published by Kensington Publishing Corp.

FIVE BELLES TOO MANY

Debra H. Goldstein

Kensington Publishing Corp.
www.kensingtonbooks.com

In memory of my mother and father, Erica and Aaron Green, who lovingly gave me and my sister, Michelle, the tools to succeed. Hopefully, we successfully pass them on to our children and grandchildren.

ACKNOWLEDGMENTS

Despite the best efforts of many to educate me, I fully take the blame for any mistakes found in this book. What is accurate, I attribute with thanks to Lucy Hansson Zahray, the Poison Lady; Micki Browning, who clarified the difference between a shotgun and a rifle, as well as the different sounds each makes; and Robin Facer, who patiently answered my questions about reality television shows, casts, crews, and other behind-the-scenes procedures.

As always, I appreciate the sharp eye of my beta-readers, Fran and Lee Godchaux, and the brutal honesty and skill of editors Barb Goffman and Lourdes Venard. A special thanks to Dawn Dowdle for agenting this series from its inception through what are now five Sarah Blair books.

Finally, my thanks to my readers. Not only have you supported this series by purchasing books, leaving good reviews, attending my events, and following my newsletters and other social media, you have given me encouragement and joy from your emails, Facebook and Instagram comments, postcards, and letters. Interacting with you is an honor and a delight.

CHAPTER 1

"You can't do this! We have a contract."

Jane Clark threw a wadded piece of paper at Alan Perrault and Sam Tolliver, the director and segment producer for the Southern Belle Perfect Wedding Competition. Sam bent and picked the paper up. He didn't return it to her.

Sarah Blair stood in the doorway of the Southwind restaurant's recently added outdoor dining porch, her back pressed against the frame, and smiled. She knew what she was seeing was not funny, but Jane was her nemesis. Time and again, Jane had caused so many problems for Sarah and her twin sister, Emily.

Her pleasure, however, was short-lived. As she scanned the room, Sarah knew she would soon be facing someone's wrath too—her mother's.

At almost sixty-three, Maybelle Johnson might not be

what people typically thought of as a Southern belle, but she'd been picked as one of the show's five finalists. Sarah had found her mother's selection amusing until her mother declared that she needed Sarah to be her designated chaperone.

Sarah had rolled her eyes at the idea of a woman with two grown children being required to have a chaperone to make sure she had no company at night during the week the show filmed. It had become more onerous when Sarah learned that, unless she wanted her mother disqualified, she'd have to accompany her to certain scheduled events. Tonight's first official full cast and crew dinner was one of the events. And Maybelle had expected Sarah to be on time.

No, her mother wasn't going to be happy.

Maybelle would be even more upset if she learned Sarah had lost track of the time because Sarah was busy playing with RahRah, her Siamese cat, and Fluffy, her rescue dog. Maybe, Sarah hoped, if she held her breath and blended into the doorway, she could avoid becoming part of whatever Jane's dramatic clash with Alan and Sam was.

It didn't work.

Spotting Sarah, Jane, her face matching her flaming red hair, whipped away from Alan and Sam and made a beeline toward her. Jane jabbed her finger into Sarah's chest. "I bet this is your doing. Whenever things start going right for me, you or that fancy chef sister of yours ruin everything."

Sarah couldn't imagine what Jane was talking about, but her tone and words got under Sarah's skin. She certainly didn't want any of the people in the room, who didn't know Emily or her, to think either of them had done anything evil to Jane in the past. "The only person who ever ruins things for you is you."

Before Jane's finger connected with Sarah again, Alan stepped between the two women. The director shielded Sarah with his lean but toned physique. His gaze met Jane's. "That's enough."

He paused, as if to give Jane and Sarah a few seconds to get a grasp on themselves. His intervention was partially successful in that the break in the tension was enough for Sarah to softly inhale and exhale and not continue to engage with Jane, but it didn't stop Jane from turning her rant back against him.

Alan cut her off in midsentence. "Jane, our contract only specified breakfast and the craft table. If you'd read the small print before signing it, you would have seen that other than the network renting out your bedrooms for the belles and their chaperones and requiring provision of a daily craft table and breakfast buffet, Sam and I have the authority to decide where and what we'll be doing for everything else."

"But I've dedicated every aspect of Jane's Place to the Southern Belle cast and crew this week."

"That's not our fault, Jane. You need to get used to Southwind not only regularly being on the shooting schedule, but it being the designated location for dinners. Most of the formal taping will be at Jane's Place, but with your two restaurants competing to be the perfect wedding venue, we intend to feature both establishments."

"But you can't do that. Not after I bent over backwards for the show. Besides . . ."

Jane wildly glanced around the room. Eventually, her gaze rested on Sarah's mother. Jane pointed to her. "It's a conflict of interest for Southwind to be a venue finalist.

Maybelle Johnson and George Rogers are finalists for the perfect wedding *and* she's the mother of two of the owners of Southwind. Having Southwind as a finalist too gives an appearance of . . ." Jane took a breath while she searched for the right word.

"Impropriety," Chef Bernardi, the pastry chef from Jane's Place, said as he joined the fracas. "Considering that you're featuring Maybelle, having Southwind as a finalist—not to mention having Southwind's pastry chef be the other finalist competing against me to make the best wedding cake—everything reeks of impropriety. I can't believe your audience isn't going to figure the show is rigged when you have so many coincidentally appearing conflicts." He crossed his arms and scowled at Alan.

"Roberto Bernardi," Alan said, drawing out each syllable of the chef's name. "We're in complete compliance with the network's rules for segments like this. We even have a compliance person on set every day. Jane's Place and you will either win or lose on merit. The audience will vote on the invitations, dress, and things like that, but guest judges will be evaluating the competitions involving tasting of food and cakes. Their judging will be based on your abilities and final products."

Chef Bernardi continued to glare at Alan, but he didn't offer a response.

Alan continued speaking. "There is one thing I can tell you, though. After having dinner here last night, including sampling two of Wanda's delectable Southwind desserts, if I were a gambling man, I'd bet your former protégé's cake is going to give you a good run for your money. Roberto, you're no stranger to culinary competitions. Figure out the odds. If you think the oven is too hot, you can concede now."

Jane clenched her fists as she stood as straight as the line of her tightened jaw. "Chef Bernardi and I can hold our own against Southwind or anyone, but you can't deny you've stacked the deck, from contestants to food choices, in Southwind's favor."

Alan's facial expression didn't change, but he uttered his words in a more clipped manner than before. "Jane and Roberto, there's nothing further to discuss. In a small town like Wheaton, there are only so many possible contestants and so many things we can use to make it interesting. It isn't likely that the older couple is going to win, so any appearance of a conflict of interest is no big deal. Besides, incorporating the rivalry you have with her daughters is good TV. Good TV means higher ratings. Higher ratings and increased viewers will bring a greater awareness in and out of Wheaton for both of your restaurants. Believe me, when our show airs, Jane's Place and Southwind will benefit in the long run."

Chef Bernardi didn't press the issue, but Alan's point seemed lost on Jane. She dropped any pretense of control. Stomping her foot, she stuck her face close enough to Alan's for them to breathe the same air. "You and Sam are weasels. You won't get away with double-crossing me. You'll hear from my lawyer."

Alan smiled. "I'll look forward to that."

Sarah glanced over to where Sam stood, holding the wadded paper but staying out of the fray. To her surprise, like Alan, Sam was grinning. She turned her gaze back toward Jane, and as she did, Sarah saw there was a cameraman positioned just outside of Jane's peripheral vision, filming everything. From his angle, Sarah realized he probably had caught her smiling at Jane's tirade too.

As the cameraman took a step closer to the doorway,

Jane either heard or noticed him. She reactively shielded her face and yelled, "Turn that blasted camera off!"

He didn't obey her.

Instead, he kept his shot focused on Jane until she left the room and then panned his camera toward Sarah. Uncertain whether he'd caught her on film when she was smiling, Sarah forced herself, as she turned her head away from the camera, to keep her expression as blank as possible. Even though this wasn't technically being called a reality TV show, she'd seen enough of them to know that film often was edited to make perfectly nice people appear to be villains. The last thing she wanted was to be lumped with Jane as one of the bad guys because she looked pleased at someone else's misfortune.

Peeking back, she was glad to see the cameraman had lost interest in her. Instead, he was filming the cast and crew, who were seated at the tables. Even if he didn't focus on the empty seat at her mother's table, Sarah realized her tardiness was permanently recorded. Crud.

Sarah had forgotten that she, like everyone in the cast and crew, signed an agreement that any location where an activity tied to the show took place was subject to being filmed. Her tardiness was something the show's editors could use to make her stand out from the others.

Eager to not be the focus of any more singular attention, Sarah started toward the seat her mother had saved, but her path was blocked by Chef Bernardi effectively using his body to corner Alan and her. He glanced from Sarah to Alan. "I'm sorry for the extent of Jane's outburst, but she's right, you know. The way Sam and you are rigging things behind the scenes is downright rotten."

Instead of waiting for a reply from Alan, Chef Bernardi brushed past Sarah. The cameraman filmed his exit.

Lest she be captured on film again, Sarah hurried toward her seat, already turning the events of the last few minutes over in her mind. Sarah couldn't disagree about the obvious conflicts of interest Jane and Chef Bernardi raised, but she understood Alan's point that the five square miles of Wheaton, Alabama, only had so many locals to choose from for anything. But, then again, the more metropolitan and newly christened foodie city of Birmingham was a mere fifteen minutes away.

Perhaps what surprised her most about Chef Bernardi standing up for Jane was that the culinary world's gossip line was reporting that, after working together for only a few weeks, there already was tension between Chef Bernardi and Jane, both with alpha personalities. According to Emily, everyone thought their working arrangement would end once the Southern Belle segments were filmed.

As she slipped into the chair next to her mother, she heard Alan loudly observe, "That, my friends, is reality TV."

CHAPTER 2

With a quick squeeze of her mother's hand, Sarah leaned back in her chair. Sarah knew if she glanced in her mother's direction, Maybelle would give her an evil eye for being late. She kept her gaze focused on the director.

Sarah was struck by Alan's attire. His fancy suit looked like what she'd expect to see on a Wall Street banker, rather than someone hanging out in Wheaton. What amazed her more was that—despite the Alabama humidity oozing into every one of her pores, even with all the fans on the screened-in porch running at full blast—there wasn't a wrinkle to be seen on Alan's pants or jacket. She assumed his wasn't an off-the-rack suit, but she wished she knew his secret for looking so impeccable. Everyone around him was a bit rumpled and several of the dinner guests were glistening in the Indian summer heat.

"Listen up, everyone." Alan held up his hand for silence. He waited for everyone to look at him, and they did, except for a diminutive gray-haired woman—a chaperone—who was seated at the next table. Her back was to him. She still didn't respond when he said, "Granny, I need your attention too."

It was only when the young blonde sitting next to Granny—her contestant granddaughter—touched her arm and pointed toward Alan that Granny turned her body in his direction. Granny was the perfect nickname for her. Deep lines were etched in her face and the woman wore her gray hair pulled back tightly.

"Sorry," Granny said. "I don't hear as well as I used to." Stone-faced, she stared at Alan, but he ignored her explanation.

"Each day, we expect all finalists and vendors with a sequence being taped to be ready to go at eight a.m. We will have a breakfast buffet open to everyone at Jane's Place beginning at six thirty. I'll have a little more to tell you later, but Sam has a few things to say before the Southwind staff serves you dinner."

Sam stepped forward. "Thank you, Alan. As most of you know, I'm Sam Tolliver, the segment producer. Although the Wheaton Southern Belle segments will air every afternoon this coming week, we're going to tape most of the competitions over the next two days in order for our production crew to have enough time to edit them. Today, we taped the contestant introductions, a few of the vendor head-to-head competitions, and the car wash charity sequence. As you learned today, it takes a lot more time for us to shoot the footage for any segment than will ever be shown."

"You're not kidding," one man said.

Sam smiled. "We'll be airing three segments tomorrow: your introductions, the two invitations the public will vote on, and the car wash event. After the show ends, the public will have a five-hour opportunity to vote for which wedding invitation design should win. Normally, our guest judge will announce the couple leaving us before the segment goes off the air, but because we'll have just introduced you and we want to build up a bit of tension with promos on Monday night, the first announcement will be made at the beginning of Tuesday's show. When we're filming, unless we are announcing your elimination, I want you to smile and look like you're having fun. After all, we're giving you a perfect wedding— that is, if you're the couple lucky enough to win."

This time, the laughter in the room was thinner.

"Whether you're the last couple sitting in a heart of love on screen will depend upon your success with the viewers, but as set out in the agreement you signed, there are a few rules you're going to have to honor or you'll be out of here without the public needing to vote you off."

He straightened out the paper Jane had thrown and held it up. "In case you didn't look at everything we gave you, which Jane apparently didn't, this is a call sheet. Every night, each one of you will get one. It has everything you'll need to know for the Southern Belle show being shot the next day, from times, shooting locations, activities, who is involved, and even the local weather."

Sarah whispered to her mother, "I left the papers they gave me with my suitcase in our room at Jane's Place. Do you have yours here?"

Wordlessly, Maybelle reached into her purse, pulled out her call sheet, and handed it to Sarah. Sarah quickly skimmed it. "It says cast and crew members will be at Jane's Place, the car wash, and the group dinner. I don't see anything that should have irritated Jane. Am I missing something?"

Maybelle raised her eyebrows in exasperation at her daughter. She pointed to the bottom of the call sheet. "Look at the line about the dinner location."

Sarah focused on the bottom of the page. In smaller print it read *Location 3: Southwind*. Scanning the page earlier, she'd caught that the crew was arriving at six thirty, dinner was at seven, and the wrap was scheduled for eight thirty, but her eye had missed that the dinner was taking place at Southwind.

"Emily and Marcus didn't find out until late last night that they were going to be doing the cast and crew dinners for the week," her mother said. Emily and her boyfriend, Marcus, were both chefs who co-owned Southwind with Sarah, who was most definitely not a chef. "Until then, Emily thought Southwind's involvement was going to be for only the venue finalist segment."

"What changed things?"

"My understanding is that Alan got into town yesterday morning and had lunch at Jane's Place, but a little birdie suggested he try Southwind for dinner. He did and by dessert he had Sam moving all dinners here for the duration of the Wheaton shoot."

"For everyone?"

"Crew, cast, vendors, you name it. Marcus and Emily scrambled all day today making sure they could take care of their regular customers, plus this group. Besides ordering extra food, they enlisted Grace's help in the kitchen and asked her to bring some of her students from the community college's hospitality program to help out with serving."

Sarah was delighted to hear that Grace Winston, her friend and Emily's former sous chef, would be helping in the kitchen for the week. "No wonder Jane was upset."

She focused again on what Sam was saying. Because his voice was softer and he mumbled more than Alan, Sarah struggled to catch his words. Realizing he wasn't talking about anything that applied to the chaperones or that she hadn't already heard, she let her mind wander to his physical appearance. With Sam's blue jeans, red-plaid flannel shirt, and scraggly salt-and-pepper-colored hair curling over his collar, he didn't project the same suave persona as Alan. She couldn't decide if he was deliberately going for a scruffy look or if he was simply growing his beard out. As he announced he was summing up his remarks, she snapped back to listen.

"If you can remember to be on time for our shoots and that there are no guns, fighting, or sex at Jane's Place, you should have no problems. Any questions?"

"Yeah, I have one."

Everyone turned their gaze toward the man who dared ask a question. Because he stood, Sarah could see he was a solidly built guy wearing a red-and-white shirt with an *A* embroidered on it. Must be an Alabama football fan.

Good chance he'd played football in high school or at Alabama, she figured, considering how large his hands were and that his neck was probably the same size as her thigh.

"Yes?" Sam said.

"I'm Trey Taylor. We understand the rules about fighting." He pointed to another guy in his twenties seated at the table next to his. In Sarah's opinion, this man, whose shirt was navy blue trimmed with burnt orange, was even physically larger than the one speaking, probably because of how petite the woman encircled by his arm was. "Lance and I vowed to avoid fighting because our teams aren't playing each other this week, but I assume there's no restriction on a little cussin' between friends?"

Sam deferred to a grinning Alan. "None at all. We even brought tapes of this past Saturday's Alabama and Auburn games so anyone can watch them again during some of our downtime. Remember, a lot of us have skin in those teams too."

As some of the chaperones and contestants reacted with shouts of "Roll Tide" and "War Eagle," Sarah glanced at her mother.

"Alan graduated from Alabama," Maybelle whispered. "Sam went to Auburn."

That was all her mother needed to say. There was nothing more important in Alabama than college football—especially the rivalry between the University of Alabama in Tuscaloosa and Auburn University.

"Okay," Sam said. "If there aren't any more questions, Alan and I want to show you the dailies."

"Daylilies?" Granny turned to her granddaughter. "Lucy, why would we want to see daylilies during dinner?"

Someone at the table behind Sarah's not only snickered at Granny's misunderstanding, but also made a rude remark.

Lucy ignored the person. She put her hand on Granny's arm and leaned forward until her mouth was near the older woman's ear. "No, Grandma. Dailies, not day-lilies."

"Oh." Granny chuckled at her mistake.

Lucy shrugged in Sam's direction. Rather than making a funny out of Granny's misunderstanding, he took the moment to explain how folks, in the old days, reviewed the unedited film shot that day. "Nowadays, filming and editing processes are different and there normally aren't dailies done for television, but Alan and I thought you should see some of what we shot today." He pointed to two monitors set up in the corners on the far side of the room.

Considering how often Sarah had been in this room during the past few weeks, especially because she'd been part of planning its addition to Southwind, she was surprised she hadn't noticed the recent placement of the monitors.

Sam walked back toward the wall near the doorway and dimmed the lights as he called to a man standing near a small table beyond where the guests were seated. There was a laptop on the table. "Flynn, cue up the introduction segment."

Sarah assumed the computer was the tool of the trade to share whatever film clips Alan and Sam wanted this audience to see. Sarah didn't know who Flynn was, but she was impressed with his well-chiseled features and excellent head of jet-black hair. Over the years, as people commented at the contrast between Sarah's thick, dark mane and her twin's much lighter and finer hair, she'd come to appreciate the value of having thick hair.

With a quick salute in Sam's direction, Flynn did as he was told. After a moment, he was the first person on both screens. "Welcome to Wheaton, Alabama. I'm Flynn Quinn, your host for the next week as five Southern belles compete for what each hope will be their journey from Wheaton to a perfect wedding. You're about to meet the five couples who are our finalists, but first, let me explain how you, the viewers, will not only help choose the winner, but will select most aspects of that winner's perfect wedding. That includes the invitations, venue, menu, flowers, and the dress. We've narrowed each vendor category to two finalists . . ."

Having heard this before, Sarah half-heartedly listened to Flynn. She periodically checked the monitor as she glanced at the others seated in the room. The people at the back tables had to be crew members, based upon their jeans, T-shirts, and the fact that the cameraman she'd previously encountered sat with them.

While Flynn droned on about the rules of the competition, Sam and Alan joined the table where Sarah, her mother, and George were, still leaving one seat empty. The other two nearby tables were filled with two finalist couples, their chaperones, and a few, Sarah presumed, vendors.

Sarah's attention was drawn back to the monitor as Flynn began doing a voice-over while the camera focused briefly on each couple, sitting behind a giant heart cutout that had their names on it. Although Sarah had heard their names mentioned when everyone was in the greenroom, she still was having trouble remembering who went with who. Sarah grabbed a pen from her purse and, as Flynn announced them, she jotted the contestants' names and whatever he said about them on a napkin.

"Lucy Aynsley and Jed Howard dream of a destination wedding in Mentone, Alabama, which is on top of Lookout Mountain. They believe its lush forest and nearby river provide the perfect location for a barn-styled hoedown. Lucy wants to wear a white dress, complemented by red cowboy boots."

On screen, Lucy clutched Jed's arm and snuggled closer to him. Sarah was sure the plastic smiles plastered on their faces were in response to the directive to make sure they looked like they were enjoying themselves. From seeing Lucy interacting earlier with Granny, she had a feeling Lucy's natural smile was like a sunbeam shining on the mountain area where she wanted her wedding to be.

"Veronica Wilson and Trey Taylor met in high school. He was the team's quarterback, and she was head cheerleader. Trey went on to play college ball and in the Canadian football league, but now they're back in Alabama to put down roots. Being die-hard Alabama fans, they want a red velvet wedding cake with white icing topped with an elephant bride and groom."

The camera next zoomed in for a close-up of Maybelle and George. Their facial expressions were neutral, but Sarah could tell George was nervous. His Adam's apple, showing above one of his beloved bow ties, was more prominent than usual. "Maybelle Johnson and George Rogers want a Christmas-themed celebration, even if it isn't December, with friends and family at a ceremony performed by Pastor Dobbs at Wheaton's Little Brown

Church. After a fine meal at Southwind, they hope to take a honeymoon trip to Disneyland."

George's bow tie and button-down shirt seemed like casual attire compared to the next couple's formal black dressed-for-success business suits. "Natalie Flores and Ralph Rhodes share not only their work at the accounting firm of Flores and Rhodes, but also their passion for anything to do with the Day of the Dead. Their dream is to combine attending Day of the Dead festivities in Mexico with celebrating the occasion of their wedding."

Slowly, the camera moved on to Starr and Lance. "Our final contestants, Starr Babbitt and Lance Larson, want a traditional wedding in every sense of the word, but it can't be during hunting season or on a Saturday when Auburn is playing football."

After a loud "cut" was heard, the monitor went black. One of the people closest to the light switches jumped up and turned on the overhead lights. Immediately, the noise level in the room rose as the waitstaff began serving pre-plated chicken dishes, one complete table at a time. At Sarah's table, everyone was served simultaneously except Alan.

He encouraged everyone to start eating, as he was sure his would arrive any minute. "I ordered a vegetarian meal," he threw out to those sitting near him. He drank from the insulated water bottle he'd brought with him to the table. "Eating healthy and my special herb tea is what's going to keep me going during this shoot."

Knowing her sister's insistence that everyone at a table be served at the same time, Sarah looked around the room to see if there was an errant server, perhaps one of the college students, who needed to be flagged over to their table. As Alan continued drinking his tea, Sarah spotted a waiter looking lost. She waved to him. He immediately came to their table and with a relieved expression placed a vegetable plate in front of Alan.

Veggies and herb tea weren't what she expected from Alan. Maybe Sam, but not Alan. Sarah scolded herself for judgmentally pegging Sam, because of his freer spirit look, as more likely to be a vegetarian than Alan. Somewhat irritated with herself, Sarah looked down at her plate. When she raised her eyes again, she saw Cliff Rogers—George Rogers's nephew and Sarah's on-again, off-again boyfriend—take the empty seat between his uncle and Alan.

For a moment, he gazed across the table at Sarah before turning toward Alan. She thought he looked as uncomfortable as she felt. Saying things were awkward between them would be a more-than-kind way of describing their present state of interaction. Since she'd opened the door for them to break off their relationship a couple of months ago, when she'd felt the urge to go on what proved to be a less-than-successful first date with RahRah's veterinarian, they'd never regained their easygoing friendship.

Since then, they'd exchanged pleasantries at meetings about the animal shelter—they both were on its board—and during the construction of Southwind's new room, which Cliff's company did. But there had always been other people around, like now, precluding any intimate discussions. Because they had an audience, she wasn't surprised he didn't greet her, but it did seem a bit strange that instead of saying something immediately to his uncle, he addressed his comments to Alan. "Sorry to be late. Have I missed anything?"

Cliff must be here because of Alan or the show, rather than to cheer his uncle and Maybelle on. She could have smacked her head. That's why the chair next to Alan had been left open. It also explained why Trey and Lance were at different tables. Seating for dinner tonight was another thing the show was controlling. Something told her it wasn't going to be Alan and Sam's only power move this week. Alan's reply to Cliff confirmed her fear.

Chapter 3

"You didn't miss anything of importance. We only showed everyone a rough version of the first segment we'll broadcast. It introduces everyone." He laughed. "Wait until Sam and I run another tape during dessert, that's when you're going to see some fireworks."

From the furrow of Cliff's brow, she didn't think the vibe he took from Alan's comment was any better than the one she got. She decided a change of subject might lighten the moment. "Cliff, I didn't expect to see you here tonight. I thought only the Belles had to have chaperones. You're not a surprise contestant, are you?"

He laughed. "No. And I'm not chaperoning either. I'm here as Alan and Sam's guest."

Alan slapped Cliff's back. "Cliff's more than a guest. He's our general contractor."

"You're using a Wheaton contractor?" She waved her

hand toward the tables in the back of the room. "I thought you brought your entire New York crew to town."

This time, Alan clapped a hand on Cliff's shoulder. "All but Cliff, here. We flew in our own technical and camera crews, but because most of the filming is being done at Jane's Place, Sam and I decided it was more cost-efficient to hire someone local to handle our few construction needs. Chef Bernardi told our advance crew that Cliff was the most qualified and honest contractor in town. That's true, isn't it, Cliff?"

A red flush crept up Cliff's neck. She knew that meant something wasn't sitting right with Cliff. She wasn't sure what she'd missed in Alan's comment, but there was no question Cliff was an excellent contractor.

Maybe it was simply a matter of Cliff finding it difficult to accept praise. But there was no questioning that his work as a contractor deserved to be lauded. Consequently, even knowing it might embarrass him, she wholeheartedly seconded Chef Bernardi's endorsement of Cliff.

"For a quick idea of the quality of Cliff's work, take a walk down Main Street. Not only has he done the remodeling here at Southwind, including adding on the room we're sitting in, but he and his crew were responsible for the updating of the carriage house out back, as well as Jane's Place and the veterinarian clinic across the street. Plus, after a big fire almost destroyed Wheaton's main shopping mall, he was the general contractor the owners hired to rebuild everything in it, including our Southwind Pub. Personally, though, I think some of his best work has been for the animal shelter."

"What did he build for the shelter?" Sam asked.

Sarah hadn't realized Sam was listening to the conversation, but she gladly answered him. "He built the staging to show off our adoptable animals during our first Yip Yeow Day fundraiser benefiting Wheaton's animal shelter. Now, Cliff is spearheading the changes needed to the shelter's building as a group of community volunteers work to make it a no-kill facility."

"Sounds interesting," Alan said.

Sarah leaned forward, warming to the topic that was close to her heart. "Our vision for Wheaton's shelter is a place that even when we're full doesn't kill healthy animals or those with treatable conditions. Euthanasia is reserved only for animals posing a danger to Wheaton's public safety or that are terminally ill. Even with that philosophy, a no-kill shelter can still put down ten percent of healthy animals, but our goal is to be as close to a zero-threshold tolerance level."

"How will you do that?"

"By building a bigger volunteer base, modifying the protocols involved with housing and medical service, doing outreach to promote more fostering and other ways that minimize how many homeless animals actually come into the shelter, and raising money to expand our services and educate the public."

Alan played aimlessly with his fork. "Maybe we could piggyback on what you're doing as an extra charitable activity for our show."

Sarah shook her head. "That won't work. You'll be done filming in Wheaton by the time we're ready to go public with our activities."

Alan ignored her as he punctuated his remarks with a thrust of his fork. "That's not a problem. The magic of TV can bring anything you want to do online earlier."

Sarah and Cliff exchanged a quick look before she carefully chose her words. "Having your support would be wonderful, but we still need to do a lot of preparatory education."

Alan again dismissed her objections with a wave of his hand. "Don't worry about any of that. We can handle everything. Plus, the network will make a nice contribution."

"But . . ."

"Besides, a picture on TV is worth a thousand words." Alan chuckled at his own mangling of the old saying. "Now, let's eat."

He stabbed his fork into an asparagus spear on his plate, making it clear that at least for him, the conversation was over.

Sarah looked at her plate. She usually adored Marcus's and her sister's food, but the knot in her stomach prevented her from eating. By the time dessert was served, Sarah was more relaxed. Although Alan might have a lot of ideas, she got the feeling they weren't going to happen unless Sam implemented them. From what she could see, Sam had enough to do. She doubted he was inclined to add anything—especially if she made it sound complicated.

Finishing his dessert, Alan carefully dabbed his mouth with his napkin. "Sarah, Cliff, let's talk more tomorrow about the talent show. But now, time for a little bit of work and some fun." He patted the breast pocket of his jacket. "An after-dinner Cuban cigar for me and a different type of treat for everyone else."

"Cuban cigar? Aren't they illegal? Besides, you're a vegetarian." Sarah closed her mouth tightly. Once again, she'd blurted out what she was thinking without censoring herself. She glanced over at her mother. For not the first time of late, it occurred to her that she was getting

more and more like her mother. Sarah inwardly shuddered. If she already was like this and she wasn't even
thirty, would she completely be her mother when she
reached her mother's age?

Alan laughed. "It's my one vice, other than an occa-
sional electronic cigarette, now that, with the help of my
magic patch, I've given up being a real smoker." He tugged
the collar of his shirt open enough for Sarah to see a nicotine patch. "You can't buy or sell Cuban cigars in the
United States, but you can bring them in from other coun-
tries and enjoy them. Sam, Flynn, and I occasionally
enjoy good cigars, so whenever one of us has the opportunity while traveling, we buy some and share them when
we get together."

Alan reached into the breast pocket of his jacket and
pulled out a plastic cigar case that had the network's logo
on it. "To make up for missing something in my mouth, I
chomp on a cigar during the day when we're on a set, but
I only light up after dinner." He opened the case.

There were four cigars and a pencil-thin electronic
cigarette in the case. Alan took two cigars out and handed
one to Cliff and one to Sarah. "A few weeks ago, when
Flynn and Sam got back from a job in Canada, the three
of us got together in New York to plan our Southern Belle
competition shoot. It was during that meeting that Sam
got the idea that cigars would not only be the perfect gift
for the male contestants, but could be worked into a bit
for the show."

Sarah examined the cigar he'd given her. Turning it
over in her hand, she noticed its wrapper also had the network's logo on it. She held it up. "Maybe I'm missing
something, but I don't think the network is Cuban. How

are you fitting these cigars into the Southern Belle competition?"

"Do you remember in *Gone with the Wind* and some of the other classic novels and movies set in the South, there was always a scene where the women went upstairs to rest or retreated to a drawing room while the men gathered in the smoking room or on an outside patio for a cigar, port, and man talk?"

Sarah recalled these scenes, although she had never seen any like them in real life. "Yes?"

"We thought having a beer and smoke time or two with just the men would give the audience a way to zero in on some of the grooms." Alan reached into his case and pulled out another cigar that had already been chewed on. Its label was different than the one she held.

"That's what a real one looks like. The ones with the network logo are knockoff gifts we had made for our male contestants. They'll do the trick for the few times we've scheduled men-only sessions before or after dinner during the week. Don't worry. We're also filming behind-the-scenes moments with the brides and the gifts we gave them."

Sarah went to hand the cigar Alan had given her back to him.

"Keep it as a souvenir from this week." Alan stood and rapped his fork against his water glass.

Looking down the table, Sarah saw Sam do the same thing. The high-pitch tinkling of their metal forks striking their glasses did the trick of attracting enough people's attention at each table that everyone quickly hushed. "Thank you. If you enjoyed dinner as much as I did, I think we should show a little love to our Southwind chefs."

As if on cue, Marcus, Emily, and Wanda waved from the doorway near the main dining room. Flynn, who was with them, did the introductions, using the same rich-sounding voice from the introduction segment.

"Chefs Marcus and Emily are the owners of the South-wind Pub and Southwind, where we're eating tonight. Both are CIA graduates—that's Culinary Institute of America rather than the spy intelligence group—though with the excellence of their food, they could sneak in anywhere. After training stints in New York, California, and Chicago, Marcus and Emily brought their finely honed skills to Wheaton, Alabama. Wanda, their pastry chef, recently joined the Southwind staff. Tonight, whether you ate her carrot cake or her baked apple, you had the perfect ending to a perfect meal."

Marcus stepped forward. "Chef Emily and I want to personally welcome you to Southwind. We're delighted to share our farm-to-table cuisine with you each night this week. We'd also like to remind you that if you're looking for a burger, a beer, or simply a more casual atmosphere for lunch or to kick back while you're here in Wheaton, try our Southwind Pub. Em?"

"If there is anything we can do to make your stay in Wheaton more enjoyable, just ask." As her statement was met with polite applause, she led the team out of the room.

Once the serving team left the porch, Alan addressed everyone again. "Hopefully, between today's activities and tonight's dinner, you've had an opportunity to get to know each other better. I can assure you that by the end of the week, we'll all be one happy family. For now, I'm going to take off, but Sam is going to show you some more footage we taped today. Take it as a reminder that the cameras are always on and that this is a competition."

The room quieted as Alan left. The lights dimmed and the monitors flicked on again. The setting this time was the smaller dining room of Jane's Place, which was being used as the production's greenroom. Sarah recognized that this tape must have been made this afternoon, just after Alan instructed the five finalist couples to move into the larger dining room to film their introductions.

Apparently, other than Sarah, every chaperone had stayed during the filming. In the film clip, Sarah could see three gathered around the monitor. Instead of joining them, Barbie, Starr's mother, trailed Starr and Lance as they left the greenroom. Alan stopped her before she could follow them into the large dining room.

"Only the finalists."

Barbie waved her multi-ring–covered hand in the direction Starr and Lance had gone. "I know. I'm simply going to pop in with them for a moment to fix Starr's makeup. You know how harsh the lights can be."

"Relax, Barbie. Your daughter's as pretty as a picture. Besides, we have a professional makeup person in there to do any necessary touch-ups. Why don't you get to know the other chaperones?"

Barbie grimaced but complied with Alan's directive. As she slowly moved closer to the monitor, the oldest chaperone spoke to her.

"Hi, I gather from what Alan just said, you're Starr's mom. Everyone calls me Granny."

From Sarah's perspective of the tape, Granny, as she prattled on, physically prevented Barbie from any easy means of escaping the conversation. "My late husband started calling me Granny right after we got married because he thought I resembled some actress from a TV show that was on in the 1960s. I never saw the show or, for that matter, the actress, but the nickname stuck. As you can see, I've now grown into it." She chortled at her own comment. "I'm chaperoning my granddaughter, Lucy. We live in Marshall County."

"Is your granddaughter really old enough to get married?" The icy tone of the off-screen voice posing the question caught Sarah's attention. She stared at the woman who entered the frame from behind Granny. The woman's olive skin was set off by the contrast between her black dress and a shawl of shades of gold draped around her shoulders.

Granny, who was almost a head shorter than the other woman, met her gaze in a way that Sarah thought equalized them. "Rose, I'll have you know my granddaughter is twenty-seven. Lucy may look young, but not only is she wise beyond her years, that makes her a year older than your niece."

"It didn't seem that way when Lucy started the water fight today during the car wash."

Confused, Sarah gave Maybelle a sideways glance.

"Lucy went to squirt Jed with her hose," Maybelle whispered, "but she missed. Instead, Lucy hit Trey. She yanked the hose up in the air and managed to drench Rose's niece, Natalie. Trey responded and it became a free-for-all. It was all part of the planned fun that the network wanted, but Natalie took the brunt of the soaking in the cross fire."

Sarah glanced around the Southwind dining room to see if both Granny and Rose were at dinner. They were. Seated at different tables, but both very much alive.

Granny's movement on the screen caught Sarah's eye. Granny raised her chin while planting her feet and sticking out her chest. It reminded Sarah of two children defying each other to cross a line in the playground. Sarah waited to see which one blinked first.

She was almost disappointed when neither one did. Rather than continuing their confrontation, Rose threw back her head and laughed. Seemingly unable to control herself, Rose glanced from Granny to the other chaperones.

"Why should I worry if any of these girls are ready to be married? None of them will probably go through with a ceremony—or for that matter, even want to." She gestured to the monitor. "I don't approve of this nonsense, but Natalie wouldn't listen to me. She said Ralph insisted it would be good exposure for the accounting practice they recently started. I highly doubt that, but if she was going to be here, so was I."

Rose pulled her shawl tightly around her. "Tell me, what's the real agenda of your Belle? Or are you the one with an agenda?"

By challenging the other chaperones, Rose effectively sidestepped escalating the tension between Granny and her. Sarah had to agree with Rose that it was doubtful wedding bells were the only motivation for the presence of each of the couples. She wondered which ones wanted a "perfect" wedding and which were simply there for the exposure.

Granny was the first to respond to Rose's challenge. "Lucy doesn't have an 'agenda,' as you refer to it. I resent you saying she does. She'd be happy marrying Jed in our backyard and toasting their nuptials with apple cider."

"Or moonshine," Barbie muttered.

Granny didn't respond to the remark, and Sarah tried to see if she was wearing hearing aids. She didn't see any. "Nope, Lucy's a good girl. I'm the one who encouraged Jed and her to apply. When they win, they'll get the kind of wedding they deserve and that I can't afford to give them."

The only woman who hadn't spoken yet gently touched Granny's arm. "That's not an agenda. That's love." The woman shifted her gaze to Barbie and Rose. "Don't you find it absurd that we're standing in front of a TV monitor arguing about hidden agendas? Let's just assume everyone has a reason for being here and leave it at that."

"Why should we, Heather?" Barbie said. "Are you going to tell me you don't want this exposure for Veronica and Trey? Eager to get them their own reality show? Hoping you can find him a job now that his one and done football career is over? Do tell?"

Heather didn't take the bait, but Barbie continued. "I'm honest. Starr's been winning beauty pageants since she was three. She's got one more to go and gaining a cheering squad who might come out and watch her could be to her advantage."

Heather smiled. "If I recall, the size of your cheering squad didn't get you beyond third place in the Ms. Alabama pageant twenty years ago."

"But at least I got there. I seem to remember you, after cheering our last game, sitting on the barrier wall near the football field pining for Jake."

Whoever Jake was and how he fit into the dynamics between the two women didn't seem to matter to Heather. "As my mother would say, Barbie, bless your heart. Considering how that turned out, I'm surprised you'd go there. By then, Jake the Snake was history to me. Much like you are to him now."

Rose shook her head and held her hands up like a traffic cop. "Ladies, ladies. Let's stop the bickering. We'll have plenty of time for that during the remainder of the week. You can either stay and watch the monitor or you can come with me over to Southwind. I'm ready for a margarita."

On that parting line, the tape ended, and someone flipped the lights back on.

CHAPTER 4

No one moved at first, but then Granny, Jed, and Lucy rose to leave. Before they reached the entrance to the main dining room, Sam and Flynn, who had been talking, pushed by them, accidentally jostling Granny. Jed caught Granny's arm and helped her regain her footing. As they left the room, Sarah noticed Jed kept a hand on Granny's elbow. To Sarah, Granny seemed smaller and more fragile than the feisty woman she'd observed in the film segment. Sarah wondered how old she was or if she was ill.

Because her mother, George, and Cliff were engaged with Heather, Veronica, and Trey in what looked like it could be a long discussion, she decided to see if Emily needed an extra set of hands to clear the dining room. Barbie was at the doorway leading from the porch into the main dining room, observing Granny, Jed, and Lucy leaving.

"She's beautiful, isn't she?" Barbie frowned.

Confused as to whether Barbie had been speaking to her or talking to herself, Sarah decided to answer anyway. "Yes, she is."

Barbie jumped ever so slightly and swung around to face Sarah. The frown was quickly replaced by a crooked smile. "Now you know my bad habit. Between the pageants I was in and being on the sidelines for Starr's, I can't help but examine every woman, especially if they are competing against Starr, with my judge's eye. Lucy is a beautiful girl, but her teeth are a little bucked, don't you think?"

"I hadn't noticed." Sarah didn't think there was a problem with Lucy's teeth. If anything, her genuine look was refreshing and her smile immediately engaging. Perhaps Lucy didn't meet the beauty pageant criteria Barbie used to evaluate contestants, but she'd obviously met the Southern Belle standard. There was no question; just as Barbie had done, people stopped and looked at Lucy.

As one who didn't particularly use much makeup, Sarah preferred Lucy's natural appearance, but then again this wasn't a beauty contest—or was it? Perhaps Barbie understood something Sarah hadn't considered. While Sarah evaluated people on what they said and did, a lot of viewers might only consider superficial facial characteristics in voting for a person. Sarah hoped not.

Sarah didn't think a perfect wedding was what others picked for you, but the idea that the winner might be selected only on her looks bothered her. In a sense, though, this tied in with what Maybelle said when she asked Sarah to be a chaperone. She'd explained that much as they cared about each other, their being on the show was going to be a lark for her and George. Sarah pointed out that they might win, but Maybelle disagreed. "Honey, while people may enjoy following a geriatric couple's journey, the show's winner will be one of the more physically appealing younger couples."

It seemed apparent to Sarah that Barbie may have been a contestant in her day, but now her self-esteem was tied to the public's reaction to her daughter's physical looks. Sarah hurriedly reassured her how beautiful Starr was.

"Thank you. As her mother, I know I'm biased. The irony is that my daughter couldn't care less. Would you believe she only takes part in pageants for the scholarship money?"

"I never paid much attention to that aspect of beauty contests."

"The scholarship money can be considerable if you finish in the top, which Starr consistently has. She's going to graduate college in a few months without a cent of debt."

"That is impressive." Sarah pointed toward one of the blackened monitors. "On the tape, you mentioned Starr has a big competition coming up?"

"Yes, Miss Alabama." Barbie leaned on a nearby chair. The smile slipped from her face. "Except, at the moment, she says no matter how much I've sacrificed to get her to this point, she doesn't want any part of it."

"But isn't Miss Alabama the pageant all the other ones she competed in have prepared her for? From what you're saying, she's a natural to do well."

"I think so too. But for her it comes down to the money. She says because she's graduating and doesn't need any more money for school, there's no need to keep competing."

"Maybe she'll change her mind," Sarah suggested, although if Starr was as stubborn as Barbie seemed to be, that might not be the case.

"She'll come around. I've worked too hard for her not to go all the way."

Thinking about how over the years she often did things that were contrary to what Maybelle would have preferred, like marrying Bill instead of staying in school, Sarah wasn't as positive about what Starr would do. "If Starr is the Southern Belle winner, will it be a problem?"

"Not if Starr and Lance don't go through with a real ceremony right away."

"I'm confused. I thought the final Southern Belle show is a wedding for the winning couple."

"It can be, but like those shows where in the last episode the person doesn't give the final rose or accept the proposal, it says in the fine print that the Southern Belle couple is permitted to sidestep the actual wedding, if they agree to give the network an option to film the ceremony as a mock pledge to each other. That's what Starr will do so she can continue competing this year."

"But what about the vendors and the things like the invitations, cake, and dress?"

"The vendors won't care because they're in it for the publicity. You don't really think the invitations are going to be mailed out by Friday, do you? What's important to the vendor is all the copycat orders they'll get by Friday and during the next few weeks."

What Barbie was saying did and didn't quite make sense to Sarah. Why would a network put all this money into a Southern Belle show if the finale didn't satisfy the viewers? Plus, in the clip played at dinner, Barbie admitted wanting to build a following for her daughter, but Sarah doubted viewers would support someone who disappointed them. She knew she wouldn't.

The more she thought about it, the more Sarah decided her mother's idea of this being a lark to lose was the right attitude. Having a wedding where everything from the dress to the guests were orchestrated wasn't Sarah's idea of a perfect wedding and she couldn't imagine how it was anyone else's dream come true, either.

"A lot of pageant contestants have boyfriends," Barbie said. "Starr just has to stay single during the year of her reign and, of course, for the extra time if she goes on and wins Miss America."

"Won't that be a problem for Starr and Lance? They seem like they're crazy about each other."

Barbie smirked and dismissively flopped her hand toward Sarah. "Believe me, that won't be an issue. When Starr wins the crown, she'll be kept way too busy to even worry about the details of a wedding."

Glancing over to where Lance and Starr, with his arm once again around her, were talking with one of the cameramen, Sarah didn't think they looked like a couple who would happily stay apart for a couple of years. It dawned on her that Barbie might be questioning what she was saying too. Barbie, having followed Sarah's gaze, abruptly ended their conversation.

"I hadn't realized it's so late. I better get Starr over to Jane's Place. See you back there or talk to you tomorrow."

Sarah decided that if there was any contest Starr had a desire to win, it was the Southern Belle. She obviously had a different focus for the stars in her eyes than her mother. Plus, noting how Starr's motivation for competing in pageants was for the scholarships, what could be more perfect than having all the trimmings of a spectacular wedding to the man she loved paid for?

Sarah took stock of Barbie and her daughter as they passed her leaving the room. Both reminded Sarah of the porcelain faced dolls Sarah ignored, but Emily played with when they were children. Starr, besides being petite, truly was beauty queen beautiful. Judging by their similarly heart-shaped faces and high cheekbones, Sarah thought there might have been a time the daughter was considered a clone of her mother, but not anymore.

Somewhere along the line, a tired look that wasn't well covered by the heavy pancake makeup she wore had set into Barbie's face. Either from one facelift too many or a Botox treatment gone awry, the skin over the lower portion of her face was unnaturally tight in contrast to the crow's feet around her eyes.

Lance didn't immediately follow Barbie and Starr's exit. Instead, he took his own sweet time finishing his conversation with the cameraman. He neared where Sarah stood and she called out to catch his attention. "Lance."

He stopped and looked in her direction. "Yes, ma'am."

Ma'am? At twenty-nine, she couldn't be more than seven or eight years older than him. He might think of her as an older sister, but nothing more. You don't *ma'am* an older sister. You *ma'am* a mother. Or a grandmother. Lance couldn't possibly think she looked that old, could he? No way! He was just being polite. Plain old Southern politeness. She'd stick with that belief until her dying breath—which he apparently thought could be coming any day now.

"I was wondering about something they said about Starr and you in the introduction."

"What was that, ma'am?"

He'd done it again, but she couldn't dwell on that. "They mentioned you didn't want to get married during football or hunting season. I know when football season is, but I thought in Alabama, the time for deer hunting overlaps football time. Do you hunt something else?"

Lance shook his head and grinned at her. "Not one single thing. I hate guns and killing innocent animals, but it's a different matter for my bride-to-be. Her dad wanted a boy, but all he got was Starr. Jake decided to make the best of it by introducing her to his number-two pastime. Starr may be slender and slight, but she hunts with the stealth of a tiger and is an expert shot. She's also quite adept at fishing. I enjoy catch and release, so that is something we do together between May and July. The intro probably should have been hunting and fishing, but we didn't have any final control over what Flynn said."

Without covering his mouth, Lance yawned. His hand belatedly went up to his face. "I'm sorry. I didn't get much sleep last night. Starr and I stayed up late with Trey and Veronica. We figure with the show's silly keep-the-brides-to-be-protected-at-night housing scheme, we probably won't have any time alone this next week."

"I guess that's true for everyone."

"It's worse for us. Most chaperones will only be on duty during the lockdown hours. In our case, even during the daytime, my future mother-in-law is going to stick to Starr like flypaper. And we all know what that means for anyone who gets too close."

"Barbie seems like she could be a bit domineering," Sarah said. Lance let out a deep-throated laugh that Sarah found herself joining in with. "A mamazilla instead of a bridezilla?"

He nodded. "Exactly. Barbie developed a long-range plan for Starr years ago and she's sticking to it."

The laugh was gone. Where a moment ago, she could read the amusement in his face, now his staid features were unreadable. "If the plan was made when Starr was a child, has it been modified to include you?"

"Not really. According to Barbie, I'm in the next facet of the plan. For now, according to her, I'm allowed to be a close friend, or with this show, the man she wants to marry, but nothing can be formalized until the year after Starr competes and wins the title."

"But what if you win this competition?"

He smiled. "That would let us throw a monkey wrench into Barbie's plan, wouldn't it?"

CHAPTER 5

Seeing that the regular waitstaff assisted by the students from the college's culinary program were quickly clearing the dining room, Sarah joined the group clustered around her mother. Maybelle was in her element. She had George, Cliff, Trey, Veronica, and Heather in stitches.

"Sarah," Veronica said, "your mother is adorable. She was just telling us how George and she decided to try out for the show as a last-minute lark because she was sure they'd need to cast a geriatric couple."

"Being a decade older than Maybelle, I may be geriatric, but she's far from it," George said. "That's why I never dreamt we had a chance of being interviewed, let alone being chosen as finalists. But, as she usually is, Maybelle was right."

Cliff cupped his ear. "Uncle George, did I just hear you correctly? Maybelle is usually right?"

Taking Maybelle's hand, George ignored his nephew and continued his narrative. "We were watching the six o'clock news with a group of our friends in my TV lounge when a story came on announcing how the mayor and city council finally worked together on something—bidding Wheaton to be the Southern Belle perfect wedding town—and that to everyone's surprise, their joint proposal won."

"Maybe they should try working together on other things," Sarah observed. She highly doubted that would be the case for the next few months. The president of the city council, Anne Hightower, who Sarah well knew didn't believe in taking any prisoners, had recently announced she was running against the incumbent mayor.

George nodded. "That was the subtle point the newscaster made when he talked about the benefit of their cooperative efforts creating an economic boon for Wheaton's hotels and merchants. At the end of the piece, the station flashed a web address for anyone interested in applying to be a vendor or one of the contestant couples. Just for something to do, Maybelle and I decided to enter. Who knew?"

Maybelle retrieved her hand and shot a wry grin in George's direction. "I did. It was obvious to me that, for diversity's sake, they'd need an older couple, but one still young enough to participate in the charitable activities they were going to do. We were perfect for our demographic."

Sarah had to agree with her mother's casting assessment. Except for her mother and George, it didn't appear any contestant was older than Sarah. "Other than all being young, from the looks of your competitors, it appears the show picked a pretty diverse group of contestants."

Her mother chuckled. "You nailed it. From backwoods folk to stodgy accountants to us old fogies, there is a couple for everyone in the viewing audience to root for. The producer and director knew we'll interest a large share of the viewers, even though they won't want us to win."

Cocking her head, Sarah stared at her mother. "Is this the woman who has always told me I could do anything if I tried? Why shouldn't you win? Being older doesn't automatically make you a loser. Age doesn't mean you can't have a perfect wedding."

"Honey, that may be true, but that's not showbiz."

"Are the rules of show business different than those in real life?"

Heather and Maybelle simultaneously nodded. "Everything is done for a purpose," Heather said.

Maybelle agreed. "The facts of TV life are simple. George and I will be portrayed as underdogs in the challenges. Subliminally, the audience will be encouraged to root for us. At one point, we'll even look like we can win the whole enchilada, but about the third day, a twist in a challenge or something unforeseen will take us out of the competition."

"I don't know, Mom . . . Maybelle. I've always heard reality TV is scripted, so how much influence can they really have behind the scenes? Either you win a challenge or you don't."

"You'd be surprised. Camera angles, what gets shown, all work to manipulate the audience. Think about the cooking shows where someone is shown usually in a more villainous light and others are highlighted as talented, but helpful and kind."

"Sort of like they might do with Jane and her outburst?" Sarah couldn't help thinking it would be delicious if Jane were portrayed as the manipulative, husband-stealing person she was—especially if Sarah, Maybelle, and Emily came off as the good guys.

"Exactly. Did you know they taped a short segment about how Marcus and Emily are business partners and a couple? When it comes to George and me, the network executives don't want a couple of retreads to win. They want to send a couple in their twenties, who've never been married before, off on their dream honeymoon still talking about their perfect wedding."

"Sometimes," Heather said, "the network, if the public really becomes invested in the couple, will do a spin-off with them. For example, they could take a couple like Veronica and Trey through their first year or years of marriage."

As Heather continued explaining that this was exactly the kind of reality show networks loved making because they were low budget, Sarah bit her tongue not to say it was exactly the type of show she avoided watching.

"Often," Heather said, "the shows run for years because the viewers became devoted to watching every episode, even in reruns. The couple becomes almost an extension of their own family."

As Heather prattled about how long a reality show could go on, Sarah noticed Trey and Veronica exchange a look she interpreted as disgust. Trey took Veronica's hand and pulled her to him. Veronica's shoulders visibly relaxed as she curled closer to him. It was almost the same reaction Sarah had when she cuddled with RahRah.

"I guess you both have a point there," Sarah said. She remembered her wedding to Bill Blair. She'd been eighteen and so eager to be Mrs. Blair that she dropped out of college after only two weeks to be married in front of a justice of the peace. There hadn't been any fanfare, but it hadn't mattered. Being with Bill made up for a lack of wedding trimmings. She still felt that way when, almost two years ago, the rat told her he wanted a divorce because he'd fallen in love with someone else—Jane Clark.

Ten years of marriage and all Sarah had gotten out of the divorce was RahRah, her Siamese cat. Not that she was planning to, but if she ever got married again, the idea of letting unknown viewers choose the perfect invitations, wedding venue, flowers, and dress for her seemed absurd. She also couldn't believe she'd let her mother rope her into spending five nights under Jane's roof.

Sarah had objected she couldn't leave RahRah and Fluffy alone all night, but her mother was ready with an answer. "That's not going to be a problem. You can take care of them before our nightly lockdown. Emily will check on them after the Southwind dinner rush and then sleep at your house. They won't even realize you're not home."

Considering how her mother avoided pets of any kind most of the time, claiming an as-yet unproven allergy to all animals, Sarah didn't put any stock in her mother's last comment. She knew that the loyalty of her pets to her couldn't possibly be replaced by Emily's presence. Speaking of which, if her mother was volunteering Emily to sleep at the house, her mother evidently had already discussed this plan with Emily and won her acquiescence. Rather than challenging her mother and Emily's de facto approval, Sarah tried a different tactic.

"But I'm working too. Harlan's got a big trial coming up and with the other cases he has going, things at the office are busy. He may need me to work late some of the nights of your competition. Besides, I'm right in the middle of organizing two fundraising events for the animal shelter."

Maybelle snorted. "You have weeks until you have to do much for either of those events. I'm only asking you to be on duty at night. Chaperoning me won't interfere with your day job. Knowing how important this taping is as a revenue source for Wheaton, I'm sure Harlan will work around the hours I need you."

"But—"

Ignoring the beginning of Sarah's next objection, her mother talked over her. "Besides, you love television. This is a wonderful way for you to get an inside view of how a show works. Who knows? Maybe one of the producers or directors will cast you in something else down the road?"

Being part of another reality show was the last thing on Sarah's bucket list. Pursing her lips together, she silently gave in. As she'd learned long ago, arguing with her mother was fruitless.

The silence in the room made Sarah realize the waitstaff had finished cleaning up. The seven of them were the only ones still in the room. "Speaking of being locked in, I guess we better make our way across the street to Jane's Place before they use tardiness to disqualify two couples."

"That's not going to be the case. Like we were just saying, my daughter and Trey, as well as your mother and George, are too important to disqualify at this point. Alan and Sam need more footage before kicking either couple off the show."

Sarah furrowed her brow. Heather sounded so sure of herself. "Why?"

"They need backstory to go with today's introduction. Maybelle already nailed it when she said George and she will be played up as the competition's older couple."

"And Veronica and Trey?"

Heather laughed. "Are you the one person in Alabama who isn't a football fan?"

"Possibly."

"Well, Sarah, in our state there's nothing more important than the Alabama-Auburn rivalry. Every child or transplant to the state must pick a side. Like with your mother and George, there isn't enough film shot yet for Alan or Sam to edit and demonstrate a rivalry between Veronica and Starr or Trey and Lance, especially since they all went to the same high school but picked opposing colleges. They may even highlight that Trey and Lance were star high school football players with the possibility of SEC college playing time, but Lance blew out his knee in a stupid car accident."

Considering how big and strong Trey and Lance were, Sarah could imagine both playing football. It must have been a big adjustment for Lance to have his dream snatched away from him. Sarah knew Emily would be desolate if for some reason she lost her sense of taste and couldn't be a chef.

"The public eats up any scenes with conflict and tension. That's why Sam and Alan want to build up a mock feud between them. In my opinion, these are the three couples who will be in the final three."

"But what about the other couples?"

"Nope." Heather shook her head. "The others are too nice or too boring. My money is on age and football."

At least, Sarah agreed, the football fans would vote the way Heather predicted. For her money, she'd be more interested in Lucy and Jed or even her mother and George. That, she now understood, was the beauty of the Southern Belle competition's casting—there was at least one couple whose story could resonate with any viewer. "I get your point, but maybe those of us who need to be at Jane's Place should start across the street. Sort of a, let's all try to stay on Alan's good side . . ."

"Does he have one?" Heather asked, making a face. "You're right, though. I guess we better not push our luck. Come on, Veronica, we'll walk Trey to his car."

After Heather, Veronica, and Trey left, Sarah started to say good night to George and Cliff, but George cut her off. "Come on. We'll walk you across the street. It will be my last chance to see my bride-to-be for at least twelve hours."

Cliff held up his arm, showing the other three the face of his watch. "That's not right, Uncle George. You're always up early. If you meet Maybelle for breakfast at Jane's Place when the cast and crew breakfast buffet line opens, you won't have to wait twelve hours."

Maybelle chuckled and exchanged a knowing look with George. "Yes, he will. I don't do six thirty breakfast for anyone. A cup of coffee and a last-minute appearance is fine for me."

Sarah fell into step with Cliff, behind her mother and George, as they walked down Southwind's front steps.

"It was really great to see Emily and Marcus so busy

tonight," Sarah said. "I still can't believe Alan was so taken with their food that after one meal he shifted all the dinners to Southwind."

George stopped in front of Southwind and adjusted his pince-nez glasses. "Alan's impression of the food was part of his excuse, but not the real reason."

He waited, like a child savoring a piece of candy, until Maybelle, who with Cliff and Sarah had crowded around him to hear him, said, "George Rogers. Do you know something I don't know? Something you didn't share with me?"

CHAPTER 6

George grinned. "We've been so busy. I didn't have time to tell you." He paused again.

Obviously impatient, Maybelle put her hands on her hips and tried to nudge his story along. "Spill the beans. What's the truth behind Alan moving the dinners?"

Unlike her mother, Sarah didn't push George to elaborate any faster than he wanted. She'd known George a long time, dating back to when he lived in the home that now housed Jane's Place and Sarah and Bill resided in the big house across Main Street, where Southwind now was. She knew he couldn't and wouldn't be rushed.

"One thing about being a little older is sometimes people forget you have ears. They simply think of you as an object in the room."

"True, but what did you hear?" Maybelle persisted in egging him on.

"The truth, as I overheard Sam tell Alan yesterday," George said, warming to his topic, "is that Sam felt Alan should schedule as many meals as possible at Southwind because Sam, the advance crew, and the prospective vendors, who've been here all week, preferred eating at the two Southwind restaurants over Jane's Place."

Maybelle snorted. "That's not a surprise. Anyone with any sense would rather eat at Southwind or the Southwind Pub rather than at Jane's Place."

"But that's not the only reason Sam felt Alan needed to move the dinners to Southwind. The other part is what interested me." George didn't wait for anyone to prod him along this time. "Sam reminded Alan that they needed to focus on their numbers. The more people become invested in the outcome, the more they'll watch and tell their friends to watch too. More viewers mean they can charge more for the commercials. Sam suggested that if the Southern Belle segments engaged more people in the right demographic groups, Alan and Sam would win brownie points with the network that would stand them in good stead later."

Cliff rubbed his chin. "Uncle George, from a business perspective, I understand the advertising dollars aspect, but that still doesn't explain why Sam wanted the dinners moved to Southwind."

"Sam thought viewers would become more invested in the show if they got to see more of the vendors. By showing more of Southwind and deliberately focusing camera time on Emily, Marcus, and Wanda, Sam felt it would create two solid camps: Jane and Roberto versus Emily, Marcus, and Wanda. In a sense, he urged Alan to make Marcus and Emily so familiar to everyone that they were like a sixth contestant couple."

"Now I get it. More camera time, more familiarity, which equals more viewer investment," Cliff said.

"That's right. The bottom line is that more engagement by the viewers will heighten the competition's tension. Consequently, audience attendance will increase or at least stay solid through the entire five days of broadcasts. Sam even reminded Alan about how on those singing shows, when they only show a contestant in a montage format, that person never builds a sufficient following to garner enough votes to stay around. Alan was planning to have dinner last night with his old college roommate, who was in Wheaton yesterday afternoon to see his daughter, so Sam taking the roommate and Alan to dinner at Southwind last night was a business decision."

"You know, I've been so busy with work, meetings for the animal shelter, my dog walking, and taking care of RahRah and Fluffy, that I didn't think through the timing of how they are filming and showing the Southern Belle segments. Isn't the final show supposed to be the wedding? How can they get the invitations printed and out fast enough for guests to respond, let alone make travel plans?"

Maybelle smiled. "More reality TV. There will be a mock-up of the invitation, but the vendor's prize is how many orders the public will send in for the invitation. As for the guests, we had to turn in detailed guest lists a few weeks ago, but the show will only bring in a few of the winning couple's guests. The rest of the people at the ceremony and reception will be dressed-up crew members, some of the residents from where George lives, our Wheaton politicians, and as many other Wheatonite bodies as the show needs. Or, in other words, anyone in Wheaton who'd like a free dinner and a chance to be on television."

"Mo—Maybelle, I can't believe it. You're ruining all my romantic notions of this Southern Belle wedding."

Maybelle made a clucking sound with her tongue. "Most of us had romantic illusions of what this was going to be, but the producers and our contracts spelled out the reality of what we were getting into. The deal is that if the couple agrees to go through with the wedding, it will be an entirely legal ceremony that is filmed. Afterwards, the winners will receive the dream honeymoon they requested and five thousand dollars of spending money."

"You make it sound like there is an alternative."

"There is. If the couple prefers, they can have a commitment ceremony and take ten thousand dollars to put toward a wedding or use in any way they please. Some will simply divide the prize and go on their way, but others may go through with their own version of a perfect wedding later. If they do and the network is willing to film it then, the network will give the couple more television exposure and will pay them an additional five thousand dollars toward their honeymoon."

Her mother's description of the winners' options and the different angles the chaperones discussed when they didn't realize they were being taped made Sarah question everyone's motives. "Everything you're describing feels dirty both from the show's side and from any contestants who are simply milking the system. It's just downright sneaky."

"No more than those fixer-upper house shows that really only redo one or two rooms or the house-hunting shows where the couple has already picked and bought the chosen home before they ever start filming."

"Well—"

Maybelle made a chiding sound with her tongue and cheek. "Sarah, you didn't think everything about those shows was real, did you? Reality TV is like being out in the forest during open season with a hunter who knows the rules, but does things his way. He goes out, his deer hunting license in his pocket, his gun loaded, but then shoots whatever type of animal he pleases."

"Have you taken up hunting, Mother?"

"It's Maybelle," her mother again corrected. "No, but at least one of the contestants is an avid hunter and worked that into her wedding theme. Sam told us that hunting and anything people can possibly imagine everyone does in the South is what the network suits want him and Alan to incorporate into each of the segments they shoot."

Sarah felt her dander rising. "There are so many misconceptions about the South. I bet some people think we all go around barefoot, use outhouses, and spend most of the day drinking or making moonshine."

"There are those who think that way and, sadly, the show is probably going to do everything it can to make us fit those stereotypical images, plus more."

"More?"

George, who had been so quiet Sarah had almost forgotten he was standing with them, leaned his head closer to Sarah's. "Besides having cast one guaranteed mamazilla, they want your sweet mother and the others to act like bridezillas."

Sarah looked at her mother, who nodded. "It's a form of reality TV, Sarah. They expect us to make it interesting. It won't be scripted, but we're being prompted to create some moments of tension, like Lucy did with the hose. If they don't have one of us act out in some manner, the show will take advantage of our existing conflicts or manufacture some."

The idea of manufactured conflicts rankled Sarah. She couldn't believe it didn't bother her mother too. Although her mother could be tart and direct, she wasn't a prima donna. Nor was she one to let others tell her what to do, especially when she didn't agree. "You may be my mamazilla, but you're not a public bride or mamazilla. As much as you love the South, I can't see you participating in something that mocks it. You said George and you applied for the fun of it, but this doesn't sound like fun."

"Sarah, the advance team did its homework. In a sense, other than the football rivalry, George and I are part of the most obvious conflict. Remember, Jane's Place is in the house George used to own and Emily and you are my daughters. I'm sure, that's why, at least for the wedding reception and wedding cake, they pitted Jane's Place against Southwind. Someone must have made them aware of the bad blood between the two restaurants and its owners."

"You can bet Chef Bernardi played up the rivalry between Jane, Emily, and Sarah, as well as touted his own skills," Cliff said.

Accepting Cliff's premise, it was obvious that by helping the advance team, Chef Bernardi had been in the position to sway many of the competitor selections. That meant when he accused Sam and Alan of being weasels, it was merely an act. He was simply giving the show footage to help garner sympathy in his direction.

Cliff rubbed his hands together and crossed his arm in front of his face as if hiding it with a cape. "He probably laid it on about how Wanda, his innocent prize pupil, crossed to the dark side by turning on him and becoming Southwind's pastry chef."

Sarah groaned at his bad *Star Wars* analogy. "I doubt Wanda or Emily would describe Wanda's working for Southwind as going over to the dark side, but I guess if we don't get over to Jane's Place, someone may infer some truth to Jane's accusations about Mother and my relationship with Southwind."

"You're right, Sarah." George offered his arm to Maybelle. To Sarah's surprise, her mother slipped her hand into the crook of his elbow. Immediately engaged in conversation, the two, with only a quick glance back by George, crossed Main Street.

Left alone with Cliff, Sarah felt awkward. Without anyone running interference between them, she wasn't sure what to say.

Cliff broke the tension by offering his arm in the same manner his uncle had to Sarah's mother. "Don't worry. I won't bite."

In mock fear, Sarah held her hands up like a shield. "Maybe just sting a bit?" When Cliff didn't smile or laugh, she wasn't sure what to say. "You know, we're probably going to be seeing a lot of each other this week."

"Yeah."

She looked toward the sidewalk. "If we were at war, I'd say we needed to call a truce, but I don't feel that's the case. I'm sorry how things worked out and I guess, if you want us to stay like this, I deserve it."

He reached his hand out toward Sarah's chin, but pulled it back before touching her. "No, you don't. Our breaking up was a mutual decision. That night it seemed so simple. We agreed to remain friends, but since then I just haven't known what to say or what you want me to say." He swallowed. "Sarah, I've missed you as a friend."

"I've missed you too." For a moment, the two stared at each other, their conversation seemingly at a standstill.

Sarah glanced across the street. Her mouth dropped open and she started to laugh—a raucous full-throated belly laugh she couldn't control. She took a deep breath, swallowed, and then burst out laughing again.

Cliff backed away from her. Sarah, barely able to stop quivering, held up her hands and gasped out a few words. "Wait. Don't look at me as if I'm a creature from another planet."

He licked his lips and put his hands into his pockets. "Aren't you? Tell me, what's so funny? I thought we were having a serious conversation."

Sarah, overcome again with laughter, tried to regain control. She finally sputtered out some more words. "We were. We are. But do you realize what your uncle and my mother just did to us?"

"What do you mean?"

She pointed at George and Maybelle talking on the walkway to Jane's Place. "They hightailed it across the street, leaving us alone. Like they did with steak night at the retirement home, they manipulated us into having to talk to each other."

He hit his hand against his forehead, causing a lock of his tousled sandy-brown hair to fall into his face. He brushed it out of his eyes and grinned. "My uncle looked back. I thought he was seeing if we were coming, but I bet he was checking if their plan was working."

"Probably."

"Well, it's not going to work quite the same way this time around, is it, friend?"

"Not quite." Especially, Sarah thought, when he found out that after she accepted the offer of a rain check from Dr. Glenn Amos, RahRah's veterinarian, they'd had a much more successful date. Since then, they had fallen into a comfortable once-a-week date routine. She wouldn't have to worry about that this week because Glenn was out of town at a professional conference.

Sarah reached out her arm and slid her hand between Cliff's elbow and warm body. It felt as natural as in the past. "It will be nice to have my old friend to pal around with this next week."

Together, the two of them started across the street.

"Cliff, who do you think is going to win?"

"If I were in the pool, I'd put my money on either Trey and Veronica or Starr and Lance. Those are the ones that Chef Bernardi is giving the best odds on to win."

She stopped walking and stared at Cliff. "What! He's gambling again?"

"Sarah, he never stopped. This time, though, he's running the pool." With a gentle tug, he started them walking again. "Believe me, by being the bookie or house, Chef Bernardi will take a piece of the action on every bet."

"How?"

"I gather you don't know much about gambling."

"Nothing."

"Okay, Chef Bernardi makes the odds or the line and adds the juice—the bit he'll take off the bet. Probably on our Alabama or Auburn couples; the way he's handicapped them is quite low compared to the margin he's given to whichever couples are the long shots to win. The long shot couples are the ones Chef Bernardi would rather see more wagers placed on. The odds and possible win tied to the point spread for them are higher, so he stands to make more juice. Of course, circumstances will make the line shift constantly during the week."

"Now you've lost me. Why will the line shift once he's established it?"

"Because of different factors. In a horse or dog race, it may be that a competitor is scratched before the race begins or the favorite wakes up under the weather. Then, people change their bets. In this competition, Chef Bernardi's line will shift when couples get eliminated. At that point, more money may be poured in for the remaining couples or one couple may do something that generates extra interest, so there is more betting on them. Either way, Chef Bernardi won't merely hold the bag and pay it back out. He'll make sure he gets his cut."

Sarah knew people bet on anything from football to the ridiculous—like which turtle would cross a line first. To her, having the Southern Belle competition take place in Wheaton was weird enough, but betting on it felt dirty. That's probably why sports and many other types of betting were illegal—at least here in Alabama. She assumed Chef Bernardi was only taking bets from people he could trust to keep their mouths shut. "Cliff, did you bet?"

"Nah, it's not my thing. And I'm certainly not inclined to do it when Chef Bernardi is involved in setting the odds."

Joining George and Maybelle, Sarah pointed to the front door of Jane's Place. "I think we've reached the limits where you two guys can go. Good night."

To Sarah's surprise, her mother leaned over and lightly kissed George's forehead. "See you tomorrow, love." Leaving George and Cliff at the bottom of the walkway, a giggling Maybelle grabbed Sarah's arm and took the lead as they ran up the steps to the porch. Still acting silly, Maybelle pushed open the front door of Jane's Place, stepped inside, and screamed.

CHAPTER 7

Maybelle pointed to the hardwood floor in front of her. Sarah wordlessly peered over her mother's shoulder and stared at the spot beyond where her mother's finger extended. Behind her, she heard Cliff leap up the stairs to the porch. She was cognizant of softer footsteps and winded breathing as George joined him. They crowded through the doorway behind Sarah, but stopped as abruptly as Maybelle and she had at the sight of Alan lying on the floor, with Jane bent over him.

Jane raised her head and stretched her hands out to them. They were covered in blood.

"I was in the kitchen and heard a loud *bang*. I found Alan like this. I didn't do it." She looked at her hands and back up at Sarah. "Sarah, I didn't kill him. Help me, please."

Sarah simply stared at Jane, not knowing what to

think. Considering what Jane had put Sarah through the past two years, Sarah couldn't believe she had the gall to ask for her help.

George stepped forward, reaching his hand out to Jane. Sarah blocked his path. "Stop. You'll mess up the crime scene."

Jane whimpered again. "Please, Sarah. I didn't do anything. I was just trying to help him."

From the look George flashed in Sarah's direction, Sarah could see he was torn between Sarah's prohibition and helping Jane up. Apparently, his urge to be a gentleman won out because, ignoring the blood on Jane's hands, he guided her to her feet and allowed her to grab onto his jacket. As she swayed unsteadily, he braced her with his body.

"Stay put," Sarah ordered. This time, George followed Sarah's directive while she pulled her cell phone from her pocket. Rather than call 911, she punched in the Wheaton police department from her contact list. They were a permanent contact as part of her many past encounters with them. Her experience solving a few murders also explained why Jane had the nerve to ask for Sarah's help.

As the phone rang, she noticed sharp-edged ceramic shards on the floor. The large vase that normally sat on a metal stand in the corner of the entryway to the side of the hostess stand was shattered on the floor. The piece of pottery, which Jane kept filled with fresh flowers, and its stand had been knocked over. The flowers lay on the ground in a heap, but pieces from the vase had flown in all directions.

Pointing to his feet, Sarah again begged George and

Jane not to move until the police arrived. Although she was thinking of telling them to stay put rather than chance trampling some valuable evidence, she merely said, "You might get hurt stepping on those sharp, broken pieces."

Jane glanced down at Alan. "I can't stay here. I didn't do anything." She started to move closer to where Maybelle, Cliff, and Sarah were, but George held her back.

He motioned toward the phone pressed to Sarah's ear. "Tell them to hurry."

She nodded as the call connected.

She was relieved it was Officer Robinson rather than Chief Gerard who answered. She'd established a good working relationship with him over the past few months—unlike with Chief Gerard.

She didn't want to see the chief's face when he learned that, once again, she was at a murder scene. He wasn't fond of her propensity for finding bodies.

"Officer Robinson. This is Sarah Blair. I'm at Jane's Place."

He chuckled in her ear. "Sarah, you know you always get in trouble when you go over there. Is Jane trying to run you off or holding you hostage this time?"

His comment might have been funny under other circumstances, but not with Alan lying on the ground so pasty and still that Sarah knew there was nothing she could do to help him. "It's worse than that. Alan Perrault, the Southern Belle director from New York, is dead."

"What?"

She shifted her stance. Although the others could still hear her, her repositioning prevented her from looking directly at Jane or Alan. "I'm supposed to be chaperoning my mother, but that isn't important now, except to say that's why we're at Jane's Place. Maybelle and I just walked into the house through the restaurant's front door and found Alan on the ground. It looks to me like someone may have hit him over the head with the big ceramic vase that sits on the high stand in the restaurant's entryway." She stopped to take a breath.

"And?"

She swallowed. "It's Jane. She keeps repeating she didn't do it, but when we walked in, the room was empty except for Jane kneeling by Alan. Her hands are covered in blood."

Sarah pressed the phone to her ear to hear Officer Robinson asking, "Jane? We?" over Jane yelling: "What are you telling them? I didn't do anything!"

Sarah ignored Jane's outburst as she responded to Officer Robinson. "Yes, my mother, Cliff, George, and Jane are all here. Jane swears she found him like he is, but she got into it earlier with Alan in front of everyone and—"

"Stop it!" Jane shouted. "Like always, instead of helping me, you're throwing me under the bus."

"Sarah, keep the site intact. We'll be there in a few minutes." The phone clicked off from his end.

She turned back to the others. Jane, her body quivering in anger, stared daggers at Sarah.

Sarah averted her eyes from Jane's. "Officer Robinson answered. The police will be here in a few minutes. In the meantime, they'd like us to stay put and not disturb anything any more than we already have."

Except for Jane, who was continuing to deny her involvement and pointing out that there were plenty of other people in the house, the others indicated their understanding of what Sarah had said. They waited for Officer Robinson and probably the other two members of the Wheaton police force: Chief Dwayne Gerard and its one detective, as well as the county's coroner, Dr. David Smith. Sarah, despite not wanting to look at Alan, couldn't resist evaluating the crime scene.

Jane's presence and George's actions obviously had disturbed things. Slowly, Sarah dissected the room in front of her. Unfortunately, she'd been around enough crime scenes during the past few months to have learned she might see something that didn't seem relevant now, but could later be important to help the police determine who killed Alan.

Alan lay on the ground, amid the clumped flowers and pieces of shattered vase. Because she could only see the back of his head and part of his face, it appeared to her that he had fallen forward, but turned his head toward the stairwell to his left before he hit the ground. One hand was blocked by the way his body lay, but the one she could see clutched a piece of white paper with words or lettering on it. Although the way he held the crumpled sheet only let her see a little of each side, she thought it might be a call sheet with something scrawled on what would have been the paper's blank side.

Staying on the outside perimeter of the room near the front door, Sarah moved back and forth, trying to ascertain what she might be missing. The angle at which Alan lay made her think he might have been walking toward the greenroom or the kitchen. Other than Jane, there was no one else in the entryway. Nothing except for the broken vase and its stand appeared to have been disturbed.

She shifted her gaze from Alan's head to Jane's bloody

hands and back to Alan. From her vantage point, there wasn't a hair out of place on the back of his head, nor did she see any blood pooled on the ground near his head. She examined the hand that was visible to her. There was no apparent wound, nor were there any red stains splotching the white paper. Unless he had a knife stuck in his chest or a bullet hole in the part of his face and forehead that Sarah couldn't see, she couldn't figure out how Jane had gotten blood on her hands. Sadly, from her past experiences, she was positive it was blood rather than food coloring or tomato sauce.

The back door that led into the smaller dining room banged open and Sarah heard voices. It was Heather and Veronica. As they came closer to the doorway between the greenroom and the front hall, toward the main staircase, Sarah called out to them. "Stay where you are. Don't come into the entryway."

They froze just before the entryway threshold. Sarah wasn't sure if her words stopped them or it was the sight of Alan lying on the floor or of Jane, her face streaked with blood from where she'd touched it with her hands, clinging to George.

Heather was the first to react by starting to go to Alan, but another admonishment from Sarah stopped her as she stepped into the entryway. She stood, her eyes fixed on Alan. "What happened?"

In a monotone, Jane replied before Sarah could. "Alan's dead. I found him like this." Despite George holding her close, she shuddered violently.

"Did anyone call the police?"

"They're on the way," Sarah said.

Sarah's attention was brought back to Jane, who was

looking wildly around before locking eyes with Heather. "I didn't do it. I didn't. He was like this when I found him."

Not coming any closer, but keeping her gaze tied to Jane's, Heather spoke with a calming tone and slow cadence. "That must have been frightening, but you're okay now. We're all here with you." She waved her hand to encompass everyone.

Jane nodded, but her shaking intensified. Even from where she stood, Sarah could hear Jane's teeth chattering. George, keeping one arm on Jane, eased out of his sports coat and wrapped it around Jane's shoulders.

"Thank you." Jane pulled George's jacket tightly around her. Again, she stared at Alan. "I'm so cold."

Not as cold as Alan flitted through Sarah's mind. Shaking the thought out of her head, she peered into the next room, where Heather and Veronica waited. "Are you just getting back? You left way ahead of us."

Sarah caught Veronica give her mother a side glance.

"Veronica and I walked with Trey back to his car," Heather said. "It was blocked in by Sam's car. He and Flynn were sitting inside with the windows rolled down, talking, so we joined the conversation. To tell the truth, Veronica and I were in no hurry to be locked up for the night."

Seemingly surer of herself than she'd appeared a minute earlier, Veronica picked up the story. "We were outside talking and cutting up for quite some time when Sam mentioned Alan was here, going over some things for tomorrow. Sam sort of winked at us and said the real reason Alan was here was that he wanted to check if every bride-to-be and her chaperone was accounted for and if the second film upset anyone. Once we heard that, Mother and I decided we'd better hightail it inside or fear the wrath of Alan."

Heather gestured toward where Alan lay. "I'm sorry about this, but in so many ways, he wasn't a particularly nice person."

Wow. She knew Alan before she got involved in the show, Sarah realized. Before Sarah could home in on their previous connection, Heather observed, "At least, when the police arrive, they won't need any of us for long, except for Jane."

"They'll still need to check out where Alan is lying and get statements from each of us," Sarah said.

"But it shouldn't be a big deal. We can all alibi each other. Veronica, Trey, and I can attest to our whereabouts until we joined up with Sam and Flynn behind Jane's Place. The two of them can vouch for each other before the five of us were together. The four of you can cover for each other because you were together after we left you, right? It seems to me that, except for Jane, we all have pretty airtight alibis."

Sarah had to agree. Assuming what Heather said was true, it seemed like Chief Gerard would easily be able to rule out the nine of them, and maybe some of the other contestants and chaperones if they had believable alibis. But, she wondered, if Sam and Flynn knew Alan was in Jane's Place, had either of them ever been alone with him? If so, they would have a problem fully alibiing each other.

From experience, knowing Chief Gerard's investigative forte was jumping to conclusions, Sarah could easily predict what he would determine when faced with at least nine people with alibis and one possibly without. Alan's killer theoretically could be anyone involved with the show, as well as everyone who crossed paths with Alan since he came to town. But the chief would assume the person who threatened to sue Alan just a couple of hours ago and then conveniently found his body was the likely person who killed him.

Hopefully, though, Chief Gerard would at least check where the other chaperones and brides-to-be were at the time of death, as well as the behind-the-scenes people. Hopefully too Jane had an alibi for the time of death. She was alone when she found Alan, but where was she when he was killed? Once the time of death was determined, then they could really start to figure out who could have killed him.

It was odd to Sarah why no one else had come downstairs to see what the ruckus going on was. Based on the size of the house, it seemed impossible that some of them hadn't heard Maybelle scream, let alone the crash when the vase fell. Then again, she realized it depended on who was assigned to what bedroom. Except for the rooms her mother and she had, Sarah wasn't sure who was occupying which room on the two sleeping floors.

From having walked through Jane's Place with Cliff during its remodeling, she knew both floors could be reached from the front hall stairway that ran up the middle of the house. One could also use a narrow set of stairs to go directly from the kitchen to the second and third floors. On the second floor, the original family bedroom and sitting rooms had been redone to create four nice-sized guest rooms with individual bathrooms.

The third floor once consisted of the children's playroom, nursery, and rooms used by the family's help. Cliff's remodel had knocked out walls, resulting in the floor having four bedrooms—two on each side of the hall, each set sharing an adjoining bathroom—as well as a private bridal suite, with a room that could be locked off and rented out by itself as a bride's dressing room.

Maybelle and Sarah were assigned to the two smaller third-floor bedrooms facing Main Street that shared a bathroom. Sarah hypothesized, seeing how many of the show's decisions seemed to revolve around convenience and expediency, that Maybelle and George were expected to be voted off the show more quickly than some of the other couples. Consequently, they'd have fewer days to need timely bathroom access to be ready for the morning shoot. Once she found out who were in the two rooms across the hall, she'd see if her assumption was right.

Sarah could understand the possibility that the other third-floor occupants might be too far from the front door to have heard the vase shatter or voices downstairs, but Maybelle's scream had been loud. Giving those two third-floor rooms the benefit of the doubt or the possibility that they were Veronica and Heather's, it still seemed peculiar to her that no one from the second floor had come downstairs to investigate.

It wouldn't matter in the long run. Being all too familiar with the procedural methods of the Wheaton police, she knew, besides jumping to conclusions, one of Chief Gerard's first moves would be rousing everyone for questioning. Veronica might think that nine of them having alibis would speed things along, but taking statements was one area of investigative work where the chief took his time.

Sarah studied Jane. For only the second time since Sarah had known her, Sarah saw a fragility in Jane. Even her coloring, which earlier in the evening had matched her fire engine red hair, was now washed out. Once again, Sarah pulled her cell phone out of her pocket.

This time, the number she called was on her favorites list. "Harlan," she said to her lawyer boss when he answered on the second ring, "you're not going to believe this because I really don't. After everything that's gone on between Jane and me, I'm calling you because I think she needs your help."

CHAPTER 8

The Wheaton police force—all three of them—finally arrived in its entirety. Chief Gerard gave Sarah a cold stare but didn't say anything to her. Instead, he banished Maybelle, Sarah, and Cliff, as a group, from their place in the front doorway of Jane's Place to one of the front patio tables Jane used for outdoor seating. Maybelle and Cliff did as they were told. Sarah didn't. Instead, she carefully stayed within hearing range, but just far enough away from the chief to avoid drawing his attention and ire to her. She couldn't help herself. She had to see if she was right about the chief jumping to conclusions and if Dr. Smith seemed to find anything she hadn't observed.

As Chief Gerard and Officer Robinson put on the protective blue booties and gloves that Dr. Smith handed them, the chief began giving the detective and Officer Robinson their preliminary instructions.

"Robinson, when I stopped by here yesterday, Alan introduced me to his segment director and host. The brides-to-be are staying here, but the crew and male members of the cast are being put up in a hotel nearer to Birmingham. George can tell you their names and which hotel to call. Get the director and host back here, pronto. When they arrive, have them wait on the patio until I'm ready to talk to them."

"Will do." Officer Robinson followed Chief Gerard into Jane's Place. "Anything else?"

"Yes." He pointed to where Heather stood with Veronica in the doorway to the smaller dining room. "I want you to make sure they stay in there. Leave George and Jane in the larger dining room for now. Once you have all of them settled and contained, go through the entire house and bring down anyone you find. There should be some who already turned in for the night in the bedrooms. Have them use the back stairs and separate them from each other, as best you can, either in the kitchen or the small dining room until we can get their statements. Inform anyone you find that under no circumstances are they to leave the premises until we have talked to them."

Finished giving Officer Robinson directions, the chief beckoned to Dr. Smith, who had been getting other things out of his bag. Steadying the camera he'd put around his neck, Dr. Smith joined Chief Gerard inside the building at the periphery of the crime scene. With the three no longer standing near the front doorway, Sarah eased closer to watch what Dr. Smith and Chief Gerard were doing. From the prior instances where she'd stumbled across a body, she was all too familiar with the protocol Dr. Smith would follow.

As she figured, today was no different. Dr. Smith, true

professional that he was, was taking pictures of the scene, working from the room's exterior perimeter toward the body. She was glad to see Chief Gerard slowly circle the room, this time touching nothing. In the past, when he was still a desk officer, that hadn't been the case. There was no question that he'd absorbed some of the information in the classes he'd taken since being named acting and then full chief of the Wheaton police force.

Chief Gerard reached the far side of the room, viewing Alan from the side she hadn't been able to see. He paused and frowned. He squatted, stared, and stood again. Arms crossed, his lips pressed tightly together, he didn't move.

After what seemed an interminable amount of time, Chief Gerard uncrossed his arms, raised his hand, and re-peatedly beckoned with his forefinger for Dr. Smith to join him. He pointed toward something near Alan's head. "What do you make of this?"

"I'm not sure." Dr. Smith picked up the camera that hung from his neck and began shooting pictures of Alan, the floor area near where he lay, and the room in general from his new vantage point. As Dr. Smith moved closer to the body, he went around it. He took pictures from the back and of the top of Alan's head before moving to the side where Chief Gerard still stood. He snapped several shots that Sarah assumed were of Alan's face. Maybe that's where the wound was?

Done taking pictures, Dr. Smith carefully kneeled, making sure to miss any of the pointed shards on the ground. He shook his head. "I'll run some tests. I'm quite sure they'll confirm that that's blood on his jacket and shirt, but I see what you mean. I don't see an obvious en-trance or exit wound or any evidence he was bashed over the head. He spit up a bit and his lips are a little blue, but

I don't see anything else that's visually out of the ordinary. Until I do an autopsy and get the tests back, I can't fully rule out natural causes, but that's not what my gut says." Dr. Smith took a few more pictures from different angles.

"I've been taught to follow the money or the blood," Chief Gerard said. "Jane's got blood on her hands and he's got blood on him. Two plus two in my book equals four."

"That might be too simple an equation. I saw some blood smudges on George's hand, shirt, and the jacket he put around Jane. I feel certain any blood on him was transferred from Jane, but I never take odds on any conclusion before I test and prove it."

"That's a good philosophy, but in this case there's a lot of circumstantial evidence."

Sarah wasn't sure what evidence Chief Gerard was referring to. She hoped it wasn't only from her telling Officer Robinson that Jane had threatened Alan earlier in the evening. Jane might have a sharp tongue and usually picked the wrong way to achieve a goal, but Sarah couldn't picture her as a killer.

As if he had read her mind, he continued espousing his theory to Dr. Smith. "George just isn't the kind to commit murder. He's too good a soul. Always trying to help someone out. It makes sense that any blood on him was transferred from Jane or the victim. If we accept what Sarah told Officer Robinson over the phone—that Alan was lying on the ground with Jane kneeling by his side, but with blood on her hands—well, we know Jane and her temper. And you told me Sarah said Jane threatened Alan earlier in the evening."

"You may be right, but until I finish here at the scene and have an opportunity to fully examine the body, as well as collect evidence from George, Jane, and the rest of this scene, I'm not willing to opine anything."

Chief Gerard cleared his throat. "We'll see."

"You know my philosophy, Chief. Better to be a little cautious than to be wrong. It just feels like there is more going on here than meets the eye."

"We'll play it your way for now." The chief pulled a roll of yellow crime scene tape out of his pocket. Nodding his head toward where Alan lay, he said, "I'll tape off this area, so no one interferes with your examination of the evidence. But first, maybe you should check out those bloodstains on Jane and George, so we can let them out of the big dining room. After I secure this area for you, I'll get the ball underway taking statements. When you see Sam or the host guy arrive, let me know, but have them wait on the patio."

"Okay." Dr. Smith snapped another picture of the shards on the floor. Carefully moving to the side Sarah could see, he removed and bagged the piece of paper Alan clutched. From the floor on Alan's other side, he bagged what looked to Sarah like a cigar and appeared to take samples of whatever was on the floor near Alan's mouth. After a final moment of looking around and taking one more picture, Dr. Smith went into the big dining room as the chief had instructed.

Alone in the entryway, Chief Gerard tore a piece of the tape he needed off the roll with his teeth. He quickly blocked entry to the crime scene from the main stairwell. As he bit off another piece of tape, Sarah heard a woman's voice coming from the small dining room. By the way its pitch was quickly rising, it sounded as though Officer Robinson had roused at least one person in the wrong way.

"I don't care if there is a problem. You have no right rushing us down here without letting us get properly dressed. Your boss is going to hear about this!"

Without finishing what he was doing, Chief Gerard stepped into the greenroom. Happily, he stopped within the part of the room Sarah could see from the front door. "You wanted to tell me something?"

Making sure not to step over the threshold, Sarah leaned forward, craning her neck to ascertain who he was talking to. The woman stepped forward, thrusting her face in his direction while pointing her finger to something or someone to her side. Sarah wasn't surprised to see it was Barbie. Although she couldn't see who or what Barbie was pointing at, Sarah presumed from her words that it was Officer Robinson.

"This officer invaded my privacy. He didn't have the decency to let me get dressed before insisting I come down here."

Having observed Chief Gerard many times in the past, there was no question from the side of his face that Sarah could see that he was stifling a grin as he listened to Barbie's tirade. Sarah was sure it wasn't Barbie's words or even her spider-veined legs showing out from under a tattered floral print bathrobe that prompted his smile. No, she was certain it was the two big pink rollers affixed on either side of her head, topped off by the remainder of her hair being wrapped around a giant, empty soda can.

If the only thing Sarah could think was how Barbie managed to sleep at night, she knew it had to be going through Chief Gerard's mind as well. Because Barbie's full face wasn't turned toward Sarah, she could only imagine the full impact of Barbie without makeup.

Considering everything, Sarah was amazed that Officer Robinson had succeeded in getting Barbie to come downstairs, where she'd be seen au naturel by everyone in the house. Then again, when faced with the polite invitation of a uniformed police officer, who was a former linebacker, declining might not have felt like an option.

"We may have to be in this house as part of our contract with the show, but we didn't agree to be harassed by the police. I'm going to file a complaint!"

"Can it, Barbie." The interrupting voice was Heather's. "This isn't the time for your shenanigans."

Barbie spun around in the direction the voice came from. "You stay out of this, Heather. This discussion is between this policeman and me."

"Chief Gerard," Officer Robinson interjected.

"At the moment," Heather said, "he has far more important things to do than listen to you run your mouth."

"What! Don't you start with me, missy." Barbie took a few steps in Heather's direction, but she stayed just within Sarah's view.

Rose joined Barbie, but her gaze was on the arch leading to the front entryway. Rose's night outfit of soft, silk golden pajamas was as striking against her olive skin as the shawl she had worn earlier in the day. She put her hand to her throat. "There is evil here. I can feel it."

"Oh, don't be so dramatic," Barbie said.

"No, it's suffoca—" Rose's hand fluttered to her side as her eyes rolled back and her body swayed. Sarah held back from crossing the line and offering to help only because Officer Robinson jumped forward and caught Rose before she slipped to the floor. Supporting her with one hand, he stretched his long reach to snag a chair from the table behind him. Gently, holding on to one of her arms, he guided her into the chair. Blinking her eyes, but still unfocused, she slowly came around.

Barbie's mouth gaped open, but she no longer was having a hissy fit. Chief Gerard remained fixed in place, staring at Rose and Officer Robinson. Veronica, having apparently run to the kitchen, handed Officer Robinson a glass of water. He took it and she backed away, out of Sarah's line of vision, in the direction where she thought Heather was standing.

Officer Robinson offered the glass to Rose, but she waved it away. He set it on the table. Although Rose sat slumped against the back of the chair, he was apparently convinced that she no longer needed his support, because he released her arm and took a step backwards.

Pulling herself ramrod straight in her chair, Rose pointed a long finger, tipped with black nail polish, toward the front hall. "There is evil there. The devil will pay."

Barbie turned to see what Rose was pointing at. Her gaze finally rested on Alan's body. She let out a bloodcurdling scream that made Maybelle's earlier one seem like a whisper. Now, it was Chief Gerard's turn to lead a shaken woman, probably to another chair, out of Sarah's view.

Someone must have relieved the chief of his burden as he almost immediately walked back into the part of the room within Sarah's vantage point. He held up his hand. "I'm sorry for the shocking way you just found out about Alan Perrault's passing."

"What happened?" Sarah wasn't sure who the voice asking the question belonged to.

"We're not sure yet. We're investigating the situation, but the reason we brought you down here or have asked you to stay is that Officer Robinson and I are going to need to take a statement from each of you. Not only do we need to know when or how long you've been in the house tonight, but also if you had guests or saw someone here who is not staying on the premises. We need to know what each of you saw or heard and where or when that was. In a situation like this, we realize we are inconveniencing you, but we appreciate any help you can give us."

"Flynn and Sam were here earlier," Heather volunteered.

"We know that. We already called them to come back to talk to them." He looked in the direction of the front hall. Dr. Smith, who was now back in the entryway, shot him a thumbs-up. "Please sit where you are or take seats at one of the other tables. While I finish taping off the other room, Officer Robinson will help you get settled."

There was an undercurrent of comments in the room that Sarah couldn't make out.

"We'll both be taking statements. Once you've given your statement, feel free to go back to your room, but use the back steps, please. Thank you again for your cooperation. We'll get your statements as quickly as we can."

His thanks was met with silence. This time nobody protested having been brought down in their nighttime attire.

CHAPTER 9

As Officer Robinson took care of settling the potential witnesses, Chief Gerard came back into the front room. He pulled the yellow tape out of his pocket, but instead of taping anything, he walked to the open front door. Knowing it wasn't worth trying to retreat, even to the nearby table where Flynn and Sam sat, Sarah braced herself for her imminent confrontation with Chief Gerard.

For a moment, as he filled the doorway with his ample frame, he simply stared at her, thumping the tape in his hand against his other hand. He was so close she could smell his aftershave. Its musky odor wasn't one of her favorite scents. "What are you doing here, Sarah?"

"I'm a Southern Belle chaperone."

"For whom?"

"My mother." Speaking at breakneck speed, Sarah explained how she had been roped into being Maybelle's chaperone because of the silly rules of the competition. She made sure to keep repeating that this time she hadn't found the body on her own.

"Maybe not, but you certainly have a propensity for being at the wrong place at the wrong time."

Sarah waited for him to chastise her further or to give her a warning to stay out of police business, but he didn't. Instead, he leaned around her and called to Sam and Flynn to get their attention. "You two."

"Yes, sir," Flynn responded.

"I want the two of you to go around the building and come in through the back door by the kitchen. I'll meet you there in a minute. Then we'll talk."

Flynn again answered in the affirmative.

Sam quickly rose and did as Chief Gerard bid. Flynn followed. Because he jumped to skip the last few steps, he ended up being in the lead as they walked to the back of the building.

Once they went around the corner of the building and were out of sight, Sarah turned back toward Chief Gerard, who'd resumed taping off the crime scene. "Sarah?"

"Yes." Apparently, he wasn't finished with her after all.

He stopped his taping. "You've got to leave this to the professionals."

"Having the professionals investigate whatever the situation is this time has always been my intention." Sarah frowned. She knew from prior encounters with Chief Gerard that sometimes the professionals needed a little help.

He ignored her frown as, done with her, he finished taping the main dining room's entrance to the crime scene.

Angry at being patronized, she was about to add a more pointed response when a deep voice spoke from behind her. "I understand Jane might need some help."

Sarah whipped around so quickly she turned her foot and stumbled. She'd been so intent watching Chief Gerard that she hadn't heard Harlan come up the stairs.

Her boss grabbed her elbow and steadied her. "Whoa, Sarah. I didn't mean to startle you."

Embarrassed, but solidly back on both feet, Sarah mouthed her thanks as Harlan released her arm and met Chief Gerard's gaze.

"Where is Jane?"

"I don't remember anyone calling you, Harlan. Don't tell me—a little bird told you that someone needs your legal services?"

"Wasn't a little bird."

"No, I guess that wouldn't be the way to describe her, would it?"

They both looked at Sarah. She opened her mouth to make a pointed retort, but thought better of it. Making a snippy comment might feel good now, but it wouldn't do her any good with Chief Gerard in the long run. Instead, she took a deep breath and slowly exhaled it as she waited for the men to spar with each other.

Harlan repeated that he was there to help Jane. The chief didn't immediately acquiesce to Harlan's request. "You two must really be hard up for business, Harlan, if Sarah is calling you on Jane's behalf."

"No, it's that despite her personal feelings, Sarah believes in justice for all."

Sarah listened to their exchange, noting that as it went on the chief's voice sounded more strained while Harlan's tone seemed even smoother. She wondered if this was the end of the bromance they'd been exhibiting since the last time Sarah involved Harlan in a murder case.

Watching Harlan slip back into his calm, concerned, but hard-as-nails lawyer mode after having gently rescued her a moment earlier, Sarah marveled at her boss. After her divorce, when she was having trouble finding a job because her skills were slightly above none, he took a chance, perhaps out of pity, to hire her as the receptionist/secretary for his one-man law firm. With time she'd improved and gained confidence in herself, but she was well aware another employer would have fired her long ago for either incompetence or the hours of work time she'd caused him to lose when her various family members or friends were suspected of murder.

Now, once again, despite the big case he had pending, Harlan had responded immediately when she called. She still could not believe she'd brought him to Jane's Place to help her archenemy and that knowing Jane, he'd come. There was no question: Harlan was either a saint or a fool.

Sarah was going to be neither this time. She'd learned her lesson. No one needed to warn her about leaving it to the professionals. She knew exactly what she was going to do—give her statement and go home to RahRah and Fluffy. Surely, after this tragedy, the network folks would cancel the Southern Belle wedding competition. She felt a little bit sad for her mother, George, and the other contestants and vendors for having their showbiz dreams shattered in much the same way as the vase on the ground. Truthfully, though, she was relieved at the idea of not having to stay in Jane's Place beyond however long it took to give her statement.

This time, she didn't have to worry about who Chief

Gerard accused if he followed his tendency to jump to conclusions. Jane was in good hands with Harlan. Of course, if Jane was arrested and if by accident Sarah stumbled on anything that might be significant, she'd let Harlan track down her lead.

As Chief Gerard relented and took Harlan to Jane, Sarah decided it would be a good idea to stay out of the chief's way and line of vision until either he or Officer Robinson called for her. She opted to join Cliff and her mother at their table on the patio. She'd been so focused on Chief Gerard and what was happening in the house, she hadn't noticed they'd moved from the table near the door to a table at the farthest point of the patio.

Sarah sat hard on one of the metal chairs, not realizing it was minus the cushion that graced it when the restaurant was open. Reeling from the hard impact on her bottom, Sarah asked, "When did you change tables? I was busy watching the various showdowns going on inside Jane's Place and I didn't notice you moved. Was something wrong with the other table?"

Maybelle immediately spoke up. "I couldn't stand Flynn and Sam's cigar smoke."

Sarah glanced at Cliff. He bobbed his head in agreement but didn't interrupt her mother. "Flynn and Sam got here together. I don't know if they already knew Alan was dead or were as surprised as we were to see him lying in the entryway, but Dr. Smith talked to them. He apologized that after coming over so quickly, they were going to have to wait for a few more minutes because the chief was finishing up something else. They made some phone calls and then, when Chief Gerard still hadn't called them, they both lit up cigars. I tell you, they must have been pretty cheap cigars because the stench from them was overpowering. I made Cliff change tables."

Done with that topic, her mother peppered Sarah with questions. "What's going on in there that they're not letting us in? What are they doing with George?"

"From what I saw, nothing yet."

"Then why don't they let him come out here and join us?"

"I think because they put him and Jane in the big dining room. Remember, the only means of going in and out of the building on the main floor is through the front door, the door from the little dining room, or from the kitchen. Because you can't exit the main dining room except by walking into the front hall entryway, George and Jane were stuck in there until Dr. Smith cleared the area for them to walk through. I'm not sure if he's given them the okay to go into the other dining room to give their statements yet."

She hoped her answer was enough to calm her mother down. She didn't think it would be wise to explain that the other reason for a delay was the delicate matter of Dr. Smith needing to get samples of their clothing and from their hands because of the blood observed on them.

"That's ridiculous! I'm going to give Dwayne Gerard a piece of my mind."

Before Sarah or Cliff could stop her, Maybelle was out of her chair and heading for the front door. Sarah started to go after her, but Cliff grabbed her arm. "Let her go. She's super-upset. Even if she can't accomplish anything, she needs to feel like she tried."

Sarah settled herself back in her chair. "When did you get so wise? It seems to me that the Cliff I knew would al-

ready have stormed the castle instead of sitting here cool-
ing his heels."

"I've mellowed. What's happened this past year with
my family and everyone has taught me to be a little more
patient."

"Wow."

He grinned. "Don't be too impressed. I said it has
taught me, but you know I'm a slow learner. Not all lessons stick the first, second, or even the third time around."

"You're not the only one. Oh, look. The lights at Southwind just went off."

For a moment they both stared across the street at the
large white building, now illuminated only in spots by the
few lights left on for security reasons. "I guess Emily will
get to the carriage house before I do."

Cliff furrowed his brow. Keeping his elbow resting on
his chair arm, he held his hand palm up, his fingers aimed
across the street. "What makes you think you'll be going
home tonight?"

"Surely, with Alan's death, they'll close down the set
and cancel filming the competition. No show, no chaperoning."

"Wrong."

"What?"

Cliff gave her a sideways glance as she shook his head
slowly. "You heard your mother mention Sam and Flynn
were burning up the telephone lines while you were
watching Chief Gerard and Dr. Smith?"

As Sarah thought about the implication of what Cliff
was saying, she felt the knot in her stomach that had gone
away at the prospect of being able to go home to RahRah
and Fluffy return. "I wasn't paying attention to them. I
simply assumed that while Chief Gerard was playing the

hurry-up-and-wait game with them, they were notifying whoever their bosses are about what happened and working on creating a shutdown plan."

"Wrong. They were doing damage control to their own benefit."

She crinkled her brow. "What do you mean?"

"Before your mother made us move, I overheard Sam report Alan's death to someone and then stress that Alan, having not been part of the advance team, was barely known by the contestants or vendors. After a pause, where I guess the person on the other end of the line spoke, Sam urged whomever he was talking to to reconsider. There was too much money, time, not to mention shot film, to cancel the Southern Belle project now. Sam reminded the person on the other end of the call that he, that's Sam—"

"I know."

"Okay, anyway, reminded them that he was more than capable of finishing this gig alone, but that he'd already talked to Flynn about handling his hosting duties and providing any needed assistance."

"That's probably true, but it doesn't feel right going forward with the show."

"Maybe not, but there was another pause and then whoever was on the other end must have agreed, because Sam assured the person it would all go smoothly because Sam could assume Alan's responsibilities and still segment direct, while Flynn would host, plus do some segment direction. Hanging up, Sam gave a thumbs-up to Flynn."

"You make a pretty good sleuth."

"Not as good as you."

Sarah jerked her head up at this remark. It was the first time she could think of that Cliff had praised her investigative efforts. When they'd been together, he repeatedly argued that for her own safety, she should leave things to the professionals. Maybe Cliff really had mellowed?

"Anyway," Cliff said, "after he hung up, Sam and Flynn started sharing stories about Alan. Flynn took a leather cigar case from his pocket, they each picked a smoke, and they then lit up in Alan's memory. That's the point at which your mother insisted we move."

"I can't say that I blame her. Alan mentioned having knockoffs made with the network's logo on the band. If they smelled that bad, maybe they were smoking two of the knockoffs."

"It's possible. Cigars don't interest me. Give me a glass of wine, some cheese and crackers, and the ability to watch a sunset over the water from my front porch, and I'm a happy man."

Remembering the many times they'd done just that, Sarah could mentally picture the impressive beauty of such a moment. "Makes two of us."

Cliff concentrated on his hand as he fingered the metal latticework of the table. "You know, Sarah, when we first became friends, I told you to feel free to come out to the bluff anytime you wanted."

Cliff had made that offer soon after they met. He'd just learned that before he bought the property and posted his KEEP OUT and PRIVATE PROPERTY signs, the bluff had been Sarah's favorite place to retreat from the world. She'd first discovered the rock landing that hung out over the water's edge while exploring the wooded lake area as a teenager.

With an owner in absentia, no one had ever stopped her from exploring the overgrown property on foot or by bicycle. From the moment she'd found the unobstructed view of the water, it had become her special spot. Over the years, she often went to the bluff to sit and stare at the water until things in her life either felt trivial or okay again. Once the signs went up, she never trespassed—even though there were times she yearned to make a trip to her bluff. That's why, after she found out Cliff was the property's new owner, it was one of the reasons she'd been delighted when he invited her to spend time there with or without him.

He looked up from the table, his hand now still. His gaze met hers. "Sarah, my offer still stands. Whether from the porch, the dockside outdoor living space, or merely from the bluff, you don't have to see me to enjoy my property."

She hesitated, stifling the urge to put her hand over his. "Thank you. I've missed the bluff."

Sarah felt the awkwardness of the moment but didn't know what to say. Her usual go-to in a situation like this would be to introduce levity by making a funny face or telling a joke, but she instinctively knew this wasn't the time for that. Why? She wasn't sure.

Cliff was the first to break their silence. "Sarah."

"Yes, Cliff."

"I know, besides sitting on the bluff, you loved getting out on the water." He turned his head away from her and then looked down at his hands on the metal table. "I'm going to put the boats up soon and I was wondering—just as a friend, of course—if you'd like to take one more spin this season?"

Her answer popped out of her mouth before she thought with her brain. "That would be lovely."

"How about Tuesday evening? We could time it to watch the sunset."

Sarah shook her head. "I'm sorry." Seeing the lines of Cliff's face tighten, she hurried to explain. "I can't because of my chaperone duties. You know how they're doing these charitable competitions? The one planned for Tuesday is floral arranging. Originally, I thought the female contestants were going to tape the floral arranging competition, but it turns out that to make it more interesting and add the element of vying chaperones, we're required to be there too. Because not all the chaperones are available until evening, they opted to tape the segment after store hours. I hope you'll give me a rain check."

From the way his shoulders and the lines around his mouth relaxed, Cliff didn't even have to say, "Of course," for her to know his answer was a "yes." Officer Robinson summoned Cliff to give his statement, cutting off their discussion before they could come up with a rain check time. It was just as well. When it came to the bluff and Cliff's water toys, a last-minute decision suited her better than deciding anything in advance.

CHAPTER 10

With Cliff inside giving his statement to Officer Robinson, her mother who knows where, and Chief Gerard still interviewing Sam and Flynn, Sarah wondered how long she'd have to wait for her turn to come up. It felt strange to be the only one left on the patio. She pulled out her phone and scrolled through her messages. Most were advertisements or spam.

"Is anyone sitting here?"

Sarah jerked her head up. Flynn stood next to the chair Cliff had recently vacated. She made a pretense of checking out the other patio tables. "I do believe it's one of the few remaining available seats. Would you like to join me?"

"If you don't mind."

"Please."

"Thank you." Flynn settled himself gingerly into the ironworks chair. "I made the mistake earlier of plopping into one of these chairs. Luckily, no one will see my bruised hip on camera tomorrow."

"Makes two of us. Of course, in my case, it's another part of my anatomy that I'm hoping no one sees." Sarah winked, wondering where that came from. As Flynn smiled, Sarah continued: "When Jane's Place is open, she has cushions on the chairs. I didn't even think to check if one was here before I sat."

"Ouch. Big mistake."

"Definitely." Sarah could understand why he was on TV. He was charming. Easy to talk to. "I thought you were in the house giving your statement to Chief Gerard."

"I was, but he finished with me fairly quickly. I guess the chief didn't think I had much to add after I told him I didn't see Alan again after he left our dinner at Southwind. Chief Gerard has Sam in the hot seat now. Because we rode together from the hotel, I need to wait for him."

"Do you think he'll be long?"

"Longer than me. After dinner, Sam ran back by here to check out something on the set with Alan, but Sam swears Alan was alive when he left him. Are you waiting for someone too?"

So, they hadn't been together for the entire time. "No. I'm in the somewhere-down-the-line-to-give-my-statement holding pattern. I know we've met in passing, but I don't think we've been formally introduced. I'm Sarah Blair, Maybelle's daughter and chaperone."

"Flynn Quinn."

Even in general conversation, Flynn's voice was rich and full. "You have a beautiful voice," Sarah said, pleasantly surprised by her own forwardness. At least she hadn't complimented him on his rugged handsomeness. She could understand how the contrast of his cobalt-blue eyes, auburn hair, and sensuous lips, plus the sound of his voice, attracted women viewers even if he talked gibberish. Sarah forced her hand into her lap. "I bet you get told that all the time in your line of work."

"Often," he admitted. "And I'm sure, no matter what your line of work is, you've been told a million times that you have beautiful eyes."

"Thank you." Sarah decided that rather than continue the mutual admiration society they were quickly falling into—though she was enjoying herself—it might benefit Harlan if she had a better understanding of what Flynn and the other production team members did, just in case Jane did become the prime suspect. "I know you're listed as being the Southern Belle's host, but what does that mean?"

"Normally, my job is to introduce everyone and everything in the show."

"Normally?"

"Sadly, the circumstances of this shoot have changed my responsibilities."

Although he cast his eyes down in the way one should when a death was the root of the changes, she could feel his excitement. It was obvious Flynn was barely able to hold back talking about it. Playing dumb was probably going to get him to reveal more information than direct questions would.

"Now that Alan is, well..." Sarah hesitated, deliberately letting her tongue roll over the words. "You know, gone, I guess you'll have to discontinue shooting."

His gaze flicked upward as he barely shook his head. "Oh, no."

"No?"

"The network agrees that the show must go on. Sort of as a tribute to Alan."

Sarah wrinkled her brow. "But how? As the director, wasn't he"—she searched for a metaphor—"the engine or the captain of this ship? Won't it sink without him?"

He took a deep breath and used the latticework of the iron table for illustration. Pointing to one of the diamond-shaped holes, he explained that Alan was the designated director for this project. He touched the diamond to the right, but one level down. "This one is Sam, the segment producer. Unfortunately, because this was a quick shoot, we don't have anyone in the subordinate slot—the associate producer—who could step in to handle Sam's duties if Sam has to step up to do other ones."

"Like Alan's?"

"Right." Flynn moved his hand to a slot about six places over, but parallel to the missing associate producer. "All the slots in this area are camera people or directors of photography. We have several on this shoot, plus a data management person who takes the memory cards from the cameras, organizes them, and backs up the digital footage." He waved his hand generally over the same area of the table. "There also is an audio engineer, a compliance person, and some other miscellaneous folks."

"Where do you fit in?"

Flynn drew a line going directly below Alan's, but into a diamond that fell to the left and below where Sam's was. "That's me, the on-camera host slot. I answer to Alan and Sam. Usually, I'm just the on-camera presence. With Alan's tragic death, Sam is formally assuming most of his duties as well as those he presently has, with me helping out."

"With the network flying in every crew member except the construction work that Cliff is doing, why didn't they simply fly in another director?"

Flynn sat up straight and puffed his chest out. "At one time, Alan was a wunderkind, but during the last few years, since I came on the team, he had evolved into more of a figurehead for the various projects the network sends us out to shoot. Last year, when we did a perfect wedding segment set on the West Coast, Sam did the scouting, location choosing, and other hands-on tasks, and I did the miscellaneous pretaping things like making room assignments, ordering novelty gifts, and picking meal menus. Now, I'll assume more of Sam's day-to-day responsibilities while he officially does Alan's."

"Sounds like a lot of work."

"It is, but without knowing it, the network is simply formalizing the way our team has operated on our last few shoots."

"Sounds like you've figured out a good teamwork approach. But why do you want to do behind-the-scenes work? Surely a talented guy like you enjoys being in front of the camera."

"I do, but there are only a limited number of host jobs and a limited time one can be an on-the-air presence."

Sarah thought his last reference applied more to women than men. It seemed to her that men grayed and stayed on the air forever, but wrinkles or signs of age often meant a female anchor was shifted over to doing feature stories if her on-air career continued.

"I've been fortunate. A small network affiliate gave me a news anchor position and then the big network brought me in to host segments a few years ago. But I see the handwriting on the wall for my career as a host. When they began a third hour of the morning show, the network promoted the weekend anchor, which meant they needed to replace him. The suits passed me over for both jobs, although I've been a contributing segment host for during the week and on weekends. I'm no fool. I either need to prove myself behind the camera or be satisfied with where I am."

"From what I understand Sam and Alan were good people to learn from."

"The best. Losing Alan is horrible. He may have slacked off some in doing things, but he had an eye for making sure everything we did was right. Sam and I were afraid the suits would cancel this shoot, but Sam brought them around because we already had two contestant and almost all the vendor segments in the can. If we pull this off, we both stand to be fair-haired for a while."

"What happens if it doesn't work?"

"For me, nothing. I can continue hosting and building my behind-the-scenes skills. It's Sam who will have a problem. The network is putting its money on him to come through for them. If he fails, it will make it more difficult for him to move up to Alan's level and maybe raise questions about his abilities in general."

Officer Robinson was signaling Sarah from the bottom of the patio stairwell. She acknowledged him with a wave. Flynn turned in his chair to see who was there.

"My turn," Sarah said. "Best of luck to Sam and you. You've got a crew of bridezillas and mamazillas to train."

CHAPTER 11

Sarah still couldn't believe it. She wasn't going to get to go home even for the remainder of the night! As almost the last person to have her statement taken, she'd finally been released to go to her room. Reluctantly, she trudged up the main steps to the third floor.

During the almost three hours it took Chief Gerard and Officer Robinson to take everyone's statements, Alan's body was removed, the broken vase swept up, and the tape taken down. Things looked normal. In fact, it seemed as if the clock had been turned back to before Alan's death.

But it hadn't. It was now almost two a.m. and at least five hours since Alan died. Counting each step, Sarah thought about how she would much rather be counting the steps between Jane's Place and the carriage house. Even if she would have to wake them, cuddling RahRah and Fluffy would be a lot more comforting than spending the night alone in her assigned room.

She locked the door behind her and, as she had done earlier in the day, absorbed the room's sterile environment. A bed covered with a plain yellow comforter and a white throw at its end was the main focal point. Because the room was tiny, there was only one nightstand, a modern piece on which one could hang or rest clothing, a chair, and a desk. The pièce de résistance was a television, almost as wide as the bed, hanging on the wall with the door to the bathroom that connected her room to her mother's.

Her suitcase sat next to the bed, waiting to be unpacked. Sarah debated whether to unpack now or tomorrow. If she waited until tomorrow, she could always hang the outfit she was going to wear in the bathroom while she showered in the morning. It would get enough of the wrinkles out to start the day. Even if her outfit wasn't perfect, she'd be running home to check on RahRah and Fluffy for lunch and could change then.

Brushing the papers she'd left on the bed to the side, she lay on it fully clothed. Sarah knew she needed to sleep, or she'd be off her game at work, but she was too keyed up. Giving in to her pent-up energy, Sarah tried focusing on what had transpired since the competition began, but her mind kept returning to Jane.

Considering all the trouble and heartache Jane had caused Sarah in the past few years—from breaking up her marriage, trying to keep Emily and Marcus from succeeding, and doing everything in her power to get control of RahRah and the carriage house—something had made Sarah call Harlan on Jane's behalf. But what? It wasn't pure kindness, because if the truth was known,

there were many times Sarah had entertained more than un-
kind thoughts about Jane. It obviously wasn't because
they were friends or even frenemies. Putting it bluntly,
Jane often was like a stone around Sarah's neck. No, it
was because things didn't add up.

The vase was broken, but there hadn't been a hair out
of place on Alan's head. He obviously hadn't been hit
over the head and killed with the vase. Sarah had promised the chief she'd leave the investigation to him, but she
couldn't turn her mind off. Maybe if she tried to make
sense of things, she could get a few hours of sleep before
work. Knowing she did better with pen and paper, Sarah
sat up and grabbed a pen from her purse and the call sheet
lying on her bed. Turning it over, she started making a
list.

1. Alan's hair wasn't mussed. He couldn't have
   been hit over the head with the vase. How had it
   shattered?

One thing that might be important in determining how
it shattered was whether the shards were under him, which
might indicate the vase broke before he fell, or around
him. If Jane were accused, this could be important in
matching her alibi to the timeline of the events. Harlan,
if he needed to, could probably establish this through Dr.
Smith's pictures.

2. There was vomit or froth next to Alan's face.

Something had caught Dr. Smith and Chief Gerard's
attention on the far side of Alan's face that was enough to
make Dr. Smith sample whatever it was. The position of

Alan's head had blocked her view of what they saw. Again, the answer of what it was and how much should be visible in Dr. Smith's pictures.

3. Jane's hands were covered with blood and there was blood on Alan, but Dr. Smith hadn't observed an entrance or exit wound on his first examination of the body. Was it Alan or Jane's blood? Where had it come from?

No entrance or exit wound sounded like Dr. Smith had ruled out a gunshot or knife wound. She thought about other things that might cause bleeding that had been in the different novels she'd read or TV shows she'd watched. If there had been a wound from a knitting needle or an arrow, Dr. Smith would have spotted it. The amount of blood visible on Alan might also have made Dr. Smith think that, in the same way Jane transferred blood to George and his jacket, she'd done the same to Alan.

Possibly, when, as Jane alleged, she'd bent to check Alan, she had put her hand down and been cut but hadn't realized it when she touched him? There definitely were a lot of sharp shards on the floor and, if Jane was focused on Alan, she might have not even been aware of touching one.

Even without seeing Dr. Smith's report or notes, in her heart of hearts Sarah had instinctively understood the existence of the small traces of blood on Alan were because Jane accidentally cut herself. Much as she hated—was that too strong a word?—Jane, Sarah could no more let her be railroaded by one of Chief Gerard's quick conclusions than she could her sister, mother, or a friend.

Putting her pen back to the paper, Sarah dashed down

key words and thoughts as she brainstormed for a few minutes. Finished, she examined her scribblings. Three questions jumped out at her: A) If there was no wound, could Alan have been poisoned? B) Could Alan have had a convulsion or attack, causing him to knock over the vase himself? And C) Looking at her scribblings on the back of the call sheet, was the paper in Alan's hand a call sheet and what were the scribblings on the back of it?

Subconsciously, when she found Jane and called the police, she must have considered these questions and realized they might never be addressed or answered by Chief Gerard unless prompted by others. Dr. Smith, by his hesitancy to confirm Chief Gerard's hypothesis, probably also realized Alan might have been poisoned or that Alan might have knocked the vase over himself, but Chief Gerard was his boss. If the evidence went in a direction that Chief Gerard thought was wrong, how much power would Dr. Smith have to push it? Sarah feared it wasn't enough.

That's why she'd called Harlan to help Jane. That was also why, despite her wanting to leave this case entirely to the professionals, if she noticed anything, she'd still try to help Jane. No matter her personal feelings, she didn't believe Jane was capable of murder.

Certain she was right and feeling relieved, Sarah sat up. She decided to unpack and let the wrinkles in her clothes hang out overnight rather than trying to steam them when she took her morning shower. For tonight, at least, once she got into her pajamas, nothing would disturb her catching up on her sleep. She was sure she could turn off her mind now. And with Emily taking care of RahRah and Fluffy in the morning, Sarah could sleep until the very last minute before she had to be at work.

Like her mother, she wasn't going to be one of those early birds who took advantage of the breakfast buffet. No, this was one morning she'd grab an extra hour of sleep rather than, as usual, try to be at the office at eight to give herself an hour to ease into the business day with a cup of coffee.

Clothing unpacked, pajamas on, teeth brushed, Sarah crawled into bed and shut her eyes. Sleep came almost instantly, but it wasn't restful. She dreamed she was in the middle of a sign shop wanting to buy STOP, NO SMOKING, OPEN, and BACK IN A MINUTE signs. The problem was that she didn't have enough money for more than one.

Frustrated, she was weighing where it was most important to put a sign. Her choices were the corner of Main Street closest to Southwind, the greenroom at Jane's Place, on the door of the Southwind Pub, or wrapped as a gift for the veterinarian clinic. In her dream, Sarah couldn't prioritize one sign over another, so she was reaching out to her favorite sounding board. Sarah had just punched in Emily's cell phone number to run her dilemma by her twin when the sound of a giant boom woke her.

For a moment, Sarah wasn't sure if the sound was part of her dream. She waited to hear if there would be another explosive noise. None came. She was about to write it off as part of her bad dream when her mother came through their shared bathroom, shouting to find out if Sarah was all right.

Trying to fully get her bearings as her mother opened the door into Sarah's room, Sarah sat up and grabbed her cell phone. It was only five o'clock. "Did you hear that boom?" her mother asked. "It sounded like a gunshot. Where do you think it came from?"

"I don't know." Sarah debated her options: leave the safety of her room to find out what was going on or burrow down under her blanket. Her decision was made for her by her mother.

"Well, I'm going to find out."

"Not by yourself, you're not."

Maybelle headed toward the door of Sarah's room. "Maybelle, wait. I need to call the police."

"Call them, but I'm not waiting. Someone could be hurt."

Reluctantly, Sarah grabbed her cell phone and followed her mother out the door without making the call.

CHAPTER 12

Using the back staircase, Maybelle and Sarah eased their way downstairs, deliberately trying not to make any noise lest it was a gunshot and the shooter decided to fire at them. As they neared the kitchen, Sarah heard voices. She and her mother were obviously not the first ones who'd come running in reaction to the noise. Comfortable that it was safe to enter the kitchen, they moved more quickly.

The sight that greeted them was bizarre. The kitchen counters, floor, and Chef Bernardi—who was cowering behind the island, clutching a large wooden spoon—were covered in flour. From the bowl and other ingredients on the island, it appeared he had been in the process of preparing to bake something. Granny stood across the room from him, the shotgun in her hand still raised in his direction. Apparently, having used the main stairwell, Rose and Natalie, from a point of safety just outside the kitchen, were yelling, "Put down the gun."

As Sarah tried to take in the entire scene, Lucy rushed into the kitchen from the greenroom entrance and went to her grandmother's side. "Granny, I'm here."

Lucy rested her hand on the gun's barrel, leading Granny to lower it. Gently, she eased the shotgun from Granny's hand. "Granny, what did you do?"

Granny put a hand to her ear. "What did you say?"

Rising from behind the island, Chef Bernardi didn't even make a pretext of trying to wipe the flour off. Instead, he pointed the spoon first at Granny and then at the wall behind where he must have been standing when the gun went off. The kitchen's otherwise smooth Sheetrock was peppered with small indentations. "She tried to kill me. That's what she did."

"What? Granny . . ."

"I was thirsty. I came downstairs to get a drink."

Chef Bernardi, again using his spoon, pointed at the shotgun Lucy now held. "With a shotgun? What kind of an idiot is she? She could have killed me."

Lucy met his gaze, her eyes flashing. "She's not an idiot. Considering what happened last night, all of us, including Granny, have reason to be edgy." As she held the gun up so everyone now crowded in the kitchen could see it, Sarah heard the front door's opening chime and Natalie's voice, but her attention was on what Lucy was saying.

"There's no way Granny could have killed anyone with this gun. It's loaded with birdshot."

"Birdshot?" Officer Robinson repeated as he came

into the kitchen, returning his own gun to its holster. He glanced toward Sarah as he carefully took the shotgun from Lucy. "We got some 911 calls that there had been a shooting."

Officer Robinson turned to Sarah. "Why don't you tell me what's going on?"

"I'm not quite sure. Mother and I were awoken by a loud boom. By the time we came downstairs to investigate, everyone else who's here in the kitchen or the entryway was already here. My impression is that for some reason Granny shot her gun in Chef Bernardi's direction, but that other than a bag of flour exploding and the wall being hit with pellets, there isn't any damage."

With the hand not holding the shotgun, Officer Robinson rubbed the back of his neck. "Remember what we did earlier with taking your statements? We're going to have to do it again, folks."

"Why?" Natalie said. "Most of us didn't see anything. Having heard the boom, my aunt and I came downstairs to see what it was, but we were after the fact. When we saw Granny holding the gun, we called 911. Other than the fact that the others didn't call for help, our statements are going to be identical."

"Actually," Starr said from the front hall, "I called 911 too. I recognized the sound of the gun."

Natalie acknowledged Starr's comment and made it part of her argument. "That proves my point. We all reacted to hearing the gun blast but didn't see it happen."

Squaring his broad shoulders, Officer Robinson asked, "Who, other than Chef Bernardi, was here when the gun was fired?"

No hands went up, confirming what Natalie said.

Officer Robinson pulled a notebook and pen out of his pocket. He tore a page out of the notebook. "Okay, tell you what we're going to do. Rather than keep you from going back to bed or getting dressed, I'm going to give Sarah this piece of paper and pen to make a list of your names for me. Don't leave until you check in with her. If I feel I need to talk to you, I'll be in touch."

"But—" Chef Bernardi interrupted.

Raising one of his giant linebacker hands, Officer Robinson hushed him. "Chef Bernardi and Granny, you two, I want to talk with now. Everyone else in the kitchen can go once you've given your name to Sarah."

Lucy, who was holding Granny close to her, spoke up. "May I stay? From all the years of shooting birds, rabbits, and other things for us to eat without ear protection, Granny doesn't hear well. I'm sure having been near the gun when it went off, she'll have even more trouble hearing you right now."

Officer Robinson nodded his acquiescence, and Lucy led Granny to a stool near the flour-covered island.

A small line formed in front of Sarah. As quickly as Sarah took down each name, the person giving it to her left the kitchen. Sarah looked at the last person and frowned with her eyes. "Mom, I know who you are."

"Maybelle."

"Not at five a.m., you're not." Maybelle went upstairs as Sarah dutifully added her mother's name to the list. Finished, Sarah carried her piece of paper over to where Officer Robinson stood viewing the kitchen. "They sure made a mess, didn't they," he said.

"Yes. Here's the list."

He didn't immediately take it from her, but instead glanced at the big clock on the kitchen's wall. "I know you probably want to get a little sleep before work, but I'd like you to stay too, please."

"Of course." She handed him the list. Thanking her, he put it in his pocket. He walked across the kitchen to where Chef Bernardi, having thrown out all the ingredients he'd had at his workstation, was frantically scrubbing the counter area where he'd been working before Granny's potshot.

Trying to decide the best place from which to observe, Sarah finally settled on a seat at a small prep table in the corner of the kitchen. It let her be out of the way but still see everyone's faces.

Despite Officer Robinson's presence, Chef Bernardi continued preparing his workstation.

"Chef Bernardi, I know this was very traumatic for you. Would you like to take a break while we talk?"

"I can't. I have to get the breakfast buffet ready."

"At this hour?"

"It takes time to make everything from scratch. When Jane got back from the station, she woke me up to tell me that, because of cutting her hand, she wouldn't be able to make breakfast this morning. The entire breakfast buffet is on my shoulders. Do you know how much time it takes to make enough biscuits from scratch for the crowd we're feeding?" He continued wiping the island's counter.

"I don't, but I'm sure everyone will understand if there isn't a buffet this morning."

Chef Bernardi stopped for a moment, his rag poised midair. "No, they won't. But I must clean everything before I start over." He reached in front of Officer Robinson to scour the final portion of the counter.

Officer Robinson put his hand on the counter, blocking Chef Bernardi from resuming his circular cleaning motions. "I need you to stop so I can get your statement. Now."

"Look, I was making biscuits when that woman shot at me. Our contract calls for the buffet to be ready to go early. I'm way behind. If I don't keep working while we talk, I may not finish before the cast and crew arrive."

"I thought the food and lodging contract was between Jane's Place or Jane and the network."

Chef Bernardi put the rag aside and turned the oven on to preheat it. He took a large bowl out of one of the cabinets and placed it in the center of the island. As he talked, he gathered various ingredients and brought them to his workstation. Once he had everything lined up, he put flour, baking powder, sugar, and salt into the large bowl, but Sarah couldn't tell how much of each he used.

Chef Bernardi worked, seemingly oblivious to Officer Robinson. Officer Robinson turned toward her, making an "I can't believe this" face. Sarah stifled a giggle. From having observed Emily in the kitchen and making biscuits, she recognized that Chef Bernardi's concentration was so intense that he'd zoned out of anything around him. Because of Emily, she knew his next step was cutting butter into the mixture. She was impressed by the fluidity of his movements and his sudden resumption of talking to Officer Robinson as if no time had passed.

"No, the contract isn't just between them this time. Because I'd known Alan for years, he called seeking some guidance on whether there were enough decent establishments in Wheaton to hold the Southern Belle contest. After I told him about Jane's Place, the Southwind restaurants, and Little Italy, he asked if I would like to be a paid consultant working with Sam and the rest of the advance team on the different aspects of the show. Because I was working here, I was glad to steer them to Jane's Place. For the last few months, Jane's kept this place going out of her own pocket. There's no way she can do that forever." Chef Bernardi rolled out the dough and picked up a small biscuit cutter.

"Why do you think Granny shot at you?"

"I honestly don't know. I got up early and was getting everything ready to make the biscuits and other things I'll be serving. She must have come in while I was in the walk-in refrigerator because she was standing near the sink, holding that shotgun, when I came out. My arms were full of ingredients. I acknowledged her as I dropped everything onto the island. The next thing I knew, she whipped around, and I was staring into her gun. I put my hands out toward her, trying to wave off her insanity."

"My grandmother is not insane!" Lucy rose from where she'd been sitting by Granny, but stopped when Officer Robinson waved her off. For a second, she peered down at Granny, who was looking up at her with a quizzical expression, then sat down again. Gently, she rubbed Granny's back.

"Insanity?" Officer Robinson said.

"Her eyes were blank. Emotionless. It was almost like she was looking right through me. Time slowed. Instead of stopping, she pulled the trigger."

"But she didn't hit you?"

"No. I don't know if I realized she was going to pull the trigger or if it was the expression on her face, but I hit the deck."

"You fell behind the island?"

"Yes. I was afraid that she would fire her shotgun at me again."

"Did she?"

"No. Everything was silent. I eventually peered around the side of the island. She was simply standing there, the gun pointed in my direction. She didn't make a sound before the others who heard the shot came running in. Either just before or when her granddaughter took the gun away from her, she said something about having come downstairs for a drink of water."

Chef Bernardi buttered the bottom of a pan, positioned the cut biscuits, and placed the pan in the oven. He stood and pulled at his earlobe. "She was so close to me that my ears are still ringing from when the gun went off."

He waved his hands around the kitchen. "Officer Robinson, if I'm not going to make a mistake, I've got to pay full attention to what I'm doing. I think from that point on you already know what happened. Look, I'm okay. Jane can fix the wall, but this old lady is crazy."

Sarah glanced over at Lucy, still rubbing Granny's back. She had to agree with Lucy: Granny wasn't crazy. From her observation of Granny earlier, there was no question she was hard of hearing and therefore prone to making some mistakes.

Although Chef Bernardi was almost finished with his biscuits, he wasn't finished sharing his impression of Granny. "She's a menace. You need to do something about her."

Sarah shook her head in Officer Robinson's direction. She was sure, hearing issues aside, Granny had all her marbles.

"Officer Robinson, right now, I need to get breakfast

ready." Chef Bernardi put his batter bowl in the sink. Almost as an afterthought, he looked up and addressed Officer Robinson again. "If you want to talk later in the day, we can."

"Thank you." Officer Robinson slipped his notebook back into his pocket.

CHAPTER 13

Back in her room, Sarah hurried to get dressed. It was a good thing she'd ended up unpacking and giving her clothing time to hang out. Being pressed for time, she decided to skip taking a shower and washing her hair. As Sarah rushed to put on a touch of makeup—eye shadow and lipstick—her mother opened the door from the other side of the bathroom.

"You didn't come back upstairs right away. Why?"

"Officer Robinson wanted me to listen when he informally questioned Chef Bernardi and Granny."

"For that he didn't let you go back to bed?"

"Not exactly. After he finished interviewing them in the kitchen, he took me back into the greenroom to get my impression of whether either one of them was lying or seemed to have left anything important out."

"And?"

"I thought both were telling the truth about everything that I was aware happened."

"Good." Maybelle put the back of the toilet seat down and sat on the throne. She leaned forward, resting her arm on the edge of the bathroom vanity. "Tell me, why did Granny shoot at Chef Bernardi?"

"The best anyone can tell, it was an accident. Granny hadn't slept well and was feeling skittish. Just before the sun came up, she decided to go downstairs and get a drink of water."

"With a gun?"

"With a shotgun filled with birdshot. Being older and living alone, she keeps it with her at all times in case she needs to defend herself."

"But we're not in the backwoods here. We're in Wheaton, Alabama. People don't go around carrying guns. Besides, one of the rules of the show that Alan reminded us of yesterday was that guns were prohibited."

"That's true. Lucy told Officer Robinson that their agreement with Granny, after they learned of the rule, was that Jed and she let Granny keep her shotgun in her room so she'd feel safe at night, as long as Granny promised the gun would stay in her closet during the competition. She reluctantly agreed, but Alan's death changed things for her. Granny was afraid to wander around alone without her gun when other people weren't awake yet."

"I can understand that reaction, but that still doesn't explain why she shot at Chef Bernardi. He's someone she knows."

"It was a horrible mistake. Lucy explained that from all the shooting Granny's done in the past, without ear protection, she's had a significant hearing loss that can't be compensated for with hearing aids. Because Chef

Bernardi was in the walk-in refrigerator, she didn't see him when she came downstairs to get her drink."

"Oh, no." Maybelle rested her hand on her cheek.

"Yup. Best we can figure, because Granny had her back toward the walk-in and the sink water was running, she didn't hear Chef Bernardi until he dropped a bunch of ingredients on the bar with a bang. Startled, she swung around, raised her gun, and fired."

"She could have killed him. He's lucky he wasn't injured."

"It was buckshot. Officer Robinson didn't think, even if he was shot, she'd have been able to kill him. He commended Chef Bernardi on his reflex reaction. Most people wouldn't have been able to drop to the ground in time to avoid being shot."

"What's going to happen now?"

"I'm not sure. Sam and Flynn came into the building and were headed toward the kitchen when I came upstairs. Guns were one of the things that Alan and Sam stressed were grounds for an automatic elimination. The question is, because it was Granny who had the gun, if they will disqualify Jed and Lucy or let them stay with a new chaperone. It's not like they caught Granny drinking moonshine—this was a gun. Everything about the situation, with Alan's death, makes what they and the suits above them do a big *if*."

"If? You didn't stay to find out if Lucy and Jed were going to be disqualified?"

"Mo—Maybelle, I couldn't. By the time Officer Robinson finished talking to Chef Bernardi, Granny, and Lucy, I had to get up here and get ready for work."

"You could have been late one day."

Sarah put her last dab of lipstick on and gave her mother

a quick peck. "Remember, we agreed chaperoning wasn't going to interfere with my day job."

Maybelle followed Sarah into Sarah's bedroom. She plopped down on Sarah's unmade bed. "How can you leave without knowing?"

"Because it doesn't really matter. This is a game that, not counting today, will be over in four more days. My job, which I will remind you that I need, hopefully will still be there after this week." She grabbed her purse from her bed. "Besides, with Harlan being tied up with Jane last night instead of being able to work on his case, I'm sure he'll be on overdrive today as he makes up for the time he lost. Considering I'm the one who called him, I want to be there to make sure that whatever he needs me to do, I'm available."

Pouting, Maybelle crossed her legs and rearranged her robe. "Well, I would have stayed, but I understand your reasoning about Harlan."

Giving a little, Sarah decided to soften the moment for her mother. "I'll be at the office all day, except for when I go home during lunch to take care of RahRah and Fluffy. Let me know if you hear anything juicy. I saw from the call sheet, which you'll be happy to know I read this time, that you've got a full day. You're not only filming the invitation reveal segment and personal interviews, but you've got a big event at the Mudbowl with the Wildcat motorcycle group. The notation next to it said the event will benefit the Wheaton Food Bank."

"Yes, they've got us hopping today so we can have enough, as they say, 'in the can.' The personal interviews won't be long, but they'll take time to shoot."

"I don't remember seeing a mention of personal interviews on the call sheet."

"They weren't on there. Apparently, yesterday they taped quick pieces with Marcus, Emily, and Jane, and someone realized they were a great way for the viewers to build some empathy with us. Because they had the time this morning, someone decided everyone should film a thirty-second to one-minute interview. Not only can they use them for promos or intersperse the bits with our longer segments, but edited correctly they could make them into exit pieces."

"A final way to connect with the audience."

"That's right. If anything gets announced, I'll let you know." She held her face up toward Sarah. "Love you."

Sarah bent toward her mother. "Love you too." She gave her mother's uplifted face another quick kiss before rushing off to work.

CHAPTER 14

At the office, Sarah found two surprises waiting for her. The pleasant one was the smell of a pot of coffee being brewed. The unpleasant one was that Jane, with a bandaged hand, was in the break room, waiting for the coffee she'd made to finish gurgling through the machine.

Sarah steeled herself for what might transpire next. She was glad Harlan had been able to keep Jane from being railroaded, but seeing her at the office first thing this morning made the pity she'd felt for Jane last night dissipate, only to be replaced by their usual nemesis dance.

Knowing she needed to temper her feelings before she said or did something she'd regret or that would trigger a negative response from Jane, Sarah bypassed the break room and her coffee. Instead, she went straight to her desk in the front room. She hoped its location, behind a low wall barricade that separated her workspace from the rest of the waiting room, might shield her from Jane. Sarah hung her jacket, put her purse in her bottom desk drawer, and powered on her computer.

Glancing at her in-box, she was amazed it was empty. Usually, first thing in the morning, it was full of things her night owl boss had drafted. Harlan was a brilliant lawyer, an excellent employer, and a good human being, as evidenced by his volunteer work at the animal shelter and helping people quietly in the community, but he couldn't type to save his soul. He counted on Sarah for her quick turnarounds of the letters and briefs he dictated or wrote in longhand on page after page from yellow legal pads.

Jane being in the break room making coffee, Sarah's empty in-box, and Chef Bernardi having mentioned Jane woke him up to say she couldn't make breakfast, meant they'd probably gone home for a few hours of sleep and only returned to the office in the last hour. Obviously, Harlan hadn't had a moment to work on his big case or any of the little matters that needed addressing.

Resigned and desperately needing her caffeine fix, Sarah swallowed. It was time to be a mature adult and face Jane in the break room.

Her goal of ducking in, retrieving a cup of coffee, and returning to her desk was aborted when Harlan stuck his head out of his private office and, using a hand gesture, beckoned her into his office. She started to reply, but he put his forefinger up to his lips. Confused, she obeyed and hurried into his office.

He quickly closed his office door behind her.

"You're being awfully mysterious this morning," she teased.

He didn't laugh. "Sarah, I need some information, which may put you in an uncomfortable position to answer. Asking you this isn't how I usually operate."

This wasn't typical of Harlan. Always a straight shooter and aboveboard, it almost felt like he was asking her to be complicit in something sinister. "What is it? I gathered Jane being in our break room means the blood on her hands was her own. Didn't that resolve everything and get her off the hook with Chief Gerard?"

"Only for the time being. And it might not only be Jane who could be in trouble, but she's still Chief Gerard's number-one suspect."

Without elaborating, he walked to the conversation area in his office and sat in his preferred big winged brown leather chair. He picked up a yellow legal pad and pen from the coffee table. Harlan not saying anything or gesturing as an invitation for her to take the identical chair opposite him demonstrated exactly how distracted he was.

"What is it, Harlan? What do you need to ask me?"

"Do you know who at Southwind would have made the vegetarian plate Alan ate?"

"I'm sorry. I didn't go into the kitchen last night, so I can't be sure. Grace was helping. If Emily, Marcus, and Grace divided tasks the way they usually do, Marcus would have been the one handling the vegetable, sides, salad and sauce stations, Grace the meat, and Emily everything else, plus expediting. Why?"

Sarah barely got the words out. She'd thought about it in passing last night, but she'd been too tired to put two and two together—that if Alan had been poisoned, the police would suspect his dinner at Southwind might be the source. Sarah's throat tightened up at a flash of déjà vu, back to when Emily was accused of poisoning Sarah's ex-husband with a taste of her rhubarb crisp. "Do they suspect Alan was poisoned?"

Harlan nodded. "Dr. Smith, who you know is as conservative as they come before he'll render a judgment, seems to think that's the case. The little bit of vomit, a bluish tint to Alan's lips, and the fact that the vase was broken but Alan wasn't struck over the head, makes Dr. Smith think Alan was the one who bumped into the stand, causing the vase to fall and shatter. He won't be sure about that theory until he does an autopsy and gets the toxicology reports back."

"But someone else could have bumped into the stand."

"Possibly, but Dr. Smith didn't see any obvious signs that Alan was in a fight or involved in any kind of physical confrontation. That's why he's leaning to the theory Alan was poisoned and the shattered vase has no bearing on the case."

"Poison." Sarah let the word roll around on her tongue. Now she understood Harlan's discomfort at asking her about who was doing what in the Southwind kitchen. "You know Marcus wouldn't have done anything to Alan's food."

"I'm inclined to agree with you, but Dr. Smith isn't ruling anyone or anything out."

She caught Harlan's reference to Dr. Smith rather than

Chief Gerard. For once, she was pleased that Chief Gerard wasn't thinking in terms of someone in her almost immediate circle. In her mind, it was simply a matter of time until Marcus became family. Still, if there was even a chance Marcus might have his name associated with food and murder, it could really hurt everything Emily and he had achieved in the past two years. There had to be another possibility.

"Harlan, what about the special tea Alan was drinking? He brought it with him to Southwind in his own water bottle."

"That's one of the reasons Jane isn't out of the woods as a suspect. She made the tea."

Sarah's mind worked feverishly, trying to recall anything else that might exonerate Marcus or, for that matter, Jane. When it was only Jane involved, it had been easy for Sarah to wipe her hands clean and agree she would leave it to the professionals. But now, the chance of Marcus or Southwind being tainted by innuendo made everything completely different. She couldn't sit idly by. Sarah pointed her forefinger into the air as an idea came to her. "There was a server."

"There had to have been a lot of servers."

"There were, but this one stood out. Between their regular customers and finding out at the last minute they were going to have so many extra cast and crew members to serve and feed, Marcus and Emily called on Grace to give them an extra hand. You remember, when she took the job at Carleton, she offered to help when needed. Well, when they called, Grace accepted. She easily fell back into the role of being Emily's sous chef in the kitchen. The big difference was she brought several of her students from the junior college to supplement the waitstaff."

"That simply confirms that, as I said, there had to have been a lot of servers."

Gesturing impatiently as she talked with her hands, Sarah continued her thought. "You don't understand. Emily is a stickler for waiters being prepared. Her actual service rule is that all guests at a table must be served simultaneously, even if it takes more than one waiter. Before dinner, when she explained every item on the dinner menu to the servers, she would have made sure every member of last night's waitstaff understood her service rule."

"So?"

"Harlan, everyone at our table, except Alan, was served at the same time. I remember specifically reflecting on the fact that Emily would not be pleased. I thought the problem was that one of the junior college students was confused as to which table he was to serve. You know, someone who hadn't caught on to how the Southwind tables are numbered."

"And was this server confused?"

"I thought so because I saw a waiter, who I didn't know, looking aimlessly around the dining room. I waved him over. He had a vegetarian plate in his hands. That's the one he served Alan." She leaned forward in her chair. "Harlan, we need to find that waiter. Not only did he not follow Emily's serving protocol, but he would have been the last person to touch Alan's food. Maybe he slipped something into it or onto the plate. I've read about foxglove or poisonous mushrooms being mixed into salads."

"It's far-fetched to think a random waiter would have managed to be the one to serve a deadly salad to just the right person."

"True, but not impossible. What if he wasn't one of the student waiters, but someone hired to pretend to be a waiter?"

"I think you're getting a little far afield. You're going to hate me saying this, but let's leave it for the professionals."

Sarah bristled simply hearing that phrase. She relaxed a bit when he explained that Dr. Smith, who she respected, would check the contents of Alan's stomach, as well as Alan's tea container. "Knowing Dr. Smith, he won't have anything definitive to suggest how Alan died until there's an autopsy and the toxicology reports come back. As of now, there is nothing to directly tie Jane to Alan's death."

"And Marcus?"

"I'm not worried about Marcus. You and I know he wouldn't have poisoned Alan. More importantly, Chief Gerard doesn't see Marcus as being a viable suspect to pursue. No motive, nothing in the dumpster or garbage that looked peculiar to the chief, and the way Marcus was sending the food out, he wasn't expediting the orders. He might have recognized the table numbers, but they were so busy the chief doesn't think Marcus would have been focusing on the people at the table. It's not like that television show where everyone in the kitchen goes crazy during restaurant wars when the judges come into the restaurant and are seated at a specific table."

As serious as their discussion was, Sarah thought it

funny that while she didn't watch reality TV, Harlan apparently did.

"Besides, Chief Gerard likes Marcus. He accepts that he can be like a bull in a china shop, but he doesn't see Marcus as being mean-spirited or vindictive like Jane. Finally, Marcus doesn't fit Chief Gerard's theory of following the blood or the money. Since there's no blood, he'll be focusing on the money."

Harlan's words were encouraging to Sarah, but from past encounters she knew how fast Chief Gerard could change his mind if he thought a possible solution would expediently solve his case. No, until Alan's killer was found, there was no way Sarah could leave it to the professionals. "I'm not comfortable simply going with how the chief feels about Marcus today."

"There's more to it than the chief's gut feeling about Marcus."

"Oh?"

"The money I just mentioned. When the chief ran credit checks, he found Marcus has a few restaurant-related loans, but Marcus and Emily are easily servicing them. Plus, Alan's change of dinner plans for the show and the probability of extra guests at the pub during lunch hour potentially was a small windfall for the Southwind Group. No, the one financially behind the eight ball is Jane."

"Chef Bernardi indicated to Officer Robinson that Jane was hemorrhaging money."

"Let's just say that you've kidded in the past that, like a cat, she has nine lives. I'm getting the feeling she may be nearing the end of those when it comes to Jane's Place."

"Did she tell you that?"

"Not directly. When the blood trail didn't pan out, Chief Gerard went after her on the money angle. She was so shook last night that, for once, instead of being belligerent, she answered his questions about Jane's Place and her contract involvement with the Southern Belle competition. Jane admitted that after the great start Jane's Place had, things have been difficult, but she swore this contract and show were going to turn everything around."

"But you don't think they are?"

"Somewhat. Knowing Jane, there must be a twist. Even providing breakfasts and the craft table, as well as renting rooms to the advance team and now the contestants and chaperones, I don't see enough of a revenue stream for long-term success. One week of profit isn't going to stop the flow of red Jane's Place has been having. It's not like the TV show is going to turn Wheaton, and her B and B, into a big tourist destination, no matter what the mayor might hope."

"Was Chief Gerard on your wavelength?"

"I think so, but without the toxicology reports and the fact that it was established that Jane apparently cut her hand on a broken piece of the vase, so the blood was hers, he didn't push it. He will, though. That's why I brought her back to the office. To satisfy myself she isn't hiding an ace up her sleeve."

"What kind of an ace are you looking for?"

"I don't know. What's bothering me is that she was adamant that the Southern Belle show is going to put Jane's Place back in the black. She never managed to explain that to my satisfaction. I'm hoping I can get her to clarify or open up to me whatever it is that I'm missing here."

What Harlan was saying made sense. Sarah was very much aware of the various schemes Jane had tried to keep Jane's Place viable. In the end, each had had a major flaw. If Jane was skating on such a tight margin and things continued to go haywire, it might well doom Jane's Place.

CHAPTER 15

Sarah steeled herself to leave the Janeless environment of Harlan's office. She had two choices: confront her nemesis in the break room or try to find a way to avoid Jane for a few more minutes. Sarah decided her need for caffeine outweighed anything else.

To her delight, as Sarah stepped out of Harlan's office, she heard the office's main front door bang shut. Whether Jane was leaving without talking to Harlan or had another reason for going outside, Sarah didn't care. She wanted her coffee.

Happily, the pot was still half full. Sarah poured herself a cup, added two natural sugars, took a sip, and exhaled. Come what may, she was ready for it. Sarah doubted anything could top the excitement and tragedy of the past day.

As Sarah walked toward her desk, she heard the office's front doorbell. Normally, she checked the monitor that sat on her desk and only then, if everything was okay, buzzed the visitor in. But now, from where Sarah stood in the waiting room, she could see through the side windowpane of the door that the person repeatedly punching the doorbell button was Jane.

Rather than going to her desk to formally buzz Jane in, Sarah opened the door. A whiff of pungent perfume made her take a step back as she held the door open for Jane.

"Thank you," Jane said, passing Sarah.

The intensity of Jane's perfume was overpowering to the point that Sarah choked. Rather than simply closing the door, she left it open, but made sure the outer screen door was latched.

She wondered, once Jane left for good, how long it would take for the sickeningly sweet-sour stench to dissipate. Having not smelled a lingering scent of perfume in the break room, she realized Jane had probably gone to her car, in the hope that before meeting with Harlan a dousing of perfume would mask the stale odor clinging to her. Sarah felt the urge to tell her, but didn't, that even an entire bottle of perfume couldn't hide her ripeness. She felt sorry for Harlan being closed in his office with Jane.

It bothered Sarah that the kindness and pity she'd felt for Jane yesterday seemed to have fled her pores faster than the stink of the perfume would.

Jane pointed to the door's glass side panels. "I've never understood why you usually keep us waiting to be buzzed in while you check your monitor. After all, you can see clear as day anyone who approaches the door through the side windows. Sometimes, it's a real pain waiting on you."

Sarah bit her tongue. There were things to get into it with Jane over, but this wasn't one of them. "It's part of Harlan's security system."

"Well, when he converted this house into his office, if he wanted to be secure, he shouldn't have left the original glass windows on either side of the front door."

Although Sarah technically agreed with Jane's point, she knew from typing Harlan's application for the house to receive an historic designation that part of his not changing the panes was tied to the need to keep the original building preserved. In the end, from a security viewpoint, it didn't matter that the glass remained. If someone broke it and stuck a hand in and around to unlock the door, every motion would be caught on the state-of-the-art security cameras Harlan had installed.

Opting to change the topic and tone of their conversation, Sarah decided a little white lie was in order. "Harlan popped out to tell you he'll be with you in a few minutes. He had to take a phone call and it's running longer than he anticipated."

"It just doesn't make sense to me."

"That he's on the phone?"

"No. Why he left the windows."

Obviously, Sarah's plan to divert Jane's attention and topic of conversation had failed. This time she gave Jane a neutral response. "I guess he wanted to keep the original architecture intact. You know, based on the history of this house, he's applied for it to be designated as an historical home on the National Register and our state historic commission register."

Jane threw back her head and laughed. "He wasted his time on that? Whatever makes him think this house would qualify? It isn't even on Main Street. Most of those homes, like mine, belonged to the town's pioneers and none of them qualified. Believe me, I checked. Did someone famous sleep here?"

"I think it was something other than that. Harlan has the details."

Having typed the application forms, Sarah was as equally familiar as Harlan with the architecturally significant grounds for the historical designation, but she didn't want to get into it with Jane. She had the feeling that trying to explain to Jane that houses can be on the National Register for things other than a famous owner or an event could trigger a tirade of some kind. Much easier to be silent and let Jane have the last word respecting what would be approved for a historical designation.

She hoped Harlan would fetch Jane soon. In the meantime, Sarah thought it best not to chat with Jane, like she might with most of Harlan's clients when they were in the waiting room. Figuring that if she started working, Jane would get the message and entertain herself with a waiting room magazine or her phone, Sarah walked around the partition to her desk.

As Sarah put her coffee on her desk, a stronger whiff of Jane's perfume informed her that, rather than getting Sarah's message, Jane had followed her. Sarah glanced back over her shoulder. Not only was Jane there, but she was trying to sneak a peek at Sarah's computer screen.

Rather than striking a key, Sarah left her screen saver in place. "Jane, is there something I can help you with?"

"No, I'm simply passing time." Jane pointed at the monitor. "What are you working on? Anything interesting?"

"Not particularly. Although things might have seemed exciting to you last night, most of the work in a law office is mundane. Harlan cares about each of his clients, but in the end, their needs all translate into things like letters, wills, and briefs. Cut and dried, but necessary." *And private to each client*, Sarah thought.

Anything else Sarah was going to say was cut off by her cell phone playing "Edelweiss," the ringtone for her mother. She debated whether to answer it, especially since Jane was looking and listening, but considering everything going on with the show, she took the call.

"They did it." Maybelle spoke quickly. "They let Jed and Lucy go."

"Really. How?"

"Before they started taping our individual interviews, they had us all take our seats in the big dining room to tape the invitation reveal. Jed and Lucy's bench was empty, and their names were removed from the heart-shaped sign in front of their bench. They shot some footage of it as Flynn announced that because of a family problem, they sadly had to leave the show. Then, with the two finalists for the invitation design standing with him, Flynn announced the winner and noted what made it bittersweet was that the chosen invitation was based upon the premise Lucy and Jed submitted."

"You're kidding." She glanced at Jane. Sarah wondered if she should repeat what her mother had said for Jane's benefit or if Jane was close enough to hear everything herself. When Jane took a side step but stayed within the same area in Sarah's cubicle, Sarah had her answer.

"Once Flynn let that sink in, he announced to the audience that because Jed and Lucy left, no one, including the couple who came in last during the car wash challenge, would be eliminated."

"Who do you think was at the bottom after the car wash challenge?"

"Well, the guys mainly washed while the Belles tried to attract people to stop. I don't have that little extra allure that Starr, Natalie, and Veronica can demonstrate. Or Lucy, for that matter. They gave me a bucket and told me to go around to those people waiting for their cars to be washed or who simply stopped to watch and see if I could solicit extra donations. You know, 'Give to the poor and the old.'"

Sarah could just envision the look her mother gave whoever had the lucky task of conveying the assignment to Maybelle.

"I think Natalie and Ralph would have been the losing couple. After Lucy grabbed the hose and started the water fight, it was poor Natalie who ended up drenched. We'll never know, though."

Her mother paused rather than saying goodbye, and Sarah knew there had to be something else her mother wanted to tell her. Sarah point-blank asked Maybelle.

"Well, we're supposed to finish the personal interviews by eleven-ish and then have until one to get lunch from the craft table, change into Mudbowl-appropriate clothing, and report to the Mudbowl challenge. Want to come watch? I think there are going to be some fireworks worked into the challenge."

"Whoa." Sarah marveled at how her mother could jump from something as important as two contestants being unceremoniously kicked off to fireworks in the Mudbowl.

"I'll try, but I really need to work." She hit *end* and looked up. Jane was still behind her.

"Something to do with the show?"

"You didn't hear?"

"How could I? I wasn't on the phone."

Only close enough for the phone to be in your ear too, thought Sarah. "Apparently, the show's management exercised the no-gun provision and sent Lucy and Jed packing."

"But Granny had the gun."

"I guess they are treating the contestants and the chaperones as one entity."

"You don't understand. They can't do that. Lucy and Jed need to still be in the competition at least through tomorrow. Have they already been sent home?" Jane backed up and bumped her hip into the edge of the partition between Sarah's area and the waiting room.

Jane, her face heating up, more carefully maneuvered around the partition.

Sarah decided to throw Jane a bone. "My mother said to expect more fireworks when they film the Mudbowl segment."

Jane didn't pick up on her fireworks comment. Instead, her reaction was still tied to Lucy and Jed being sent home.

"He can't do this. I've got to go." Jane glanced from Harlan's closed door to the front door. "Tell Harlan I'm sorry. We'll have to talk later. I've got to go now."

Jane fiddled with the screen door's latch. Finally, she

got the door open. She stepped through the doorway at exactly the instant Harlan opened his door.

"Jane." Sarah pointed at Harlan.

Shifting her gaze between them, Jane finally rested her eyes on Sarah, but spoke to Harlan. "I'm sorry, Harlan. Our conversation is going to have to wait." With that, she left.

Harlan turned from watching Jane's rear disappear through the door to where Sarah sat, her mouth open. "What was that all about?"

"I'm not sure. She was bored waiting for you, so she was trying to see what I was working on." Touching her monitor, Sarah took on a serious demeanor. "Don't worry. I left my screen saver on while she peeked. Anyway, my mother called on my cell. I wouldn't have taken it, but with everything going on, she promised to call if there was anything juicy."

"Was there?"

"Yes. Apparently, the powers-to-be stuck to their guns about guns."

"They kicked Granny out of the house?"

"And Jed and Lucy off the show. When I told Jane, she lost it. She muttered something like 'he can't do this' and 'not today,' then, as you saw, she took off without saying what she was agitated about."

Harlan took off his glasses and rubbed his eyes with the back of his hand. The words "that's interesting" came out of his mouth, and she could almost see the wheels in his head turning.

"Do you think there's some importance to Jed and Lucy being eliminated first?" Sarah suggested. "The fact that Jane got so upset makes me wonder if there is something significant about the order in which the contestants are eliminated."

"Not that I know of. In the end, four of the five couples are going to be eliminated," Harlan said.

"Well, maybe the ogre has a heart? Perhaps she merely liked them better than the other couples. From what I could tell, Jed and Lucy are good people."

"That was my impression too. Did your mother have anything else to say?"

"Only to expect more fireworks when the Mudbowl segment is filmed. Mother wanted me to come, but I told her I need to work."

"I appreciate that." He leaned on the waiting room partition and ran his hand through his hair, skipping the bald spot at the very top of his head. "You know, this time I think it might be a good idea if we both went and watched them film the Mudbowl segment. It might help answer some of the questions nagging at me and you'll get brownie points with your mother."

"But your case?"

He glanced at his watch. "It's coming along. With my day cleared today to work on it, and with light days tomorrow and Wednesday, I'm in surprisingly good shape for Thursday morning's hearing. Why don't you combine your lunch hour and the Mudbowl? Make your mother happy and give Fluffy her walk at the same time."

"Okay, but just so you understand: As soon as I take Fluffy home, I'll come right back to the office and stay until just before I'm required to be on chaperone duty at dinner."

"That's fine, except you better leave yourself a little time before you need to be at Southwind. Otherwise, a very hungry and lonely puppy and cat will be jealous when you get supper, and they don't."

Sarah laughed. "They never have to worry about that. They're first on my list ahead of chaperoning or anything else."

Chapter 16

By the time Sarah hugged on RahRah, loaded Fluffy into the car, and parked near the Mudbowl on the Carleton Junior Community College's campus, it was nearing one o'clock. After leashing Fluffy, Sarah allowed her to meander near the edge of the Mudbowl. Sarah looked for Harlan or any of the contestants, but didn't see them in the crowd of people she was standing with.

When she spotted three kegs and looked more closely at the people near her, Sarah realized she was in the middle of the student section. Giving Fluffy a light tug, Sarah started around to the other side of the bowl, where she caught sight of her twin, Emily, standing with Harlan and some of the members of the Wheaton Wildcats, the community motorcycle group who the Southern Belle show was partnering with for today's charitable function.

For years, Sarah had thought motorcycle groups were

gangs, but during the past year she'd learned that although some people were like the stereotypical bikers on TV or in books, most could be your next-door neighbor. The Wheaton group had started as educators and their friends, joining together to take a cross-country ride each summer vacation. As more people joined them, the group expanded to become a weekly weekend gathering of bikers who divided themselves by who wanted to take a long or short ride. What they all did together was fundraising for charities, including Wheaton's animal shelter, or, like today, Wheaton's Food Bank.

Making sure she stayed where the ground was solid, Sarah held tightly to Fluffy's leash. The last thing she wanted was for her white powder puff to scamper down the bowl's sloping sides into the bottom, filled with squishy, soggy mud thanks to water piped in for the past twenty-four hours.

Sarah greeted Harlan, Emily, and friends who were there representing their motorcycle group. She gave one of them, Eloise, who not only was a Wildcat but also the newest member of the city council, a hug. Sarah pointed to the bottom of the Mudbowl, faking a shudder. "Are all of you going down there?"

Eloise laughed. "Of course not. We're staying up here collecting donations."

Sarah glanced around. Other than one basket perched on the seat of a completely tricked-out motorcycle being attended to by two members of the club, she didn't see any other points of collection. "Most of this crowd is students. How much can you raise from them?"

"Not much," Eloise admitted. "This is a fun way for us to interact with the students and hope to get them involved with our group and some of the charitable groups we raise funds for. The kids may not have extra money now, but they can offer volunteer time."

"How is this being billed as a major fundraiser?"

"The network made a generous donation that, coupled with the collections our group gathered from other sources this week, will end up being a sizable cash contribution to the Food Bank."

"That's nice."

Eloise agreed. "Plus, to get the students out here today, the Southern Belle show made a nice donation to Carleton Junior Community College's Student Government Association's charitable foundation."

Now Sarah understood. The network had bought the Southern Belle competition's way into a partnership with the Wheaton Wildcats, giving the show instant credibility and a voter base. Similarly, the donation to the school's charitable foundation, plus the purchase of three kegs, guaranteed the presence of lively participants during today's filming.

Although Sarah knew the money given to both groups would be well used, the partnership-for-money concept still bothered her. It seemed dishonest and disingenuous in much the same way Alan's proposal that the show take over the animal shelter's fundraiser hadn't sat right. She shook her head, hoping to clear her mind of these thoughts and move on. "Where are the Southern Belles?"

Emily pointed to two trailers behind the Mudbowl. "In there. Getting ready. From what Mother hinted, this should be good."

Cornered between two buildings, the Mudbowl was a gully that when the college was initially built was deemed too misshapen and small and therefore too expensive for the college to build on. Later, it was found to be too shady for successful seeding for a grassy park or student sitting area. Consequently, the depressed land became a campus reference point when giving directions for anything near the two buildings or the nearby intersection.

It would have sat abandoned forever but for a student noticing how rainwater pooled in the bottom of the gully, causing the mud to bubble. Being a pre-engineering student, he decided if the volume of water was enhanced, the resulting mud would create a perfect place for a student government–sponsored challenged game of Mudbowl football. Hence, a now thirty-plus-year-old tradition was created. Today the Southern Belle show was taking advantage of it. Although the show's contestants weren't going to play football, they were going to get in the mud for a tug-of-war. Afterwards, some of the student groups were going to take advantage of the mud for a rematch of Mudbowl games.

"Em, I thought you'd be at Southwind or the pub instead of here."

"Marcus and everyone have the final part of the lunch rush under control without me. Mom called and told me I really needed to come to today's competition. She was insistent; plus with what happened last night I wanted to lay my own eyes on her."

"Are you saying mine aren't enough?"

"Not at all. Just that, well, you know how close Mom and I are."

"Unlike me." Sarah waited a beat before adding a kicker. "You always were the favorite child."

Emily batted her eyes. "But Dad always liked you better."

Both sisters cracked up. Growing up, Emily might have been the more popular blonde cheerleader type who knew exactly what she wanted to do when she grew up. But Sarah, who was shy and awkward, was the better student who had better hair. Even today, Emily openly envied Sarah's luxuriously thick dark hair, while Sarah admired her sister's focused drive to be a chef and restaurant owner. But there was no distance between them. They adored each other.

"It must have been horrible for Mom and you to find Alan's body."

"We were shocked, but it was Jane and my reaction to her that was strange." Sarah brought her twin up to date on everything. "How's it going taking over the cast and crew meals while juggling your regular customers?"

"*Juggling* is the right word. We couldn't have pulled it off without Grace's help. In the kitchen, we fell back into our old rhythm immediately. Between Grace and her students, Marcus and I will make it through this delightful onslaught of business without slighting our regulars."

Sarah's follow-up question about whether there was a signed contract for the meals being served to the crew and cast was interrupted when Harlan observed, "They're coming."

Sarah looked in the direction of the trailers. Flynn and Sam, with a cameraman shooting Flynn in motion and another one taking still shots, were making their way to the less sloped edge of the bowl. Sarah assumed someone on the show's staff had determined that was the side that would be easier for the contestants to enter. The presence of a third cameraperson, with her camera perched on a tripod, waiting at that point, confirmed Sarah's assumption.

Harlan and Sarah moved closer to the entry point to hear Flynn better. He was introducing this as the first head-to-head competitive team challenge for the contestants. "For our tug-of-war in the mud, we were going to break the teams into the would-be grooms against the Belles, but we were afraid we might destroy a budding romance when our brides-to-be bested their guys."

There was a polite titter from the audience. Sarah guessed because of the payoff or the beer, some of the students felt an obligation to react.

"Instead, we decided to divide everyone up a little more evenly. And here they come." Flynn made a sweeping gesture with his arm. Both trailer doors opened. As the contestants stepped out, a genuine wave of laughter went through the crowd. The women all wore *Gone with the Wind*–type ruffled hoop-skirted gowns. Sarah craned her neck and was relieved to see that rather than heels, her mother was wearing high-top sneakers.

George and the accountant, whose name Sarah couldn't remember, had on dark tailcoats, gray trousers, and at their necks a piece of red-colored fabric that replicated a cravat. Whether it was a tailcoat-size issue or to give variety to the costuming, the much larger Trey and Lance were jacketless. Instead, they had on button-down shirts open at the neck, collarless single-breasted waistcoats, and neckties tied in a loose bow. All four wore different hats: a bowler, a Lincoln stovepipe, and two Clark Gable–like Western hats.

The women reached the edge of the Mudbowl and stopped, as if following directions, then faced the camera on the tripod. Flynn stepped into the shot with them and introduced each by name. He also reminded the audience of a salient factor about each one. Flynn finished the introduction and Sam yelled "cut."

"Maybelle," Sam said, "if you'll join me over here,

please. The rest of you ladies go to Rod. He's the one waving over there. He'll help you take your places at the bottom of the Mudbowl."

Rod, clad in rubber rain boots and a yellow raincoat, again waved to the remaining three Belles. Sarah figured the cameras were rolling again. She was sure of it when, with a show of chivalry, he took off his raincoat and laid it over one of the muddier areas. With care, he guided Natalie and Starr down via the least-sloped point of the bowl.

As Rod was coming back up to help Veronica, she stepped away from the Mudbowl's edge. She batted her eyes at Sam and Flynn. "Surely, you don't expect little ol' me to go down there."

"Ah, yes we do," Sam said, with a Southern accent almost as strong as the one Veronica was putting on.

She fluffed her hands against her dress and then placed her right hand over her heart. Veronica pushed her hand deeply into her chest. "Bless your heart. This dress is simply too beautiful to step into that mud." She fingered one of her dress's elaborate hooped puffs. "My gown will be ruined. I simply can't bring myself to do that to this gorgeous creation."

Sam walked over to Veronica and gently put his hand on her shoulder. Sarah couldn't hear what he said, but she could clearly see Veronica frown. Sarah wasn't positive, but she thought she saw Sam squeeze her shoulder and nudge her in Rod's direction.

Veronica shook free of Sam's hand and marched toward Rod with her head held high and a smile pasted on her face. Sarah awarded this round to Sam, but something told her that Veronica, like any traditional Southern belle, would prevail in their next showdown.

Without George joining them, the remaining male contestants were left to slip-slide down the steeper side of the Mudbowl on their own. The accountant didn't make it. He landed with a large plop. As he scrambled to his feet, his heated face almost matched his cravat.

As the crew members already in the bottom of the bowl positioned the contestants, Sarah shifted her attention back to Flynn, her mother, and George. Flynn raised his hand to hush those around him. Once it was quiet enough, he turned toward the camera. At the count of three, Flynn began speaking, introducing the challenge. He motioned for Maybelle and George to join him. As they did, a cameraman stepped back to get a wider angle to include them in the frame with him.

"By the luck of the draw, Maybelle and George have been named our honorary captains for today. Maybelle's team will be the Alabama fans, Trey and Veronica, and our Day of the Deader, Natalie. George's team is comprised of Auburn lovers, Lance and Starr, as well as Natalie's better half, Ralph."

Ralph. That was the accountant's name Sarah couldn't remember. It was interesting to her how the teams were divided. In a sense, the distribution matched Heather's prediction the other night as to which couples and rivalries would be highlighted. Ignoring Natalie and Ralph, the viewers technically were watching Alabama vs. Auburn duke it out in the mud. Camera angles would help the public develop an affinity to one of the two sports couples. Keeping George and Maybelle safe on the sidelines, while managing to feature them as the captains, also was a smart idea of Sam or Flynn's to help the older couple get screen time and build their own following without endangering them.

If Sarah had to make a prediction, Ralph's fall in the mud might be the best part of his highlight reel because there probably wasn't going to be more than another day's worth of filming time for Natalie and Ralph. Sarah wondered, had Jed and Lucy stayed in, would they or Natalie and Ralph been the first to go? She wasn't sure which scenario would have enhanced the drama or helped the ratings more. Looking around, Sarah observed that those standing on the edge of the Mudbowl were now engaged.

The tug-of-war was on.

From the sidelines, George and Maybelle cheered their teams on. Down in the Mudbowl, there was no question from their faces that Lance and Trey were the most into it. What was more interesting to Sarah than the actual pulling was watching the different angles from which cameras were filming. She never imagined that, unlike dinner the other night, there would be more than one film camera and one still camera shooting. Shots were being made in the bowl and from different angles from the rim above. An additional cameraman was catching audience reactions, as well as focusing in periodically on those of Flynn, George, and Maybelle.

A sudden yell as Lance's feet slipped out from under him and he lost his grip on the rope gave all the cameramen something to film. With him on the ground, it was only seconds until the rest of his team was pulled forward. Poor Ralph, only face-forward this time, was on the bottom of the heap in the mud.

Sarah's own yell came when her white powder puff rolled down the side of the Mudbowl. Engrossed in the final moments of the match, she'd loosened her grip ever so slightly on the leash and Fluffy was gone.

Rather than continuing her slide in the mud, Fluffy took that moment to literally jump into the action. Trey's quick reaction, catching Fluffy midair, demonstrated his football prowess. Holding the puppy up, as if he'd just caught a touchdown, he let the crowd give him a cheer before he gently passed Fluffy to a chain of crew members who handed the squirmy dog back up from the bottom to Sarah. She held him gingerly.

Except for Fluffy's dark eyes and the flick of her pink tongue laying kisses on Sarah, there wasn't much to identify Fluffy as the pristine pup who'd come with Sarah to the Mudbowl. Looking at her blouse and her mud-speckled pet, Sarah didn't know if she should laugh or cry.

"I guess you'll be a little later than you planned getting back to the office," Harlan said.

CHAPTER 17

Not putting Fluffy down, Sarah dropped her keys in the glass bowl on the table near the front door of the carriage house and carried her puppy straight into the laundry room. She reached into the cupboard above her washing machine. As she pulled out three puppy bath towels, a rubber mat, a container of doggie treats, and Fluffy's sponge, comb, and brush, she kept up a running patter of what she was doing for Fluffy's benefit.

Putting one of the towels on her washing machine, Sarah stood Fluffy on the towel. Keeping one hand on Fluffy's back, she gently brushed the squirming dog's coat, trying to remove some of the matted tangles and dried mud. "If you're this dirty, I wonder how things are at Jane's Place? Especially in terms of hot water. Everyone was covered with mud."

Satisfied she'd done the best she could before beginning Fluffy's bath, Sarah laid the rubber mat on the bottom of her laundry sink. Turning on the water, she kept her hand under the tap until the water was regulated to being a drop warmer than lukewarm.

Gently, she placed Fluffy in the sink. Still talking to her, Sarah shampooed the dog, working from back to front. Using a shower attachment, she rinsed the soap out of Fluffy's fur. The moment she turned the water off, Fluffy shook herself, sending water splashing against Sarah.

Soaked, but finished, Sarah replaced the dirty towel on the machine with one of the clean ones. She grabbed Fluffy, who was still looking for a means of escape, and wrapped the remaining towel around her little dog. Sarah stood her on the machine and dried her. Once Fluffy was pretty much dry, Sarah combed out her puppy's fur. She sat the clean white powder puff on the floor and gave her a doggie treat for being good throughout the bath process.

As Fluffy devoured the treat, Sarah quickly cleaned up the laundry room sink and threw the towels into her washing machine. Fluffy yipped. "Oh, no. I'm not picking you up again until I get myself cleaned up. Between the Mudbowl and your bath, you did a number on my blouse."

Taking the wet and mud-splattered blouse off, Sarah threw it in the machine too. She gave Fluffy another treat and headed for her own bathroom to shower and make herself presentable before she went back to work. Carrying her treat, Fluffy ran ahead of her to Sarah's bedroom. Just beyond the doorway, she dropped her treat, lay on the carpet, and rubbed her still somewhat wet body against it. Coming down the hallway, Sarah called to Fluffy, "Are you trying to get rid of the dampness or the nice shampoo smell?"

RahRah was lying on the hallway floor outside Sarah's bedroom preening himself. Sarah stopped when she reached him.

"Ah, that's where you've been. I guessed you were too smart to come into the laundry room and take a chance on getting super dirty too." Sarah bent down and stroked her Siamese cat. "Between you and me, I'm glad you stayed out here. Bathing Fluffy is one thing. Giving you a bath is like the football game the college boys played today—a real contact sport."

With a purr, RahRah stretched himself out, his tan head cocked in a way that made Sarah think he not only knew what she was saying, but he'd enjoyed creating havoc the few times he'd gotten into something that required her to bathe him. Sarah left RahRah in the hall while she showered and dried her hair.

Finished and clad in clean clothing, she walked back into the hall. RahRah sidled up to her and brushed his body against her leg. He stretched himself out in front of Sarah, covering the tips of her shoes with his body.

"Ah, you want some more attention." Sarah bent and stroked his fur. "I'd like to stay and cuddle you longer, but I need to get back to the office."

RahRah stood, shook himself out, and walked away.

"It's not that I don't love you," Sarah protested.

RahRah kept walking.

"Be like that. I love you anyway." Watching him disappear into the kitchen, probably to his favorite sun-drenched spot on the linoleum floor, she felt a twang of guilt at neglecting RahRah and Fluffy this week. She assured herself that despite work, the show's dinner attendance requirement, and the rest of her chaperoning duties, she would try to squeeze in some extra time with her pets as soon as possible.

CHAPTER 18

At the office, the rest of the day sped by. Without interruptions, a rare occurrence at Harlan's law firm, Harlan and Sarah were able to accomplish enough that she left the office at her normal quitting time. With her unplanned free time, Sarah knew exactly what she wanted to do before she had to be on chaperone duty at tonight's dinner at Southwind. She hurried to the carriage house to keep her promise of giving RahRah and Fluffy a little extra attention.

Once her puppy had a decent walk, RahRah and Fluffy had food and fresh water, and both had received lots of extra hugs and petting, a happy Sarah grabbed her keys from the bowl. Fluffy sat by the door as if waiting to go with her. Sarah smiled at her. She raised her voice so RahRah could hear what she said to Fluffy too. "I'm leaving now, but Aunt Emily will be here in a few hours. Be good for her. I'll see you tomorrow morning."

After Sarah locked the carriage house door, it seemed silly to walk down the long, winding driveway all the way to Main Street just to enter Southwind through its front door. Not only was it much more efficient to go in through the door that led into the kitchen, but it should provide an opportunity to avoid another instance of being caught on tape by one of the ever-present cameramen.

As she reached the bend in the drive, Sarah heard voices coming from the big house's original outdoor back porch. She slowed her pace and listened. Most were male voices, but she immediately recognized Jane's. Once again, it was at a high-pitched decibel level. Sarah went a few feet farther and stepped behind one of Fluffy's favorite trees. It was a great spot to view the porch, but hopefully not to be noticed as she tried to ascertain what had Jane so agitated.

Chef Bernardi, Jane, Sam, Flynn, Trey, and Lance were all on the porch together. Although some held beer cans and cigars, the Southwind's porch railing had become a temporary receptacle for cans and other objects. There was some type of confrontation going on. It was simply too tempting. Sarah knew she shouldn't, but she couldn't help but stay hidden and eavesdrop. After all, she might learn something Harlan could share with Chief Gerard that would protect Marcus and help Jane.

Sarah rolled her eyes at herself. Help Jane. Considering the anguish Jane had caused her in the past, it ate at her to be going out of her way to help her. Blast her own moral code, but as much as she disliked Jane, Sarah couldn't tolerate Jane being blamed for something Sarah felt certain she didn't do.

She'd rather Jane be blamed for the things she did do.

Although Sarah didn't see a cameraman, it appeared Jane had crashed the men enjoying one of the smoke-and-drink sessions Alan had mentioned during the first South-wind dinner.

Sarah didn't blame any of them for wanting to take the edge off before they had to be Goody-Two-shoes on camera. Only, as she peered at them, she saw that instead of the jovial frat boy look she expected, none of them seemed particularly comfortable as Jane lit into them.

She was using both hands to accentuate her points. Her fury was focused on Chef Bernardi.

By their silence, Sarah couldn't decide whose side the other men were on. Sam and Flynn stood closer to Chef Bernardi, as if they were part of the disagreement. Trey and Lance were positioned to the side, almost behind Jane. But did that mean they were on her side or merely trying to steer clear of her wrath?

"I'm going to lose my business," Jane said. "You have the ability to fix this. Do it."

Chef Bernardi raised his hands in a placating gesture. "I'm sorry. Unexpected things happen."

"Considering everything, I have to agree with Jane's point this time," Sam said.

Flynn also responded, but his comment was too soft for Sarah to catch.

Chef Bernardi shook his head.

Flynn's reaction was a frown that removed all trace of his genial host face. He took two deep puffs on his cigar, tapped it so its ash fell on the porch, and laid the stogie on the railing near what looked like a flat case. He glanced at Trey, who shrugged.

Sarah was about to reveal herself to reprimand Flynn for not being mindful of Southwind's wooden porch, but stayed in her hiding place when his raised voice carried to her ears. "Well, Roberto, it seems to all of us that the circumstances have changed. Neither Jane nor any of us could have predicted any of this or the decision the network made. You've simply got to call everything off or start over again."

The others on the porch nodded or made some other agreeing motion.

Chef Bernardi picked up his beer, took a final swig, crushed the can, and threw it into the bushes next to the porch. Avoiding the cigar, he palmed the flat object from the railing and said, "They started. It's on film. What is, is." Ignoring the others staring at him, he walked into the kitchen.

If looks could kill, the one Jane shot in his direction met that definition, but so did the ones from the others, who were now grumbling among themselves. Wondering what they could all agree on, Sarah came out from behind the tree and strode quickly to the porch. From the stairs, she yelled, "Hi, everyone. Are you ready for tonight's dinner?"

All except Jane greeted her. Jane glared at Sarah, then turned the same icy cold gaze to all the men on the porch. Most looked away. Sarah couldn't decide if they were unable or unwilling to meet Jane's gaze.

"I can't believe this! When my business goes under, it's going to be your fault. You and this stupid show! You disgust me." With a sweep of her arm, Jane knocked

Flynn's cigar into the same bushes where Chef Bernardi had thrown his beer can. Pushing by Sarah, Jane stomped down the stairs and went in the direction of Jane's Place.

Sarah continued up the steps to the porch. "What was that all about?"

A few muttered "nothing," or "that was Jane being Jane."

"We better get inside," Flynn said. Not waiting for an answer, he led the way through the kitchen door.

Almost in unison the men agreed. Unlit cigars went into pockets while empty and partially full beer cans were dropped into what Sarah presumed was a discarded cardboard box that neither Emily nor Marcus had taken to the dumpster yet. Done with their cleanup tasks, the men filed into the building as if they were schoolchildren going down the hall for recess.

Sarah stayed behind, not wanting to leave the box with the beer cans sitting on the porch and nervous that the cigar Jane had knocked off the porch might not be completely out. She didn't know how long a cigar had to sit dormant before its burning ember died.

Grabbing the box, she checked the spot where Flynn had tapped his ashes. There was nothing for her to clean up. Other than a smudge, the ashes either had blown away or been smeared by a shoe. Going down the stairs, she eyeballed where in the bushes she thought the can and the cigar might have landed. Gingerly, she reached into the clump of shrubs and, after feeling around, found the can. More exploring brought her hand in contact with the damp end of what she hoped was Flynn's stogie. Feeling slightly sick to her stomach, Sarah slowly curled her fingers around the object and dragged her prize from the bushes. The cigar's flame was out. She dropped the can and the used cigar into the box and carried the garbage to the dumpster. After throwing her load in, Sarah consciously forced herself not to wipe her dirty hands on her jeans. Rather, she hurried into the building and scrubbed her hands at the kitchen wash station.

Satisfied her hands were clean because she'd used enough soap and met her mother's adage of singing the entire "Happy Birthday" song to herself to guarantee she'd washed long enough, she dried her hands. It was time to go on duty. Hopefully, tonight's dinner wouldn't be as exciting as last night's.

Chapter 19

"You made it," Maybelle observed, as Sarah bent over her mother's shoulder and gave her a peck on the head before taking the seat next to her.

Cliff, across the table, held up the arm on which he wore his watch. "She's even early."

Sarah was going to make a crack, but instead smiled at him. Being teased by her friend was something she was willing to accept—that is, for tonight. "You're back?"

"Yeah. I decided a free Southwind dinner and the company beat going home to my own cooking." This time he grinned at her. She wasn't sure how to interpret his reaction. For that matter, she wasn't sure how to interpret the warm feeling she felt.

It wasn't like they could or would pick up where they'd left off. That last night, when they'd broken up on the deck of his cabin, they'd made it clear that while what they felt was special, it wasn't the love a long-lasting relationship could be sustained on. Whether it was the baggage they both carried or something romantically missing, it was hard to pinpoint, but they'd agreed there was no question their friendship was special. Sarah was glad they were back in step with their friendship.

"Actually," Cliff said, "I'm here because I have to do a little fine-tuning on the set before they use it for filming tomorrow. You see, with taping multiple episodes in a day and Jed and Lucy leaving when they did, the show is running ahead of when we'd planned for me to dismantle part of the seating area and set up a vendor display table."

"I thought there was an area in the far corner of the room where the two finalist vendors of the day display their wares."

"There is one for taping head-to-head vendor segments, but this is to make room for a table where all the selected vendor items are displayed. The idea is that the camera will periodically scan it during the week as the table gets fuller, helping viewers get excited about the upcoming wedding. To make room for the table, I have to remove Jed and Lucy's bench and the heart with their names tonight."

Sarah nodded. "Got it." Glancing around the table, she saw they were seated with Natalie, Ralph, and Rose, but George wasn't there, nor was there an empty chair for him. "Where's George?"

"With all the episodes we taped today and yesterday and because he's staying in his own place instead of in one of the hotels, he asked Sam for permission to skip tonight's dinner. Sam agreed. I think Sam thought, considering George's age, that maybe all of this activity was too much for George and that he really needed some rest time."

"He didn't?"

"Of course not. They were having their bonus steak dinner at the retirement home tonight."

Sarah and Cliff groaned together as they simultaneously said, "Bonus steak night?"

"That's right. George loves his steak nights, and he didn't want to miss this month's bonus one. Using the number of segments we taped in the past two days and the stress of the murder was merely his excuse."

Sarah chuckled. "Good for George."

Ralph, who evidently was listening to their conversation, joined in. "I can't believe George traded an opportunity for a Southwind dinner for the retirement home's steak dinner."

"George is a creature of habit," Maybelle said. "Besides, eating at Southwind isn't a novelty for him."

Her mother put her hand to her mouth. Happily, it appeared that the slight insult conveyed by Maybelle's words and tone was lost on Ralph.

"We're just getting our business off the ground. Dinners out anywhere are a treat for Natalie and me. Isn't that right, Natalie?"

"Yes." She bent forward as if confiding a secret. "Our energies and money have gone into opening our practice, decorating our new office, obtaining necessary equipment, and taking a minimum draw."

"I understand that," Sarah said. "We didn't put together an office this year, but getting Southwind off the ground required some of the same planning and prioritizing of the assets we had. Not to mention investing in ways to let people know Southwind exists."

"I had no idea you were part owner with your sister," Natalie said. "Do you cook too?"

"No way. To me there's nothing more frightening than being in the kitchen. I own the building, but I leave all the cooking to Emily and Marcus."

"Thank goodness," Maybelle muttered. Sarah shot her a sideways glance while continuing to listen to Natalie.

"That's the point Ralph and I are at. We met when we were getting our MBAs and paid our dues working for big firms. Last year, we celebrated our twenty-fifth birthdays by going out on our own. We're solid accountants, but we're still only a two-person firm without much in the way of cash assets. That's why Ralph wanted us to come on this show, hoping we, and therefore our practice, would get more exposure."

Sarah thought about Ralph face down in the mud and wondered how that was going to instill the public's confidence in him. It also dawned on her that their stated interest in the Day of the Dead might surprise some of their clients. "How did Ralph and you become interested in the Day of the Dead?"

Natalie touched her hand to her chest and smiled at her aunt. "The Day of the Dead is part of my culture. It's really a Mexican holiday that has extended beyond its original geographic boundaries. Aunt Rose grew up in Mexico with the true traditions, but here in the States she's modified her observance. Still, raising me after my parents died, she taught me to remember them by celebrating their memories on the Day of the Dead."

"I'm sorry about your parents."

She placed her hand over her aunt's. "Don't be. They died in an accident a long time ago, but while I remember them every day, Aunt Rose has been a loving mother and father to me. She made celebrating them on the Day of the Dead something special. You see, the belief is that on that day the barrier between the living and the nonliving world drops, allowing the souls of those who have gone before us to return to the living world to sing and dance with the living. Our family does that for my parents and our other loved ones, plus we leave food for them and follow other traditional practices."

"That's lovely."

Natalie leaned closer so only Sarah could hear her. "Over the years, the holiday has evolved, and I guess I view it through a different lens than Aunt Rose. She's a lot more spiritual and, I'd say, even mystical, than I am, but the Day of the Dead means a lot to me."

Natalie glanced toward Ralph. Seeing him involved with talking to Cliff, she continued speaking softly. "I'm afraid that in that segment Alan showed, Aunt Rose, who tends to be more truthful than she should be at times, correctly pegged part of the reason why Ralph and I are in this competition. Ralph is Irish Catholic. The Day of the Dead means nothing to him, but he knows it is important to me."

"But you both claimed to want to do a Day of the Dead wedding and honeymoon?"

"Ralph thought using the Day of the Dead as our hook would be a good gimmick to get us into the competition."

"It is unique." Sarah doubted any other applicants had tied their wedding plans to the Day of the Dead. She had to give Ralph credit for analyzing the casting process in a similar manner to her mother's consideration of demographics and age. Maybe he was a better analytical accountant than he was a Mudbowl participant. "You said business was only part of the reason Ralph and you wanted to compete in the Southern Belle competition?"

Natalie lowered her chin and concentrated on the silverware for a few seconds before glancing at Ralph. "Like I said, we don't have much in the way of cash assets, but we have a long-term business plan. We thought this might help us achieve part of that sooner. And, if we got lucky, we might not have to wait as long for a personal goal we have."

"Getting married?"

"Yes. Tell me, how long have Maybelle and George been a couple?"

"They only got together recently." Considering that until they'd announced they were finalists, neither of Maybelle's daughters nor George's nephew knew they were that serious, the idea of them getting married still didn't seem real. As she answered Natalie and reflected on how many years Ralph and Natalie had known each other, it occurred to Sarah they might do better to go with a less-than-perfect wedding. The footage being shot and edited might put both their goals in jeopardy. Sarah wasn't sure if people would seek out an accountant who they remembered lying face down in the mud. Perhaps, though, if Natalie and Ralph gained enough name recognition, people would find their firm name familiar but wouldn't put a negative association with it.

The one thing Sarah was sure of after talking with Natalie was that Maybelle's assessment of how the five finalist couples were picked for age, education, and demographics was correct. By extension of her mother's analysis, she doubted Ralph and Natalie had much more time as contestants. She decided to change the subject to something a little less personal. "You've been taping so many segments today and yesterday, I've lost track of where you are in the show."

"It actually is quite confusing," Natalie admitted. "Yesterday, Sunday, the show taped our opening introductions and the invitation vendors' competition. Those two segments were aired nationally this afternoon by the network with the hope that a taste of the Southern Belle competition will whet everyone's appetite for what will be coming for the rest of the week."

"I can see that. Still, it seems like you will have too many things taped for where you are in the competition."

Maybelle joined their conversation. "The show has to tape our competitions and those of the vendors at least a day early. Some of the events take more than a day to prepare. That's why they're filming those out of sequence. In the end, some of these segments won't be shown until midweek."

"It's a good thing you have the call sheet to rely on," Sarah said.

"That's especially true if they change something from when it was mentioned earlier. By the way, I gather you haven't read tomorrow's call sheet?" Maybelle rummaged through her purse.

"No. I haven't been back to the house since this morning. I haven't picked up my copy."

"Well, there's a time change for the floral arranging competition."

Maybelle handed Sarah her folded call sheet. "The

Belles and chaperones are taping the floral arranging and delivery competition at nine."

"In the morning? But I have to work." Maybe this was her out. Flower arranging wasn't her thing and, being honest, neither was chaperoning.

"Chaperones are required or we're out of the competition. Perhaps you could take your lunch hour before you go in for the day? You don't have to do the delivery part, only the competition itself."

"That doesn't work with Fluffy and RahRah."

Maybelle pointed at the call sheet. "We can make it work. George and I have a long break after the floral arrangements get dropped off. We can run by and take care of your pets. George would love it. He misses Fluffy. I promise it won't take more than an hour to make the flower arrangements for everyone to enjoy at the retirement home."

"Whoa," Sarah protested. "There's no way we can make arrangements for everyone at the retirement center in an hour."

"We aren't. Let me remind you, this is reality TV. Each remaining Belle and her chaperone will only make one arrangement. The retirement home staff can put them in their dining room or common areas. That way, the show can claim it provided arrangements for the joy of all the residents. The delivery is simply another group photo opportunity. Chaperones won't need to be part of that, so you can go straight to work."

"What I don't understand is if they're going to be part of the delivery, why not let the guys help with the arrangements, rather than the chaperones?"

"Two reasons. First, I think the show is having us

make floral arrangements that complement our bouquets. They don't mind if the chaperones know how the colors and flowers blend with the bouquets, but they want the groom who wins to only learn the details of the bouquets, like the dress, on his wedding day."

"And the second reason?"

Maybelle struck a pose and put on her best magnolia lady accent. "Because Southern women, or should I say Southern belles, are known for their prowess at floral arranging. It's a time for us to show off our gentler sides."

"Oh, *pu-le-e-ase*," Sarah theatrically groaned. "Everything is so orchestrated. How can they call it reality TV?"

"Because, like what happened with Veronica today, there are some unscripted or partially unscripted moments within the structured setting."

"But Veronica was put up to what she did, wasn't she?"

"She was told to be a little timid about going into the mud. Veronica improvised the rest to a point that Sam wasn't happy."

"He should have been. He got a bridezilla moment." Sarah sighed. "I'll be glad when this week is over."

"Secretly, I will be too. George, though, is having a ball."

"I'm glad. Let me see if I understand the structure of the remaining days correctly. The idea is that the network will air a segment comprised of three things each day: a vendor competition whose winner will be announced the next day; a related charitable event activity by the couples, after which the public will vote on which couple will be eliminated the next day; and the moment the eliminated couple is announced."

Cliff leaned forward and spoke before Maybelle could respond. "Sarah, that was the plan, but the timing of Jed and Lucy leaving threw things off. That's why I'm having to redesign the set tonight. The way I understand the revised plan of what's on first and who's on second from the network's perspective is crazy." He took a deep breath and using his fingers for emphasis, rattled off the days and their activities:

- Sunday: The introduction, invitation, miscellaneous vendor competition, and car wash segments were taped.
- Monday: Introduction, invitation vendor competition, and car wash segments were shown. Some personal interviews and the Mudbowl charitable event were filmed.
- Tuesday: Miscellaneous vendors will be introduced to the public. The winning invitation, florist competition, and Mudbowl segments will be televised, while the floral arrangement and delivery by the Belles will be taped. The cake bakers will bake, and Lucy and Jed will be announced as having left the show.
- Wednesday: The couple eliminated after the Mudbowl will be named, the cake vendors will compete, and the floral arrangement competition will air.
- Thursday: The winning cake vendor and floral competition winners will be announced. The third-place couple will be sent home. Venue and dress vendors will be shown tailored to the final two couples. To add to the excitement, a donation in

> honor of the final two couples will be made by the
> network to a charity of their choice. The final two
> couples will be allowed to make direct last-minute
> pitches to the audience.
> • Friday: Winner is announced—dress is worn at the
>   winning venue . . . wedding is held.

Sarah pointed to the lower part of the call sheet. "This
has Chef Bernardi and Wanda's names on it for tomorrow
afternoon. Is that all the time they get to make the cakes?"

Maybelle peeked at the call sheet. "That's right."

"But they can't possibly make wedding and grooms'
cakes by themselves in—what? Four hours?"

"They're not. Chef Bernardi and Wanda already submitted sketches for the proposed wedding and grooms'
cakes. Tomorrow, they're only making a scale model of a
groom's cake associated with one of the couple's dreams.
Knowing cakes take time, they'll both be allowed, using
helpers if they like, to start making the wedding cakes for
Friday on Wednesday. The show is paying for the ingredients. A winner will be announced on Thursday and spot-
lighted during the Friday wedding. The loser's cakes will
be donated somewhere, but I don't recall where."

"Don't tell me another photo opportunity?"

"Probably."

"Are they baking in the same place? With some of the
things Chef Bernardi has said about Wanda, that could be
extremely uncomfortable for her."

"No. The plan is for Chef Bernardi to use the kitchen
at Jane's Place, while Wanda bakes at Southwind. When
they finish baking at their respective locations, the camera people will film their scale models and then blend the
tape for Wednesday."

Sarah was about to ask if the cakes were going to be judged only on looks or if somehow taste would come into play, but the unexpected tones of a xylophone being struck interrupted their conversation. In fact, the notes caught everyone's attention, bringing the activity in the room to a standstill.

Chapter 20

Sarah looked around the room to see where the melodic sounds were coming from. Flynn and Sam were standing together, near the archway. In Sam's hand was a children's xylophone. He was striking its metal bars with a hard plastic mallet. At least two cameras were in use: one on Flynn and Sam, the other catching glimpses of those in the room.

Flynn raised his hand and Sam stopped. "We thought that rather than struggling to get your attention, we might try this. It worked so well I think we should use it every time we need your attention. What do you think, Sam?"

Sam ran the mallet across the bars. "Within reason, though I must admit this is a fun way to corral everyone." His relaxed grin was replaced by a more serious look. "Flynn and I want to thank you for stepping up to the plate in a most difficult time. We could never have continued the show without your help. Out of respect to Alan, we'll run an end card in his memory after each segment that airs next week."

There was a murmur of approval.

"Thank you. And now, would everyone join me in bowing our heads for a moment of silence in his memory."

Sarah started to do what Sam requested but stopped herself. Remembering the fiction axiom that the murderer often comes to the funeral, Sarah was curious if the same might be true when one was asked to participate in a moment of silence for a person one hated. She quickly glanced around the room to see if any heads weren't bowed or eyes were open. All of the contestants were at least paying lip service to Sam's request, but none of the chaperones were.

From Heather's remarks last night, it didn't shock Sarah that Heather not only ignored Sam's request, but was fidgeting with her cell phone. Sarah rechecked the mental note she'd made to find out what it was that Heather had against Alan. Barbie and Rose also were obviously not complying. Sarah added them to her mental checklist.

Running the list through her mind, Sarah tried to think if anyone besides Heather had expressed negative feelings for Alan or if she had seen any of them interact with him in a way that might provide a motivation for murder.

Rose had experienced that séance-like episode where she kept repeating "evil" and almost fainted, but Sarah wasn't sure if her reference was to Alan as a person or to the murder itself. Barbie hadn't said anything negative about Alan, but she definitely wasn't thrilled when he stopped her from following Starr into the big dining room on the day intros were taped. It might have thwarted Barbie at that moment, but not being able to fix her daughter's makeup didn't seem like enough of a reason to murder someone.

In some ways, Jane had the best motive for having killed him because he reneged on part of what she viewed their deal to be. Still, Sarah couldn't believe it. Jane was a bimbo, a schemer, and a lot of other things, but from the few times Jane's façade had cracked in front of Sarah, she didn't think Jane had the coldhearted ability to murder anyone. The killer had to be someone else. But who?

The moment of silence over, the noise level in the room picked up until Marcus and Emily stepped to the front of the room, near where Flynn and Sam stood, and signaled for everyone's attention. Although they both wore Southwind white jackets, the contrast of Emily's simple black pants and sneakers with Marcus's baggy multicolored balloon pants and orange clogs amused Sarah. It was as if their clothing mirrored their personalities; yet somehow their differences blended.

Part of their solid cohesiveness, Sarah knew from the time she'd spent with them, came from how much Marcus and Emily admired each other. Their unselfish pride at each other's accomplishments was the big factor that made them such a great couple.

"Once again, Emily and I are delighted to welcome you to Southwind. As you can see from the menu at your place, you can choose from salmon or chicken as your main dish. For tonight's first course, your choice is between a Greek salad or minestrone soup. The sides are creamed spinach, twice-baked potatoes, and broiled Brussels sprouts. Dessert will be doubly dangerous. Using recipes and, as Chef Emily would say, a little extra love, our bakery chef extraordinaire, Wanda, has prepared a baked pear or coconut cake for you to choose from. By now, most of you have had the opportunity to eat the delicacies Wanda makes."

Marcus winked at the audience and lowered his voice, as if he were letting them in on a secret. "Emily and I repeatedly tell Wanda how good she is, but she doesn't believe us. If you have the opportunity, why don't you tell her too."

Marcus turned away from the group and zeroed his gaze in on where Wanda stood in the shadow of the door. He waved her forward. She shook her head, but when Emily stretched her hand out toward Wanda, Wanda gave in and joined Emily and Marcus. She was met with a round of applause.

Chef Bernardi stood and threw his napkin onto the floor. Without a word, he left the dining room. Sarah was stunned by his behavior and the fact that the camera caught his entire silent protest.

She saw the cameraman pan and catch Flynn following him, until Sam, with a touch to Flynn's arm, held him back. Flynn glanced in the direction Chef Bernardi had gone, but he didn't make any further effort to pursue the chef. Acting as if neither Chef Bernardi nor Flynn had done anything, Sam nodded to Marcus and Emily.

Emily took his nod as a signal to go on with the show because she immediately began speaking. "When Marcus opened our first restaurant, now the Southwind Pub, in Wheaton, our vision was to provide a casual, comfortable neighborhood dining atmosphere where the food would be of the highest quality. Some of you already have taken advantage of our big-screen TVs, burgers, and other great food, and, of course, the twenty-one varieties of beer we serve at the pub."

Marcus slid into the conversation. "But having a white tablecloth farm-to-table restaurant on Main Street was our dream. Through a combination of luck and hard work, we've been fortunate to be able to share our vision, Southwind, with you. Not only have we achieved our dream, but with support from friends like you we've traveled this road together and come out the stronger for it. Emily and I hope that, despite the competition of your contest, you find joy in this week too."

"Speaking of joy," Emily said, "please enjoy your dinner."

Marcus and Emily waved at everyone and left the dining room. Sarah noticed that as they cleared the arch into the next dining room Marcus nonchalantly wrapped his arm around Emily and Emily glanced up at him with a giant smile.

Sarah wasn't the only one who'd observed this interchange. A cameraman had caught their private moment. In fact, unlike Sarah, he didn't turn his focus away from them until they were completely out of sight. His almost silent presence while constantly filming unnerved Sarah.

Knowing her twin and Marcus as she did, Sarah knew that not only were their remarks completely genuine, but so was the respect and love they had for each other. Considering the somewhat slanted aspects the reality show was using to pull in viewers, Sarah prayed that Emily and Marcus's actions and words, if edited for the show, would reflect them as they were, rather than for some ratings purpose. Sarah feared that the contrast in their size, attire, and mannerisms—especially Marcus's colorful aspects—

would be camera fodder that would plug their restaurants but wouldn't bode well for the two of them as a couple.

Before she could continue dwelling on how her sister and her boyfriend were going to be portrayed to the American public, Sam again raised his voice above the room's conversational noise. "In a moment, dinner will be served, but Flynn and I have one more announcement to make. As you know, with Jed and Lucy leaving us, our plans for when couples would be eliminated got out of whack. Thanks to you allowing us to double up and re-arrange filming our challenges today and tomorrow, our shows will broadcast in the order we intended. Please give yourselves a hand."

Like most in the room, Sarah dutifully applauded and waited. The way things were going, she feared another bomb was about to come out of Sam's mouth. She steeled herself when he spoke.

"As I indicated, because of you, our segments will air correctly; however, because of the sequence of our shoot-ing, coupled with Jed and Lucy leaving, a couple of things are out of whack. Although the losers of our Mudbowl segment won't be announced on the air until Wednesday, we're filming the floral arranging competition tomorrow morning. Consequently, because another couple will have been eliminated by the point that segment airs, that couple won't be taping tomorrow morning, nor partici-pating in anything after tonight's dinner. Please join me in bidding Natalie and Ralph goodbye and thanking them for being such great competitors."

He clapped his hands. As the rest of the room joined in, Sarah glanced at Ralph and Natalie's shocked faces.

It was Aunt Rose's reaction, rather than Ralph or Na-talie's, that hushed the applause. Standing, she pointed a finger at Flynn and Sam. "But no one has voted. You can't arbitrarily kick them off."

"Ms. Rose," Flynn said. "This isn't our decision. It's the network's."

With a twirl of her cape, she cut Flynn off and turned to face more of the diners. "How can it be? Did we miss the viewers' votes?" She snorted. "Was it telepathic?"

"No, ma'am." Flynn paused, but again Sam didn't save him. "Based upon analytics we're not privy to from focus group audience reactions, Natalie and Ralph would have been the first couple eliminated. If Lucy and Jed . . . I'm sorry . . ." His voice trailed off as he withered under Rose's glare.

She pulled herself erect. She held her fingers together like an arrow, pointing at Sam and Flynn. "Evil permeates any room you are in. There will be more death. A curse upon your heads."

Without another word, she marched from the room. Natalie immediately followed her. Ralph, reacting a moment later, scampered to his feet so quickly his chair fell over.

Its stark clank was softened by Marcus entering through the archway, with servers behind him. "Dinner is served."

CHAPTER 21

Cliff picked up the overturned chair. His gaze met Sarah's. They didn't have to speak to know they were both appalled by what had just happened.

As the servers worked their way through the room, the initial shocked silence of the stunned guests was quickly broken. Listening, Sarah felt the remaining diners were breaking into two camps: those who felt Natalie and Ralph had been wronged and those, eager to move forward themselves, who felt that it was all part of the game. Sarah understood both positions, but as much as she felt Natalie and Ralph should have had the opportunity to be voted off by the viewers, she didn't think the voodoo theatrics of Aunt Rose were appropriate.

Her attention was diverted when one of the two waiters prepped to simultaneously serve her table paused, confused, the three dishes of Sarah's missing tablemates on his arm. He quickly recovered, but his deer-in-the-headlights look reminded her of Alan's server from last night's dinner. She glanced around the room. Alan's waiter was nowhere to be seen.

Excusing herself, she rose and walked through the main dining room, checking the face of every member of the waitstaff. None was the one who'd served Alan.

She pushed the swinging door to the kitchen open. Just as she'd predicted to Harlan, Grace was on the meat station, Emily was expediting, and Marcus was busy with salads and vegetables. Two waiters, whose backs were to her, gathered plates and garnishes to carry into the dining room. Sarah waited for them to turn. When they did, she saw that neither was the man she was looking for. The waiter from last night was not working tonight's Southwind dinner shift.

"Grace," she called to her friend. The copper-skinned woman partially raised her arm with its farm-to-table sleeve tattoo at Sarah, but she remained concentrated on the meat she was tending. Sarah moved closer and repeated her name as Grace plated two steaks.

"Hi, Sarah. Good to be back in the saddle, but I can't talk now. I didn't realize how quickly one can become rusty."

"Hey, it's only been a few months since you left Southwind to teach full-time." She assessed her friend. Grace looked happy and rested. "It looks like the new gig is agreeing with you."

"It is." Grace moved quickly to flip two lamb chops to sear their other side. She checked something on the far side of the grill. "Let's visit later?"

"Sounds good. One quick question: Are all of your student servers from last night back tonight?"

Grace plated the lamb chops. Using a towel, she dabbed a stray drop of meat juice from the plate, then passed it to Marcus to finish the plate with vegetables and garnishes before putting it on the ledge from which Emily was expediting. Amazed at the precision and teamwork she was viewing, Sarah didn't want to break their rhythm, but she needed to know whether there were any missing waiters. "Grace? The waiters from last night?"

"No, not all of them are working again tonight. Some had other jobs or plans. Why?"

She placed four steaks on the grill in front of her.

Having her answer, Sarah didn't need to disrupt the kitchen's rhythm any further. "It's not a big deal. I'll catch you later. I think you've got your hands full right now."

Grace acknowledged Sarah's statement as Sarah backed out of the kitchen and went back to her table.

"What was that all about?" Cliff asked as she returned to her seat across from him. She picked up her fork and knife and cut herself a piece of chicken.

Meeting Cliff's gaze, Sarah swallowed. She put down her fork, no longer hungry. "Nothing."

"Nothing? You ran out of the dining room as if you were looking for a ghost."

"More of a human being in the flesh than a ghost, but I didn't find him." She quickly told Cliff about the missing waiter and his possible connection to Alan's death. "I don't know if it was a lost student or someone deliberately serving Alan a tainted dinner. Between needing to be at work in case Harlan has something for me to do before his Thursday trial and now having the floral arranging time changed, so I have to take my lunch hour before I've had breakfast, I don't know when I can go over to the culinary school tomorrow to see if I can spot the missing-in-action waiter in a class or on campus."

"There's an easier way, but you're not going to like this answer . . ."

Sarah stared at Cliff, waiting for him to explain.

"This is one time you can easily let the professionals do the snooping for you." When she started to protest, he held his hand up to silence her. "Before you flip out, let me explain. Emily and Marcus run an aboveboard operation in every sense of the word."

"True. Both worked in some bad places and vowed they'd never do anything except by the books."

"Which is what helps here. Everyone who worked tonight or last night would have provided their names and contact information, as well as their Social Security numbers in order to be paid correctly. The police, or even your sister and Marcus, can match the names of the servers from last night with those working tonight to see which ones don't overlap. Those individuals can be questioned by the Wheaton police or brought by them somewhere so you can see all of them at one time. That way, you'll either be able to make an identification quickly or know that the person who served Alan his dinner wasn't one of the students."

"Cliff, you're a genius."

"That's nice to hear, but you would have thought of it sooner or later. In the meantime, why don't you share the idea with Harlan? He can prompt the police to look into this angle."

"I will. It's so noisy in here, I better go outside and call him. If everyone finishes before I get back, will you make sure Mother gets home or at least sticks with some of the folks walking back to Jane's Place?"

"Will do."

Sarah grabbed her purse and went outside to call Harlan. Her call went directly to voice mail. She was about to leave him a message when she realized he probably was at the office working on Thursday's court case. Rather than going back inside, she decided this was important enough to run by the office and interrupt his case preparation.

She was right. Harlan was impressed. "It's definitely a logical way of ruling out if the person who served Alan was one of the students or not. Good thinking."

"The credit goes to Cliff. He's the one who came up with the idea. I was going to go over to Carleton and check out students in the different classrooms or ask Grace to help me when he came up with this alternative."

"Okay, then my hat is off to Cliff. Back in the picture, I gather?"

"Harlan Endicott! When did you get nosy about my private life?"

"I'm sorry." He picked up a paper on his desk and then put it down. From the redness flushing his cheeks, she knew he was embarrassed. "That was out of line."

A year ago, she'd have been upset that he'd seemingly crossed the line between their professional and personal relationships, but now, after walking dogs together every Saturday, being involved in solving murders, and knowing he only cared about her well-being, she realized his friend side spoke before his boss persona controlled his mouth. "I'll give you a bye, this time."

Rather than meeting her gaze, he put his full attention on shuffling the papers on his desk. She decided to give him a break. "You know, we're just friends. Because he's doing construction things for the show and I'm chaperoning, we realized we were going to be thrown together a lot this week. Better to be friends than be awkward around each other."

"Ah, yes. I can see that." He blinked and met her gaze.

While he was still uncomfortable, she decided to drop her other bombshell on him. "Harlan, the show changed the time of the floral arranging competition from late afternoon until nine tomorrow morning."

"Oh?"

She hurried to get the problem part out of her mouth. "They're requiring the Belles and their chaperones to participate."

He pressed his lips together in a thin line. "I thought this wasn't going to interfere with your workday. We can't afford to have you miss most of tomorrow."

"I know. The problem is that if I'm not there, Maybelle and George will be disqualified."

This time he didn't play with the papers lying in front of him on his desk. Instead, he leaned forward. Putting his elbow on his desk, he rested his chin on his thumb while holding his forefinger just above his lips. "From what you've said, they're probably going to be disqualified anyway after the floral arranging so that the show can feature Alabama vs. Auburn as the final two competing couples. What does it matter if you're there or not? The result will be the same."

"Harlan, you know my mother. She wants to go out with her head up high. Besides, she's the ever-optimist. Maybelle really believes there's a chance George and she might make the final two."

"Doubtful."

"I know that, but if you'll let me be late, that will be

my lunch hour. She and George will take care of Fluffy and RahRah for me during the day."

Harlan closed his eyes for a moment. He let out a sigh. "Do I have a choice?"

"Do I?"

He let out a sound between a snort and a chuckle. "Just the idea—floral arranging?"

"Don't even go there. I can't believe I'm having to do this. If you thought my office skills were weak when you hired me, wait till you see my floral arranging skills—on TV, no less. All I can say is that luckily my mother is incredibly talented when it comes to arranging flowers. Let's hope they let me sit back and watch. Otherwise . . ."

They both laughed. After the awkwardness of a few minutes ago, Sarah was glad Harlan and she were good friends.

"Seriously, how's your preparation for Thursday coming?"

"I got so much done today that even with having to mind the office by myself tomorrow morning, I'm in good shape."

She ignored his dig about tomorrow morning. In the past he had told her that only 12 percent of disputed cases ever went to a full hearing. She wondered if his detailed prep would end up being for naught. "Do you really think the case will go to trial?"

"At the moment, I have to believe so. We tendered a fair settlement offer earlier this week, but the other side rejected it outright. Yesterday they submitted a ridiculous counteroffer that only took my client and me about five minutes to reject. As of now, if you make it in, don't look for me in the office Thursday."

Sarah prayed not to be hit by a lightning bolt, considering how things kept changing with the Southern Belle competition. "Don't worry," she assured Harlan. "I'll hold down the fort. When will you share Cliff's idea with Chief Gerard or one of the other members of the force?"

"Now it's my turn to tell you not to worry. Chief Gerard was at a seminar today, but I'll make sure the Wheaton police force gets this information tonight. Hopefully, they'll jump on it tomorrow morning."

She was surprised Harlan knew Chief Gerard had been out of the office. Either he'd called him about something or their bromance was back on. Her curiosity got the better of her. "Harlan, how did you know Chief Gerard took a class today?"

"Because I told him about it. It was a continuing education course on forensic evidence being taught in Birmingham that I thought might interest him."

"And help him do his job better?"

Harlan grinned. "You never can tell what you'll pick up in a class or anywhere else, for that matter, which can translate to your everyday work."

He put his hands flat on his desk, the smile gone from his face. "Speaking of picking up things, anything else happen this evening that might help me defend my client if Chief Gerard doesn't find a better suspect?"

Sarah thought back upon the dinner at Southwind. It seemed so long ago. "Actually, there were a few things that might interest you." She filled him in on the exchange before dinner on the porch and Jane's anger with Chef Bernardi. "The funny thing is that although she was the most strident in expressing her opinion, I think most of the other people on the porch agreed with her. I just wasn't sure what it was that they wanted him to restart."

Harlan drummed his fingers on the papers on his desk but didn't say anything. She wondered what idea she might have triggered. When he semi-grunted, rather than following up with a question or comment, Sarah told him about Chef Bernardi's anger after Marcus and Emily called special attention to Wanda.

"Surely, Chef Bernardi must have realized the cameras were on. He didn't say anything. He simply stood up, threw his napkin down, and walked out of the room. Flynn started to follow Chef Bernardi, but Sam restrained him by swiftly touching Flynn's arm. I think Flynn might still have wanted to follow Chef Bernardi, but he stayed with Sam. Together, they went through a series of announcements that were pretty much what we all expected until they eliminated Natalie and Ralph."

"They what?"

Sarah quickly summarized Sam and Flynn's announcement and Aunt Rose's reaction.

Harlan went into a flurry of motion, rifling papers and folders on his desk. "You're telling me Natalie and Ralph were kicked off by Sam and Flynn rather than the public?"

"Yes." Sarah nodded as she spoke, but then stopped and corrected herself. "Actually, they tried to make it clear that the decision wasn't theirs. It was based upon the reaction to the different couples of a focus group or groups after they viewed the introductory segments that aired this afternoon. In fact, they said if a couple had gone home after the car wash competition, the focus groups voted to eliminate Natalie and Ralph."

Opening a folder, Harlan scanned the notes he'd made on a legal pad. He turned the folder around so that Sarah could read it from the side of the desk where she was standing. "This was what was on the back of Alan's call sheet, but Chief Gerard and I weren't positive what it referred to. Now, I am."

As she bent forward to read what he'd written, she noticed that the folder's label was *Belle-Jane*. Harlan might now understand what they stood for, but the list of letters and numbers scrawled on the page were meaningless to Sarah. "Is there something special I'm supposed to understand from this?"

"Yes." He leaned back in his chair, a cocky smile spreading across his face.

His satisfied grin was almost more frustrating to her than what was on the paper. "Well, I'm clueless. Give me a hint."

"I gather you don't gamble?"

"You're the second person today to ask me that. Are these letters with plus and minus numbers something a gambler would understand?"

Even before Harlan replied "immediately," it dawned on Sarah that what she was looking at had to be tied to the line Cliff had told her about. "Wait a minute. I don't quite get it, but I gather this has something to do with the line?"

"It is the line, or part of it. Alan or someone apparently copied down whatever information they wanted from the line on the night he was killed."

Sarah read the list again. "The letters correspond to the different contestants' first names."

"I think so too. The real line would have more columns with the date and other things, but whoever made these notes simply jotted down the meat of the line. I assume the letters, like N and R, are tied to a couple's names, while the pluses and minuses reflect the odds or likelihood of each couple winning the Southern Belle competition. The couple expected to win has minus or negative odds while the ones projected to lose have positive or plus odds."

"The more of a long shot, the bigger the positive number, which means someone betting on them, should they win, would receive a bigger payoff?"

"That's right. Based upon the fact that N and R have the largest positive number, I'd say whoever did the handicapping for the Southern Belle decided Natalie and Ralph were the largest long shot to make it through the competition. If they succeeded, they would have paid off the most."

Sarah pulled the paper closer. "By that logic, it looks like Jed and Lucy and my mother and George were also expected to be longer shots than the Alabama and Auburn lovers." She pushed the folder back to Harlan. "Even without a line, I could have told you that."

"You could have, but you wouldn't have won any money on your hunch and you wouldn't have cleaned up if things changed and your long shot came in."

Sarah sat in one of the two chairs that faced his desk. She remembered how Cliff explained how the line was fluid—subject to moving because of unforeseen occurrences. Excited, she leaned forward and put her finger on the plus sign next to *L&J*. "Harlan, Cliff told me Chef Bernardi was taking bets on the couples. That would make him the bookie, right?"

"Right."

"Okay, but let's think about this a few different ways. If Alan was simply placing a bet, he might have written down the odds. He also could have written them down if he was going to try to influence the outcome to fit them in some way. Do you think he could have had a deal hatched with Chef Bernardi to make sure one of the long shots came in?"

"It's possible, but remember things changed the night Alan died. Granny with her shotgun caused Lucy and Jed to be eliminated out of order."

"Which took out one of the long shots and probably meant the line moved after their departure was announced." Sarah drummed her fingers on his desk, thinking for a minute. Her thoughts jumbled together. She tried to slow them down but couldn't.

"Harlan, let me try out some ideas on you."

"Okay." He sat back and waited.

"On these celebrity shows, the public is sometimes fickle. They take a liking to a person because of physical looks or something the person says or does. Consequently, it's not unusual for a long shot to stay in the game while a favorite is eliminated. From meeting them and seeing the introduction tape, I can tell you Lucy and Jed generated a kind of warmth and likability that Natalie and Ralph don't have. Something that could have been played on through editing or camera shots to keep them in the competition for the long run."

"Are you saying Alan was going to throw the contest?"

Sarah pressed her lips together. "Alan was throwing money around setting up charity events and I think he was malicious in how he showed those dailies at the first dinner. After all, this is a TV show, not a movie. Dailies, according to him, aren't usually shown. He did it to stir up trouble or simply be mean."

"But what about the gambling?"

Sarah thought about his question for a moment. She closed her eyes and tried to picture Alan when he was talking to her at dinner. He'd been relaxed and in control, almost cocky at what he was going to reveal in the second film clip. Yet, he hadn't stayed around to see the seeds of discord that he planted.

"Alan may have bet, or he may have copied down the line because he was angry that the betting was going on. He had money and was established. I don't think he needed to throw the show. In fact, his refusing to do it might somehow have been a motive for him being killed. I'm more inclined to think if he wrote down the line it was tied with him being furious to find out others involved with the show might be trying to influence things to win a wager."

"We don't have any proof of either of your theories."

"In a way we do." This time it was Sarah who sat back in her chair, waiting to see if Harlan viewed things the same way she did. Her excitement getting the better of her, she pushed herself forward, her arms on his desk.

"After Alan's death and Granny caused Lucy and Jed to be eliminated, the line shifted. People moving their bets could account for the shift if they had money to bet differently. But what if they didn't? What if they'd lost their shirt betting on Lucy and Jed to go further than they did? If there was a fix on who was going to win and that fix was Lucy and Jed, anyone who bet on them could have completely lost their money when they were eliminated because, as Cliff explained to me, it would be comparable to a racehorse being scratched."

He raised his eyebrows as he again tapped his fingers on the papers on his desk. "I doubt our competitors want to be compared to racehorses."

Sarah rose and paced his office. "But it makes sense. Think about what I overheard when Jane was letting loose on the porch. She wanted, and everyone pretty much supported her, for Chef Bernardi to start over."

"Okay, if we assume Jed and Lucy were scratched like a horse, why wouldn't Chef Bernardi have started over? As I understand gambling, if an animal is scratched before the race, it's a push and money is refunded."

She stopped in front of his desk, making herself stay still and face him even as she felt a wave of energy he couldn't see pulse through her. "But that's not the case here. The competition had started. It was beyond a push when Jed and Lucy were officially announced as eliminated."

"How?"

"Very simple. If it had just been the advance commercials teasing the segment, the gamblers probably could have claimed a push. But that wasn't the case. The introduction of the contestants and the invitation segments were taped on Sunday and aired on Monday. By the time everyone was on the porch Monday night, the competition not only had begun on Sunday, but there was film documenting Jed and Lucy's participation. For all intents and purposes, even though the introductory segment didn't air until Monday afternoon, once it did, the public had met Lucy and Jed as real contestants. That's why Chef Bernardi said 'What is, is.'"

"He said what?"

Sarah threw her hands up in front of her, as if shaking them in the air would make Harlan see things as clearly as she did. "He said 'What is, is' to reiterate that they were beyond the point of a push. You see, in the public's eye, they were still competitors because their introduction and car wash segments aired on Monday. They weren't out of the game until their leaving was announced on Tuesday."

"I get it. By that premise, despite what Jane and everyone was asking of him, there was no going backwards."

"That's right," Sarah said. "It's exactly what Chef Bernardi said. 'What is, is.'"

"Which means people lost money." Harlan stood up and walked around his desk. As he paced his office, Sarah twisted in her chair to follow his path.

"Sarah, Jane's been saying this competition was going to get her out of the hole. I couldn't see enough of a revenue stream to do that. If Jane bet on the long shot, perhaps because she had inside information or believed she did, that might account for everything."

"She could have thought she'd make enough to be out of debt. But if there's no push, she's even deeper in the hole. No wonder she wanted Chef Bernardi to start over."

"The same would be true for anyone who bet on Jed and Lucy to not be the first couple eliminated. Does anyone else have a reason to have wanted Jed and Lucy to win?"

"Or, to consider throwing the contest?" Sarah faced Harlan. "They all do. Whether it's an opportunity to assume more control on the show or to get their own show or any of the myriad of reasons that the chaperones discussed in the second tape that Alan showed, everyone has an ulterior motive for being involved with the Southern Belle competition."

Sarah glanced at her watch. "Oh my, I've got to get back to the house. I'm on duty."

"What about RahRah and Fluffy tonight?"

"I took care of them after work and Emily is spending the night, so they're okay. It's my mother who could be in trouble for lacking a chaperone if I don't get back to Jane's Place soon."

"Be careful. I'm going to get with Chief Gerard tonight for sure, but from what we just discussed, my gut says the murderer is still close by."

Sarah appreciated his concern and that even though he was cautioning her to be careful, he hadn't added anything about leaving it to the professionals. "My gut says the same thing. Believe me, I'm going back to Jane's Place, but making sure my mother's and my doors are locked. The end of this competition can't come soon enough for me."

"Or me," Harlan said quietly.

CHAPTER 22

"Every flower has a meaning, Sarah. That could be important in how we make our arrangement today."

Sarah snapped her fingers. "I'm sorry. I forgot my flower dictionary."

"Don't get flippant with me."

"I'm not, but Mo—Maybelle, flowers and anything to do with floral arranging is as foreign to me as being in a kitchen."

"If you do exactly what I tell you, we'll be fine. I see we have assigned workstations." Maybelle pointed at three six-foot-long metal tables, each with a sign naming one of the remaining contestants, set up in the middle of the floral shop's workroom where the competition was being filmed. The shop's everyday workstations and benches had been pushed out of the way against the room's walls. A giant flower cart, overflowing with brightly colored flowers and vases, was positioned across the room at an equal distance from the three tables.

With Sarah at her side, Maybelle, her hands on her hips, assessed the room's arrangement. "I'm assuming they're going to have us three remaining Belles and our chaperones do a mad dash across the room to that flower cart to grab flowers and whatever else we need to use in making our arrangements."

Sarah looked around. This wasn't a set. Suzy's Flowers was a locally owned family-run business. Although Sarah was certain that the store's owner was being paid for being closed for the time the filming would take and the flowers being used, not to mention the florist getting credit either at the end of the show or in a voice-over, it didn't seem right that they might leave the store in worse shape than they'd started.

Other than the workstations and benches being pushed back, there were still racks with ceramic and glass vases, bins with flowers, a ribbon stand, and other things that could be damaged in a melee. "Maybe they'll let us take turns. Surely they don't want us to take a chance of destroying anything in the shop."

Maybelle made a *tsk-tsk* sound with her tongue. "It wouldn't be as interesting for the viewers if we did it in a civilized manner. No, I think it will be a free-for-all."

Sarah inwardly groaned. As a Girl Scout, Sarah had been taught to leave places better than she found them. It was becoming obvious that this lesson hadn't ever gotten through to Sam or Flynn. The last thing she wanted was to be part of a chaotic activity that added to the hint of a headache she had. She wished she'd eaten breakfast or taken something for her head. If her mother was right, this entire floral arranging event was going to be a massive headache.

Part of her problem, she knew, was her lack of sleep last night. Taking Harlan's warning to heart, she'd made sure their bedroom doors were locked before she made a quick call to Emily. After the two rehashed the day and Emily assured her RahRah and Fluffy were fine, Sarah hung up. Wishing she had some of Emily's warm almond milk laced with maple flavoring, Sarah turned in for the night.

Tired as she was, Sarah should have fallen asleep the minute her head hit her pillow, but her mind wouldn't stop racing. She particularly missed RahRah. It was on nights like this that RahRah helped relax her. Matching her breaths to the even purring sounds he made when he slept or simply having him cuddle against her legs always calmed her down.

Sarah finally fell asleep, but it was fitful. At one point, she dreamed her mother and she were being chased by a person whose face was hidden by a shadow. Just as she was about to see who the person was, Sarah woke in a cold sweat. She spent the rest of the night staring at the ceiling or the bedside clock. Consequently, the last thing Sarah wanted to do this morning was push and shove for some stupid flowers.

Her lips pressed into a pout, she refrained from sharing her thoughts with her mother. She perked to attention when she realized Maybelle was in the process of dictating what she wanted Sarah to do when the moment of insanity was upon them.

"From what I can see on the cart, different flowers are divided by color and specie into separate pots. I expect most of the contestants or chaperones will grab everything in a pot, like all the red roses, to preempt the rest of us using them. That may seem like a good competitive strategy, but it isn't going to make for a pretty arrangement."

Her mother was right. Snagging the popular flowers to be defensive was exactly what Sarah would instinctively have done without her mother's guidance. Thankfully, Maybelle obviously already had an idea of what she planned to create from simply staring across the room at the cart.

"What I want you to do is ignore the flowers. I'll take care of those," Maybelle instructed. "You concentrate on getting as much greenery, in all sizes, as you can, as well as those delicate white baby's breath flowers that you've seen people use to accent an arrangement. Do you understand your assignment?"

Sarah rolled her eyes. "Yes, Mother."

Any correction of Sarah's reference to her mother was interrupted by the other contestants and chaperones joining them.

"I'm not looking forward to this," Starr said. "There are a lot of things I do well, but when it comes to flowers, I always tell Lance if he's going to bring me any, he better already have the florist put them in a vase."

Sarah laughed, but stopped when Barbie rebuked her. "A Southern lady doesn't laugh or make fun of another woman's weaknesses."

"I wasn't. I was simply commiserating with Starr. I'm in the same boat."

Ignoring Sarah's explanation, Barbie continued to criticize Sarah's behavior until Heather cut her off. "Barbie, relax. This is just one big game. Look across the room. They've given us more than enough flowers and other things to use to make sure none of us absolutely fails."

Their conversation halted as Sam entered the room and began to give them directions. "Veronica, Starr, and Maybelle, and your chaperones, please take your places at the workstations with your names on them. You'll find the different tools of the trade you'll need to make your arrangements on your tables. The flowers and vases you can choose from are on the cart across the way."

Maybelle nudged Sarah, who ignored her mother.

"When I say 'Action,' Flynn will come in from the door near the flower cart. Look excited to see him. He'll explain everything for the audience by way of giving you your assignment and telling you that you have thirty minutes to complete your task. Because we're now caught up, the audience will be the one voting for the winning arrangement and deciding which couple will be eliminated after this challenge. Good luck."

Once everyone was in place, Sam cued the action to begin. Flynn entered, smiled at everyone, but then looked directly into the camera with a red light lit on its top.

"Good morning and welcome to our floral arranging competition. As everyone knows, the mark of a true Southern Belle, besides her drawl, is her homemaking ability. One way she makes her home warm and inviting is through the different ways she uses flowers from the garden she carefully tends."

He took a step closer to the cart, gesturing at it with an open hand. The light on the camera he'd been looking at went out as another camera went live. The cameraman working the second camera moved from a distance shot of the cart to a close-up of a container filled with white roses. When the shot was complete, the first camera went live again. This time, although he kept a good part of his face turned toward the camera, Flynn shifted his angle to make it appear that he was looking at the six women.

"Part of a beautiful arrangement is having all of its ingredients blend together. That's how it is in most things in life. Today, we've asked a special guest judge to help demonstrate how blending things right can be seen in all elements of our competition." Flynn held his hand out toward the door he had previously used. It opened again. The camera followed Chef Bernardi as he entered, waved at Flynn, and walked across the room to a small-skirted table Sarah hadn't previously noticed. The table had an assortment of bowls, bottles, and small containers on it. Some of the ingredients were dry while others were liquids.

"Ladies," Chef Bernardi said, acknowledging the contestants and chaperones. "As Flynn indicated, the audience will be looking to see how you blend various flowers to make a final thing of beauty. Baking is the same."

As he gestured to the items on the table, the cameraman took a close-up of the tabletop's contents. "We start with a mix of unrelated items." He held up a bowl and a small bag of flour. "Although my flour differs from yours, it still is the basis for my end product."

Chef Bernardi continued talking while measuring the separate ingredients and mixing them together in the bowl. Finally, after holding the bowl with his goopy mixture at an angle for a camera shot, he poured the mixture into a Bundt pan. He put the pan on the table and reached under the table for something hidden from Sarah's view by the skirting. "If we had the time and an oven, I would bake this, changing its consistency into a beautiful cake, but through the magic of TV, I'll simply show you the end product." With a flare, Chef Bernardi revealed a finished cake plated perfectly.

The women and Flynn all applauded. With a mock salute to everyone, Chef Bernardi left the workroom. Flynn went over to the cake and picked at a piece of it. "Delicious. Here's hoping your arrangements will be as perfect."

Flynn wiped his hands on a napkin before repositioning himself next to the flower cart. "Veronica, Starr, and Maybelle, you and your chaperones will be making floral arrangements for the residents of Wheaton's Sunshine Village retirement home to enjoy. Once I say *go*, you'll have thirty minutes to make anything you want, but your arrangement must complement the colors you asked to have in your bouquet. Our viewers will vote on your flower arranging skills, while Judge Bernardi will vote on how well you blend your arrangement with your proposed bouquet. Based upon an averaging of their votes, one more couple will be going home. Not to add any pressure, but right now there are three of you left in the competition. After today, we'll be down to our final two who have a chance for a perfect wedding. Good luck."

Sarah reflected about how when she visited George, she often observed him and the other residents glued to the big-screen television in the home's television lounge. Perhaps, if George and her mother could mobilize his fellow residents to watch the show featuring this segment and then vote, it would help boost their vote count. Even though her mother didn't expect to win, coming in second would feel pretty good to her.

"One other thing," Flynn said. "When I say 'go,' all of you will only have forty-five seconds to make one trip to the flower cart to get the flowers and vase you'll need to make the arrangement that complements your bouquet. Because you previously gave our floral finalists ideas of the colors you'd like to see in your bouquets, we've made sure those colors are somewhere on the cart. Understand?"

Everyone made a sound or sign of acquiescence.

"Good. Go."

After a second of hesitation, the hunt for flowers was on. It was exactly the state of confusion and elbowing her mother predicted. Rather than risk her mother's ire, Sarah ignored everyone else and stuck to retrieving the two items her mother had tasked her with. It wasn't until she dropped the greenery and baby's breath on their work-station that Sarah looked to see what the other teams had grabbed.

Much like Maybelle had predicted, Veronica's team had scooped up every one of the red and white roses. Sarah assumed Veronica and Heather's flower choice had a direct correlation to Alabama's colors. She wasn't sure if Starr and Barbie had a theme in mind. The flowers on their workstation looked to Sarah like a mishmash. Sarah thought the lavender-blue flowers were lilacs or hyacinths, but she wasn't sure what the pink and yellow flowers or the orange-colored blossoms were. Sarah also noted a few pieces of greenery on their table, but nothing compared to the amount her mother and she had.

Besides the greenery Sarah had collected, her mother had gathered a variety of pastel-colored flowers. Sarah couldn't identify most of them, but even she could envision how her mother might blend them with the baby's breath and greenery. "Is there anything you want me to do, other than stay out of your way?"

Maybelle picked up the clear tall vase she'd chosen.

She handed it and a bottle of vinegar sitting on their workstation to Sarah. "Go over to the sink, wash the vase with the dish soap that's there and some of this vinegar. When you finish, dry it thoroughly and then fill the vase with lukewarm water about three quarters of the way to the top. While you do that, I'm going to strip the leaves that will be below the waterline from the greenery and flowers."

Although Sarah wasn't sure why she had to dry the vase thoroughly before putting more water into it, she did what her mother directed. By the time Sarah returned from the sink, her mother was finished stripping the leaves and was cutting, to different lengths, the various greenery stems at a 45-degree angle.

Maybelle took the vase from Sarah. She placed it in the middle of the worktable and unlike the random way Sarah would have thrown everything into the vase, Maybelle placed the largest flowers and greenery in a circular fashion. Once her bottom nest or base was established, she continued positioning flowers, from big to small, in the vase in a circular fashion. Sarah thought the arrangement couldn't be prettier, but her mother slipped a few accent pieces of the baby's breath in among the flowers and greenery.

As she admired her mother's work, there was a large crash followed by a word uttered by Barbie that Sarah knew the show would have to bleep. Glancing at Barbie and Starr's table, Sarah saw their orange-colored vase was lying on its side, flowers strewn in every direction, and water dripping over the edge of the table. Uttering another expletive that one rarely heard cross the lips of a Southern lady, Barbie righted the vase and shoved a handful of blue and orange flowers into it.

"Time," Flynn called. "Hands down."

As a cameraman zeroed in on the finished arrangements and the competitors, Sarah looked at Veronica and Heather's table. They had indeed used their roses to reflect Alabama's colors. The roses stood at different heights in a red ceramic vase shaped like an elephant, which was Alabama's mascot. A white ribbon circling the elephant's neck was tied in a bow. The ribbon's exposed ends had been cut on a slant and notched. The final arrangement was a simple, but striking, table arrangement.

Contrasting her mother's arrangement against Barbie and Starr's disaster, it struck Sarah that when the viewers evaluated the three arrangements side by side, it was more probable Starr, rather than Maybelle, would be voted off the show. From the way Barbie's mouth dropped and her gaze vacillated from the flowers in front of her to Flynn and then to Sam, Sarah realized Barbie must be sharing the same thought.

In the end, it would be up to the public, but if Sarah was, as Cliff mentioned, a betting person, she didn't know which would make her more nervous—knowing the Alabama-Auburn even-money bet was no longer safe or wondering what the impact of the dark horse coming up from behind would be on the line.

CHAPTER 23

Once the grooms-to-be joined the Belles to prepare to deliver the flower arrangements, the chaperones were dismissed. Barbie hovered near Starr and Lance, but Heather and Sarah silently walked out of the building together. Sarah realized this might be the only time she'd have one-on-one time with Heather, but she wasn't sure how to ask her about her relationship with Alan. As she tried to think how to pose her question, Sarah turned toward the parking lot. But Heather started to go the opposite way, as if she was walking back to Jane's Place.

"Heather, do you need a ride?"

"That would be lovely. I thought, like they made sure all the contestants got to the retirement home, they'd have a way for us to get back to Jane's Place. Rather than bring multiple cars, I let Trey, who came over early for breakfast, drop Veronica and me off this morning."

"I'm surprised they didn't make provision for the chaperones. Once they do the photo opportunity drop-off, I wonder if they're going to take my mother back to Jane's Place or leave her at the retirement center?"

"Would you like me to call Trey and have him make sure she gets back to Jane's Place if that's where she wants to go?"

"That would be great."

As they walked to Sarah's parked Honda, Heather called Trey. Getting into the front seat, Heather told her it was all set. "He was planning on going back to Jane's Place anyway. He figured grazing at the craft table would give him a free lunch."

"He's a growing boy," Sarah said.

"Only if it stays as muscle. I'm afraid he's going to have to cut back on his eating now that his football days are over."

"What does he plan to do now?"

"Finish school and then work. He's getting a communications degree and hopes to find a broadcasting-related job."

"He hasn't finished school?"

"No. When he was playing for the college, he wasn't taking a full load. After his eligibility ran out, he sat on the bench in Canada for a year before wising up that professional football wasn't going to be the ticket to what he really wants."

"What's that?"

"Marriage, children, and a stable home life. Trey didn't grow up with much of anything, so he's thankful football made it possible for him to attend college. He's practical enough to realize that it's time to come home, finish his degree, and move on. Trey is only a few courses short of graduating."

"And Veronica?"

"She wants the same things he does. Since they met in high school, she's supported his dreams. She even gave up cheerleading scholarship opportunities to follow him to the college of his choice and moved to Canada when American teams wouldn't take him. She's ready to settle down too. If things work out, Trey and she will both graduate a year from May."

"She's a year behind Starr."

"In school now, yes, but all the way through high school they were in the same grade."

"Someone mentioned Veronica, Starr, Trey, and Lance went to high school together, but I guess it slipped my mind."

"Veronica is only a few months older than Starr. Veronica was a cheerleader while Starr did the beauty pageant circuit, but they're friends and at one time they thought they'd both end up the wives of professional football players. That is, until the car accident." Heather clamped her teeth together and was silent.

Sarah turned on the ignition. As she slowly pulled out of her parking space, she decided to try a different tactic, for Jane's sake, before they reached Jane's Place.

"When I met Alan at dinner the other night, he made me feel uncomfortable. Later, you mentioned he wasn't a particularly nice person. I was wondering why you felt that way."

"I shouldn't have said that. It's not nice to speak ill of the dead." Heather looked out the window as Sarah stopped for a red light.

Now that Heather was being guarded, Sarah realized she didn't have much time to break down the barrier Heather was putting up. "Well, even though I wasn't there with the rest of the chaperones, I found the clip he showed disturbing. I thought you defused the situation well. Similarly, even though you were as shocked as the rest of us, it was pretty impressive how you locked eyes and calmed Jane down."

"Thank you, but it was only a matter of letting my training take over in both situations."

The light turned green and Sarah turned onto Main Street. "Your training?"

"This week I'm a chaperone. Most weeks, I'm a psychologist specializing in family conflicts." She crossed her arms over her seat belt. "Why are you suddenly curious about what I thought of Alan?"

Sarah decided honesty might get her further with a psychologist than dodging the issue. She was about to park in front of Jane's Place when she saw Jane sweeping leaves off the walkway. Sarah drove past Jane, opting for the driveway to the back parking lot. She stopped in a spot near the kitchen door, leaving the motor running, sensing this wasn't going to be a long conversation.

"Look, for a lot of personal reasons, I don't much like Jane, but I don't think she's a killer. I'm trying to get a handle on what other people knew or thought about Alan."

"Personal reasons. That's what I hear every day. There's not much to add to my story that you didn't hear in the snide hits Barbie and I took at each other on the tape. I'm sure you gathered that Barbie and I go way back. Way back is high school for us too. I was the head cheerleader, she was the dance team captain and involved in the pageant circuit. At one point we both dated a guy named Jake."

"The one you called Jake the Snake?"

"That's the one. He was that playboy every girl in the class wants to go out with. Handsome, witty, the owner of a convertible, and a year ahead of us in school. We dated during the summer of my junior year and into football season of my senior year. At that point, if you ask Barbie, she'll tell you she moved in on my territory and I sat around pining for him to come back to me. The fact of the matter was that Jake and my relationship already had run its course; he was back to dating around, but as Jake did with all of his girlfriends, we stayed friends."

Friends? This story was beginning to hit home a little too closely.

"Jake started college during the summer session after our graduation. Alan was his roommate that summer and throughout college. It was during a night of gambling and drinking, after Jake threw snake eyes twice in a row at a craps table, that Alan dubbed him Jake the Snake. It stuck at the frat and became what everyone called him from then on."

"You all ended up at college together?"

"No. I went to a small private school. It was the summer before I left for school when I met Alan at a frat party in Tuscaloosa that Barbie and I went to together. Alan took an interest in me, but he had too much to drink and got out line. Before anything happened, other than my blouse being torn, Jake came to my rescue. He got some other guys to take care of Alan and he was calming me down when Barbie came into the room. She misread the situation, blew up, and to this day doesn't believe that what she saw was perfectly innocent between Jake and me. She thought then, and still does today, that instead of the problem being Alan, Jake and I had picked up where we left off."

Having seen Barbie in action, Sarah could imagine what a firebrand a younger Barbie probably was. She also could believe that once Barbie got an idea in her head, it couldn't be changed.

"My friendship with Barbie ended that night. I went on to my college, met a great guy, married, and had Veronica. Instead of starting school, Barbie put her energy into the pageantry circuit. She married Jake a week or so after things blew up for her at the Miss Alabama pageant. They divorced when Starr was a baby. Jake moved to New York and is still a high roller. To my knowledge, Jake's always been a caring, although absent, dad, especially in the past few years."

Keeping her hands on the wheel, Sarah glanced sideways at Heather. "I gather you know that because Jake and you maintained your friendship?"

Heather laughed. "No, over the years, because of the friendship between Starr and Veronica, what I learned was from things Veronica told me. Although Jake and I parted on good terms, I hadn't seen him in years, until Saturday afternoon. I was getting us settled into Jane's Place, while Veronica, Trey, Starr, and Lance were off doing something fun, when I ran into Jake in the front hall. He'd been in Birmingham for business and had popped over to surprise Starr before he met Alan, Sam, and Flynn for dinner. Because Starr wasn't there, we talked for a few minutes. That's when I learned he was responsible for Veronica and Starr both being Southern Belle finalists."

"In what way?"

"When Alan started casting for this show, he was the one who initiated the contact with Veronica and Trey, supposedly after becoming aware of them through an alumni contact. Obviously, he already knew about Starr from Jake."

"Are you saying Alan deliberately cast the two of them against each other like he did with Jane's Place and Southwind?"

"Exactly. Jake confirmed it during the few minutes we talked on Saturday. He boasted he was the one who suggested to Alan that our daughters and their boyfriends would be perfect for his show. Not only were they all good-looking, but their existing friendships, Alabama-Auburn rivalry, and the tension between Barbie and me would make for great reality TV."

"Was he involved in the casting?"

"Not really. Alan and Jake kept in touch all the time. Apparently, during one of their calls, Alan mentioned he was going to be working on a Southern wedding segment. Jake, who's always liked offering a good joke with a twist, told me he was kidding when he made his suggestion, but Alan was savvy enough to jump on the idea."

"Neither Starr nor Veronica knew they were going to be competing against each other?"

"Oh, they did. Barbie and I may not get along, but our daughters are friends, despite us, as are their boyfriends. In talking, they realized they both were potential finalists. For different reasons, both couples thought it would be fun to do the show."

And possibly both mothers did too.

"I don't understand why, once you knew Alan was involved and what he apparently was doing, why you let

Veronica compete, especially with Barbie and you having, shall we say, a hostile relationship?"

Heather met Sarah's gaze. "Being part of this competition isn't my choice. I don't know what he told Starr, but Alan played up the idea to Veronica and then to Trey too, that being contestants would give Trey the opportunity for exposure that he might be able to translate into a media job or they might catch the network's eye and be offered their own reality show. He didn't promise them they'd win, but Alan assured them they'd have the potential to be breakout stars."

"You didn't stop them?"

"I'm a counselor. Making them question their actions and think them through, I can do, but I can't make their final decisions. In this case, I came along as Veronica's chaperone because that's what a mother does. Plus, I thought she might need some protection from Barbie and Alan."

Heather got out of the car. Rather than close the door, she leaned slightly back in. "Alan was a conniver. We had our run-ins, but sorry, none of us killed him. Remember, Veronica, Trey, and I have the perfect alibi." She slammed the door.

Sarah sat in the car thinking about Alan and Jake. If Jake had helped get his daughter and her friend on the show, which seemed like another example of rigging things behind the scenes, could he also have been involved somehow in gambling on the show's outcome? If he was, as Heather put it, a high roller, she doubted he was betting with Chef Bernardi. With Alan? Or simply running his own line on the side?

She pulled out her cell phone and started Googling Jake Babbitt and Alan Perrault. After scanning articles about Jake making political and charitable donations or discussing him in broad strokes, she hit the mother lode. She found one article talking about him being a sports handicapper and another, from a few years ago, alleging Jake had been cleared from allegations relating to an off-shore gambling scheme. As Sarah started to look for more articles, her cell phone rang.

For a moment, all she could think of was "What's next?" When she saw Cliff's name come up on screen, she truly was confused. Good or bad? He hadn't called her in months.

"Hello."

"Hi, Sarah. Cliff here."

"I see that." That was dumb, she thought, but he didn't laugh or pick up on her comment. "What can I do for you?"

"Well, I thought it might be what I could do for you. Now that you're finished with the floral arranging competition—"

"How did you know that?" Either she was more tired than she thought, or she was getting a bit paranoid.

"Because I just dropped Uncle George off at the florist."

If her head wasn't already hurting, she'd have hit it for her own stupidity. Nothing sinister here. "Oh."

"Anyway, as I was saying, now that the competition is out of your way, would you like to take that last boat ride tonight after work?"

"That sounds wonderful, but wait a minute." She reached into her purse and pulled out the day's call sheet. Chaperones were listed as being part of the floral arranging competition, but they weren't on the call list as being required to be at dinner. In fact, they weren't listed on the call sheet at all between the morning's competition and Jane's Place bedtime duties. "I'd love to."

"Perfect. Why don't you go home and take care of RahRah and Fluffy when you get off work, and I'll pick you up at the carriage house around six?"

"I can drive out to the bluff."

"No need. I'll be in town all day. It's just as easy for me to swing by and get you."

"But then you'll have to bring me home."

"Not a problem."

Considering how often she'd driven the road back and forth from the bluff, something was up. "Cliff, what's going on?"

There was silence on the other end of the phone. She could picture him standing in the middle of a jobsite running his hand through his already tousled hair. Sarah waited. She wasn't going to let him off the hook. Although she couldn't see him, she envisioned him shifting his weight and slightly shuffling his feet when he finally confessed.

"When I dropped my uncle off, your mom came out and told me about the craziness of last night and how little sleep you got. I figured if your evening was free, you could use bluff time, but I don't think it would be a good idea for you to drive home if we share some wine. I'm not trying to control you or anything like that."

At some other time, Sarah probably would have been irked Cliff was manipulating what she could and couldn't do behind her back, but this time it didn't bother her. Her friend's kindness at offering her the bluff and making sure she was safe was sweet. "No offense taken. I'd love to take you up on your offer. What can I bring?"

"Nothing. I have wine, cheese, and I'll either grill steaks I have here or pick up sushi or something we both like before I get you. With the week I think you've been having, you need a break. And knowing how you find being in the kitchen more frightening than murder, I don't want to complicate your life any more than it already is."

CHAPTER 24

Her headache, which had come and gone all day, eased completely after a few bites of the eggplant parmesan Cliff had picked up from Little Italy. Because he remembered it was one of her favorite dishes, she bet he also had picked up tiramisu for dessert.

Sitting back in the wooden chair on Cliff's front porch, she stared out over the bluff at the calm water. The work he'd done on his cabin, from its unobstructed placement to the intricate wood pieces he'd made to furnish it, all added to her sense of peace when she visited.

Cliff refilled her wineglass, put the bottle on the table between them, sat in the matching chair, and pulled the tab back on a can of Coca-Cola. "How did the floral competition go today?"

"You won't believe this, but I think there's a very good chance my mother and your uncle may be one of the two finalists." In between more bites, she told Cliff about the floral arranging and how Maybelle knew exactly what do, but Barbie and Starr couldn't get it together. "Anyway, it's crazy. They entered on a lark, but I think Maybelle and George have a fifty-fifty chance of winning the wedding of their dreams."

"That would be wild," Cliff agreed. He took a bite from the Italian hoagie he'd ordered for himself. "I wonder how they're feeling tonight."

"What do you mean?" While she drained her wineglass, she watched him sip his. That was something she respected about Cliff. His rule was not to drink if he was going to be driving a boat.

He put his glass on the table. "Let's be honest: Until a few months ago there were plenty of times that they could be like oil and vinegar."

"True, but I think that's in the past. They really seem devoted to each other now." She stared at Cliff. Had his uncle said something negative this morning? "Cliff, is there something that makes you think they're not?"

"No, Maybelle and George are a great couple. I'm glad they've found each other at this point in their lives. But like you and I know, things can change. And I guess I always worry that people get caught up in the moment of reality TV shows instead of looking down the road. Think about how many bachelors and bachelorettes get engaged at the end of their seasons but never make it to the altar. A lot of them are broken up before they even tape the after-the-rose show."

Sarah twirled the stem of her empty wineglass between her fingers. "I know, but I don't feel that way about Mom and George. I did in the beginning because I feared it was a reaction to him having been injured, but I think they've moved beyond that. Whatever they have going on now seems pretty special."

Cliff pointed at their two now-cleaned plates. "Why don't I take those into the house and then we'll go take that boat ride I promised you."

"Sounds like a plan."

He returned quickly. As they walked down to the water, using the railroad ties he'd artfully worked into the hill, she once again marveled at how Cliff had managed to build his cabin, dock, outdoor living room deck by the water, boathouse, and road to the cabin without ruining the view from any point of his land. It had taken careful planning and patience to design and execute this project so the curve of the road was at just the right spot and everything to do with the water was placed perfectly under the bluff. His attention to detail with any project he constructed was the antithesis of how impulsive he often was in things related to his life. Perhaps, that was what made him a fun friend.

"Motorboat okay? It's a little later than I thought we'd be getting on the water and I prefer its lights and speed to the pontoon boat at this time of day."

"No problem. Simply being on the water is a joy to me."

Cliff jumped aboard and helped Sarah on from the dock. As she made herself comfortable, he prepared the boat. Once it was launched, Sarah sat back, her eyes trained on the water and shoreline, her ears listening to the smooth but increasing roar of the motor as Cliff opened the throttle. They pulled out of the cove and reached the river's open water. She glanced back at him.

He was in his element; the wind blowing his hair back, the sun shining on his face. "Do you remember the first time we came out here?"

"When you showed me the bird's nest?"

"Exactly." He slowed the boat.

Sarah hadn't realized they were already in the same area where he'd made her focus on the trees until she spotted birds caring for their young. Watching the parent birds bring food to the babies while Cliff idled the boat— as he had done many times to get them used to the sound of his boat and that he wasn't a danger to them—had been one of the best object lessons about not seeing what was obvious. Once she'd finally seen the nest and the birds perched on a branch nearby, she'd realized how clearly visible they were. Yet it had taken Cliff pointing them out to her for Sarah not to gloss over their presence.

Now, she stared intently where the nest had been. She didn't see anything except an empty branch. Knowing Cliff wouldn't be idling the boat unless there was something he wanted her to find, she slowly expanded her observation in an ever-widening set of circles. Nothing. She again glanced over her shoulder at Cliff.

He sat slumped back in his seat, his captain's cap angled to shield his eyes as if napping. The grin below the bill of his cap belied that he was very much alert and apparently enjoying her search.

Sarah tried again. There wasn't a nest or any birds where she'd seen them before. Considering that the trees were beginning to lose their leaves, so she could see much more clearly than the first time, she knew she wasn't missing something. The view was simple—the water lapping up to small rocks on the shore, no real beach, the trees. She turned her head toward him. "Cliff?"

He raised the bill of his cap and glanced at his watch. "Look again. Now!"

Sarah turned back and, as she stared, the sky behind

the trees flashed green like the leaves once were for one or two seconds. As fast as the green passed, her eyes were drawn to the array of soft clouds she could see interspersed between the trees. To the west, orange and red seemed to pass through them while the ones in the east still were tinged with blue and indigo shading. As the moments passed, the red, orange, and gold became predominant. Silently, Sarah and Cliff watched the colors splay across the sky as if they were radiating from a massive ball that moved from gold to a deep red as it sunk in the distance.

It was only after the ball was gone, dropped below the horizon, and the sky reflected a smattering of light from the refraction of the rays, that Sarah broke the silence. "That was beautiful. How did you know?"

"Nautical maps and spending a lot of time on the water during the past few weeks. Early on, I caught it at just the right moment at this spot. It took some homework, but I finally figured out when to be in position to see the wonder of the sunset through the trees and water. From the predictions, I knew that if the weather held tonight, there was promise of it being spectacular. It was the view I wanted to end the season on—a memory I could hold on to until I put the boats back in the water."

"Thank you for sharing it."

"Knowing how you love the bluff and water, I thought this might be an image you would appreciate too. That's why I'd asked if you'd like to come out for a ride tonight. I was disappointed when you thought you were going to be on chaperone duty and thrilled when the shooting schedule got moved around."

Cliff hit his arm. "Time to get back before we become fodder for the mosquitoes." He engaged the motor and turned back toward his property. "Little Italy's tiramisu to top this off?"

"Sounds divine."

Because the portion of tiramisu was too large for either of them to finish, Cliff insisted Sarah take the leftover piece back to Jane's Place in case Sarah felt the urge for a midnight snack. "Midnight is four hours away. I'm not going to eat it until breakfast. Once I put it in the refrigerator and go to my room, I don't plan to come out again until tomorrow morning."

"Too many dangerous things in the kitchen?"

"Being in my own kitchen doesn't come naturally to me, but when you add in the things in a commercial kitchen, like its super-duper hot dishwashing apparatus, walk-in refrigerators and freezers with doors that lock, an array of knives, and grills and pans that get to very hot temperatures, coupled with buckshot, rifles, and tempers that are easily frayed, I'd say the kitchen at Jane's Place can be dangerous."

Cliff laughed and gestured at the bag resting near her feet on the car's floorboard. "Should I drop you at the front door and you'll run in and put that in the refrigerator or would you rather I go to the back parking lot and you go in through either the kitchen or dining room entrance?"

"Since we found Alan in the front entryway, I've been using the stairwell that goes upstairs from the kitchen. There's no need for you to drive around the building to the parking area near the dining room, when I'm going to need to go upstairs from the kitchen. Just drop me off and I'll dash in, refrigerate the tiramisu, and flee up the back stairs."

As Cliff parked near Jane's Place's kitchen door, he

observed: "Well, at least I now know tiramisu outweighs most fears you have. I'll still walk you in, though."

"You don't need to do that."

"Oh, but I do."

Despite Cliff's words, Sarah got out of the car without waiting for Cliff to make it around the back to open her door. As he reached her side of the car, she thanked him for a lovely evening. "I'll remember the sunset for a long time, especially tomorrow when I eat my tiramisu."

He laughed as she held up the white box containing her leftovers. Together they walked to the kitchen entrance where, stretching out his arm, he grasped the doorknob before she did.

"Please, this is the last of my chivalry for the night."

Giggling, Sarah let him open the door and with a flourish of his arm granted her entry into Jane's Place. She stepped over the threshold and for the second time in a week, froze at the sight of Jane standing in the middle of the room, staring at two legs sticking out of the dishwasher's conveyor belt. Jane looked at Sarah, her expression a combination of relief and *why me*. "It's Chef Bernardi."

This time, it was Cliff who called the police.

CHAPTER 25

Ignoring Jane's "I didn't do this" and "I just came into the kitchen" and "Chef Bernardi was like this" comments, Sarah gingerly stepped closer to where the chef was. Keeping her distance, she peered over the edge of the dishwasher belt. His clothing was wet, but other than a pained look on his face, blueish lips, and a little spittle next to his mouth, it was like Alan. There were no knives sticking out of him, signs of a gunshot wound, or any other evidence of anything amiss—except Chef Bernardi obviously was dead.

Sarah peered around the kitchen. It was otherwise pristine. Her gaze rested on an iced cake depicting a green football field sitting on one of the counters. She assumed his assignment had been to bake the groom's cake for Veronica and Trey's wedding.

From when Sarah heard the sirens in the distance until

Dr. Smith closed his forensic bag and Chief Gerard and Officer Robinson finished taking statements from everyone in the house, the evening was déjà vu to Sarah. She wanted to pinch herself to wake from a bad dream, but there was no question this was a new murder.

There were a few differences between the two.

When Officer Robinson rounded up who was in the house, the size of the group was larger. Besides contestants, chaperones, Jane, and Cliff, Officer Robinson also brought Flynn, Sam, two cameramen, and Trey into the greenroom. The second difference was that although people were in all stages of being dressed, from their daytime clothes to Veronica already in her pajamas, no one acted like a bridezilla or mamazilla. Sarah wasn't sure if the fear of who might be next or simple shock had replaced the belligerence of earlier in the week.

Despite hating to do it, she'd called Harlan on Jane's behalf. To her dismay, it was immediately obvious from the thickness of his voice and words when he answered that he'd already been asleep. With one more day before the trial and all the work Harlan had been putting in preparing, Sarah hated waking him, but there was no question in her mind that while Chief Gerard found Sarah's propensity for being at the scene of murders annoying, he'd have a more skeptical view of Jane's presence this time around.

Sarah's need for Harlan had been heightened when Barbie reminded Chief Gerard, in a much sweeter tone this time, that Chef Bernardi appeared to have been murdered while competing in the cake bake-off portion of the competition. "This house isn't locked. Jane had easy access to her own kitchen, but so did the other cake finalist. She's right across the street, baking at Southwind. I've heard that besides Jane and Chef Bernardi having some conflicts, Chef Bernardi was not on the best of terms with the other cake finalist since she started making desserts for Southwind. You should check her out."

Barbie's attempt to throw Wanda, and by implication Southwind, under the bus infuriated Sarah. Neither Wanda nor Southwind needed a hint of suspicion tied to them. Her body tensed, Sarah barely controlled the timbre of her voice.

"Chief, if you or one of your officers stroll over to Southwind, you'll see what Wanda's creating today is so complex that there's no way she could have run over here for even a few minutes."

Chief Gerard rested his hand on his gun. His gaze darted between Sarah and Barbie. "We'll check it out."

"You should, but don't waste a lot of time on that line of reasoning. Southwind, unlike Jane's Place, was open to the public for lunch and dinner. With prepping for the meal service, people were going in and out of the kitchen and the restaurant all day. I have no doubt Wanda will have an alibi. Jane's Place was just the opposite. Because there was no formal taping at Jane's Place, almost everyone was on location. It would have been a lot easier for someone staying here to overpower Chef Bernardi." She stared at Barbie. "Once you have an idea when he died, I'd think you'd do better finding out who has a personal motive against Chef Bernardi rather than simply wanting to out-bake him."

Harlan's arrival gave Chief Gerard a graceful way to extricate himself from Barbie and Sarah. His relief was apparent because he didn't make any ambulance-chasing accusations. Instead, the chief acted like his bromance with Harlan was back on.

Sarah walked away from Barbie to where her mother stood on the far side of the kitchen. "Did you hear anything tonight?" Sarah asked Maybelle.

"No booms or other sounds in the night, except maybe a door opening and closing near our bedrooms. It sounded like it was from across the hall. It could have been Veronica or Heather's door." Maybelle glanced around the room. "Come to think of it, it's very interesting to see who's here now."

Sarah looked around, trying to ascertain what her mother observed. She wished Maybelle would spell it out for her, but her mother apparently thought Sarah's sleuthing skills needed a challenge.

Like the first day in the greenroom, people were huddled with who they felt comfortable with. Barbie, no longer sharing her theory with Chief Gerard, stood with Starr, while Heather and Trey were with Veronica. Sarah couldn't tell if Sam and Flynn had been together when Officer Robinson brought them to the greenroom, but they were now huddled with the two cameramen.

Still not able to figure out what her mother was referencing, Sarah finally asked Maybelle what she meant.

"Just that not all of the contestants and chaperones came back here right after dinner."

"How do you know that?"

"Because I ate with all of them, except you."

"Huh?"

"Although we were given the evening off, it was announced we still could eat dinner at Southwind on the show's dime. You were the only chaperone or contestant who didn't take advantage of the free dinner. It was more casual tonight. With so few of us, Emily set us up at a big, round table. After dinner, at Sam's request, the women retired to Jane's Place and the men went out on the back porch to tape another smoke-and-drink session before they either went back to the hotel where they're staying or on to another bar."

Sarah chuckled at her mother's characterization of the distinction between the men and women's after-dinner activities. "Are you sure none of the women joined the men on the back porch?"

"Positive. Sam made it clear that this was being done because they didn't have enough smoke-and-beer footage after Jane ruined their last taping. Sam said something about either using what they filmed tonight by itself or splicing the two to make it appear this had been a regular event as the grooms-to-be became friends."

"As opposed to the brides who became cattier each day?"

"Exactly. Sam said Southwind's back porch was off-limits to all brides and chaperones or else. Like the good little lemmings we are, we trooped back to the house in unison and even went upstairs together. Starr and Barbie said good night at the second-floor landing, while Heather, Veronica, and I came upstairs to our floor. I was tired, so I took a shower and crawled into bed with a good book. I don't even think I read five pages before I fell asleep."

"What do you find so interesting?"

"I told you I thought I heard a door open and shut. It probably was about the time I got into bed. Let's just say Trey was wearing more than an undershirt at dinner."

Sarah looked over at Trey, who was wearing a white T-shirt instead of a collared shirt. Unsure if her mother's observation meant anything, Sarah debated whether to ignore it or report it to the police or Harlan. She wondered if anyone was considering whether Trey and Veronica had broken a rule that might result in their disqualification.

By the time Dr. Smith processed the crime scene and most of the statements were taken, it was late. Once again, Cliff and Sarah were two of the last statements taken. In the time between Chief Gerard finishing with Cliff and calling for her, Sarah managed to tell Cliff good night and thank him for the lovely evening.

As Chief Gerard began questioning her, she thought about pointing out that Trey had changed his shirt, but there wasn't a place to slip it in. Other than having her describe what she'd seen walking into the kitchen, the chief quickly wrapped up his session with her once he confirmed she'd spent the day at work, gone home to her pets, and been at the lake with Cliff.

Almost everyone, including her mother, had already gone to bed or back to their hotel. Because her mother's observation was nagging at her, Sarah felt she should raise it with someone. If Officer Robinson or even Dr. Smith were still in the greenroom, she would have been comfortable telling them, but only Chief Gerard remained. Sarah wasn't sure if he'd be dismissive of her information or jump to some outlandish conclusion about it.

Her decision was made when Harlan signaled from across the room for her to join Jane and him. Jane, as Sarah expected from seeing her pale complexion and glassy-eyed expression, wasn't doing well.

"Is Chief Gerard taking Jane to the station?"

"Not now. Once again, Dr. Smith convinced him to bide his time until he performs an autopsy and gets some toxicology tests done. I don't want to talk more here, but

Sarah, I need to go over a few things with Jane. Rather than wasting time going to my office, would you mind if the three of us talk at the carriage house?"

"Of course not." Having been seen in her chaperone role before everyone left, Sarah dismissed the possibility of Maybelle being disqualified if Sarah was gone for a little while. Besides, secretly, Sarah was glad for another opportunity to see RahRah and Fluffy.

CHAPTER 26

Although it was late, it was too early for Emily to have finished at the restaurant, so Sarah took Fluffy for a quick walk while Harlan, who Sarah knew was probably more comfortable than she was in her own kitchen, got the three of them water. Returning to the carriage house, she found Harlan, with legal pad and pen, in one of the oversized chairs in her living room and Jane sitting on the edge of its counterpart. A hissing RahRah sat inches away from Jane. He clearly remembered when Jane, claiming she was supposed to be his caretaker after Sarah's former mother-in-law died last year, forced RahRah to live with her for a few days.

Sarah plunked herself down on the fireplace ledge between Jane and Harlan. Fluffy went to Harlan for a pet and then to Jane. After being ignored, despite nudging her nose at Jane's leg, Fluffy made her way back to Sarah.

During all of this, RahRah hadn't budged. Although Sarah secretly loved RahRah tormenting Jane—revenge was apparently sweet—she knew if Harlan was going to get some answers from Jane, RahRah's game must end. Bending forward, Sarah scooped her cat into her lap.

He looked at her as if to challenge what she'd done, but there was no way she could verbally explain her actions to him. Instead, she cuddled him closer and slowly stroked his fur. A purring sound told her everything was okay between them.

"Are we ready to begin now, Sarah?" Harlan didn't make eye contact with her.

She stifled the same grin she felt he was trying to keep hidden. "Yes. I think all of us are."

"Good. Jane, I want you to take me through what happened tonight. Everything."

"As you know, most of today's filming was done away from Jane's Place. Consequently, after putting out the breakfast buffet, we were only required to have a small craft table."

"We?" Harlan interrupted.

"Chef Bernardi and me. Part of our deal was a hosting partnership for the competition week." She cast her eyes downward at the floor. "I wasn't completely honest with you, Harlan. You know things have been tight the past few months. Well, I'd reached a point that I was going to have to let Chef Bernardi go. He'd been getting room and board as part of being my pastry chef. When I told him, he wasn't happy. The next day, he came to me and said something had fallen into his lap thanks to an old friendship and that, if we partnered together, it could prove profitable for both of us."

"The Southern Belle competition?"

"Yes. He knew what their specifications were, so I let him work up a proposal that would be below any competitor's bid, but would leave us a thin profit margin. We got the contract, but as you all know from the first night's dinner at Southwind, it wasn't until then that I learned the contract didn't include what would have been our gravy— the dinners."

"Didn't you read the contract?" Sarah asked.

Jane pressed her lips together and shook her head. "At the point we signed the contract, I counted on Chef Bernardi to handle the fiscal side of everything while I worried about the menus and the rooms. Things didn't become tense between us until after the contracts were signed."

Harlan tapped his pen against his pad. "What did things become tense over?"

"The everyday running of Jane's Place. Remember, he hired on as a pastry chef with me a few months ago when he thought the college would make us a hospitality training site. When that fell through and we were scrounging for other business, he wanted to highlight his pastries and turn Jane's Place into a tearoom of sorts. I refused. I wanted to work on obtaining more catering contracts and trying to build back up to being a quality restaurant."

"More on the order of Southwind?"

"Exactly. He cut a few deals with vendors and for dessert events behind my back and that was the last straw. I told him he was out once the show contract was fulfilled."

Sarah was going to say something, but she saw Harlan was about to ask a question. He began, but then stopped. By the pause and change in his phrasing, she wondered what he was going to ask instead of: "Tell me about today."

"When most of the people still staying at Jane's Place went to Southwind for dinner, I stayed behind. I went into my kitchen—"

Harlan interrupted Jane. "What time was that?"

"Around nine. By then, anyone who wasn't eating at Southwind already had grazed at the table and moved on to the bars."

From what her mother had said, Sarah knew Jane's assumption was probably correct.

"Okay, you went into the kitchen. Was Chef Bernardi there?"

"Yes. He was working on his cake, but as had become our custom, unless talking was necessary, we ignored each other. I gathered up what I needed and walked into the greenroom. Except for a few paper napkins and plates, someone already had cleared everything, including the food, from the table. I went back into the kitchen and rather than being as gracious as I probably should have been, I challenged Chef Bernardi on why, when he saw me gathering up everything, he didn't tell me he'd already taken care of the table."

Sarah leaned forward, placing her now squirmy cat on the floor. "Did he give you a reason?"

"He laughed. He indicated it served me right for not talking to him. He said he would have told me if I'd asked or mentioned what I was about to do."

Knowing how belligerent Jane could be, Sarah easily could imagine Jane ignoring Chef Bernardi and then being furious with the way he played her.

"I saw red. We got into it about how he'd be lucky, considering everything, to get out of this situation without me killing him."

"Did anyone hear you threaten him?" Harlan asked.

"I don't know. I stormed out of there and went out on the patio to cool down."

"And that was the end of it?" Harlan started to recap his pen.

"No. I came back through the front entryway and walked into the smaller dining room."

"You went back into the kitchen?"

"Again, no. He was arguing with someone so loudly that I didn't want to burst in on them."

"Instead," Sarah said, "you stayed and listened to the argument."

Jane cheeks reddened. Not as much as they heated up when she was furious, but enough to either mean Jane was embarrassed or mad. Sarah didn't care to find out. She remained quiet, hoping Jane would tell them what she'd overheard. She didn't, so Harlan prompted Jane.

"He was arguing with a woman, but I couldn't tell who because the only thing I heard her say was 'This isn't going to happen with my daughter. What are you going to do?' He made some reply and then came out of the kitchen into the dining room. When he saw me, he started in on me and my eavesdropping."

"Did the other person come out too?"

"No." Jane stopped. Her face changed as if she were trying to capture a thought. "Come to think of it, whoever it was didn't leave the building because I didn't hear the kitchen door chime."

Harlan cocked his head.

"I don't have a chime on the door leading out from the greenroom, but I do on the one from the kitchen. I was always afraid food might walk. That means the person probably took the back stairs."

"You're saying at that point Chef Bernardi was alive."

"Very much so."

"Couldn't they have waited for him to come back into the kitchen?"

"The person didn't. After he screamed that I was a fool, Chef Bernardi went back into the kitchen and I followed him. I was yelling it was his fault I was going to lose Jane's Place, but he ignored me."

"Why was that, Jane?" Harlan turned a page back in his notes. "You said you were equal partners in the Southern Belle deal and that it was structured to give you a slight profit margin. Obviously, Chef Bernardi knew the dinners weren't included and therefore weren't part of the profit margin he'd calculated. As deep in the red as you were, I don't see how the profit margin, even if the dinners had been included, could possibly have been enough to keep your business afloat. But, if you were coming out in the black based upon his bid, how was it his fault you were going to lose Jane's Place?"

"I don't know. I just said it." She pursed her lips.

"Look, Jane, I'm tired. I have work to do tomorrow. I don't have time for you to keep giving me only part of the story."

She met his gaze. "I don't know what you're talking about. I've told you the truth about everything."

"Everything you've told me. Now, I want to know the missing part."

"There isn't one."

"But there is. There is no way that the revenue stream you were getting from the show was enough to save Jane's Place, even if you didn't have to share it with Chef

Bernardi. It might have kept you limping along for a while, but not enough to stay open for long."

"That's not true. The money would have been tight, but Chef Bernardi assured me people flocking to Jane's Place after seeing it on TV would make up for the revenues I lost during the past few months."

Harlan stared at Jane as if his eyes were boring a hole in her. "Chef Bernardi did more than that, didn't he, Jane? We all know he was making book on this competition. How much did you bet?"

"I didn't."

"Was your bet tied to his free rent or somehow to his partnership?"

Jane jumped up and wagged her finger at Harlan. "How dare you say anything like that?"

Harlan didn't move a muscle. He simply waited her out. "Because what I'm saying is true, isn't it? What were the odds?"

For a moment, Sarah thought Jane was about to attack Harlan, as his stillness seemed to rile her more. Instead, Jane collapsed back into the chair as if any energy had been sucked out of her. She dropped her head into her hands.

A part of Sarah instinctively wanted to comfort her by putting an arm around her and assuring her everything would be all right, if she only told Harlan the truth. The other part of Sarah wanted to smack her own face for even thinking about putting her arms around Jane, now that karma was finally catching up to her. Instead, Sarah patted her own thigh and when Fluffy obliged by putting his head in her lap, Sarah petted him. At least she was comforting someone.

"The truth now, Jane," Harlan said.

"I was going to lose the restaurant. When we started our partnership, he assured me that if we used what he knew to place a series of bets on the show, I'd have more than enough money to keep Jane's Place going, plus extra to try a new concept."

"You were betting using insider information?" Sarah was excited. There was a good chance Chef Bernardi's source either knew what was planned for the competition or was a party to how the competition was going to be thrown. If Sarah could find that person, he or she not only would clear Jane, but also any suspicions being cast on Southwind. "If Chef Bernardi was sure enough of his information, did he brag to you who he got it from?"

"He bragged about a lot of things, but not that. Our deal was that I put up the money and he would structure my bets based upon where the line was."

"Was he rigging it?"

"I asked the same question and he said 'no.' He explained that simply by being friends with Alan and having worked on the scouting team, he was using general information as to who should be the strongest team or who people would identify with." She grimaced and shook her head. "If Natalie and Ralph had gone out like they should have, things would have been fine. All of my money was on them to be out on day one. Jed and Lucy leaving ruined everything. We all begged Chef Bernardi to refund our money or start over with the bets, but he refused."

"You weren't the only one who lost big?" Sarah asked.

"Not by a long shot. Last night when you came up on the porch as I interrupted the guys during their cigar-and-drink session, it was apparent most, if not all of them, had a bet riding with Chef Bernardi."

"Do you mean Chef Bernardi was out there with the four remaining grooms?" Harlan said.

"No, not George or Ralph. Just Trey and Lance, as well as Sam and Flynn. I don't know how big everyone's bets were, but some of them must have been pretty big in order for Chef Bernardi to have covered my bet, since he'd been confident I would win, and he couldn't have afforded to pay me out of his own pocket. Anyway, we all took the position that because the circumstances were unforeseen, the bets as placed should be canceled."

"And he refused?"

"Adamantly. He reminded us that Jed and Lucy appeared in the introduction segment that aired. He said that because Jed and Lucy officially started the competition, there was no push. All our bets were lost. When Chief Gerard finds out that besides our business arrangement, I was betting with Chef Bernardi and I lost everything, he's not going to look beyond me for Chef Bernardi's death."

"When you say 'everything,' what do you mean?"

"I had to bet big to win big." Jane sighed. For the next hour, she went into detail about her financial situation, how her creditors were pushing her, and her reason for trying to grab the brass ring by gambling. She stopped talking when a key turned in the front door.

"Hi, Em," Sarah yelled, so her sister wouldn't be frightened by hearing people in the house. Emily joined them in the living room.

"Hi, everyone. I didn't expect to see you here tonight, Sarah."

"We came over here to talk for a while. I already walked Fluffy for the night."

"Thanks. I'm beat. I'll let you get back to what you were doing. Bedtime for me."

"I'll lock up when we leave. Good night."

Once Emily had gone to the guest bedroom, Jane resumed her explanation. "Absent a miracle, I only have enough cash to keep the business open until the end of the month. I know how this sounds. But Harlan, I swear when I left Chef Bernardi the second time, not only was he still alive, but he had pulled a leather cigar case out of his pocket and was going out for a peaceful smoke."

"I have one more question, Jane," Harlan said. "Why did you come back to the kitchen where you might run into Chef Bernardi for a third time?"

"I was hungry."

"What?" Sarah stopped petting Fluffy. "After everything, you were hungry?"

Jane nodded. "I didn't go to dinner with everyone, so I was hungry. When I was in the kitchen the second time, I saw he'd put the finishing touches of a little football player and cheerleader on his cake. That's why I thought I'd have my kitchen back to make myself a late dinner. I walked in and there he was—stuck upside down in the dishwasher conveyor belt. It wasn't more than a few moments later when Sarah and Cliff came in." She laughed. "It's ironic. He took me and everyone else to the cleaners, and you might say he ended up getting the same treatment."

CHAPTER 27

As Harlan wrapped up things with Jane, Sarah took their water glasses to the kitchen. She tried to piece together what she could from the tidbits Jane recounted. Sarah knew Jane's confession filled in the pieces about the money, especially the revenue stream, which Harlan felt were missing. In Sarah's mind, what Jane told them only raised new questions she wanted to bounce off Harlan.

Hearing the front door close, she went back into the living room eager to talk to Harlan. He was sitting in the big chair, snapping his briefcase closed. "Harlan, I was thinking—"

He put his hand up to cut her off. "Not tonight, Sarah. I've got to get some sleep."

"But don't you think we learned a lot from Jane that if we brainstormed together might help us figure this out?"

"Sarah, I'm brain-dead. Sadly, this will all be here to-morrow."

Although she knew he was right, she hated the idea of letting any time pass by if they could possibly steer Chief Gerard away from Jane or anybody at Southwind. Trying one more time, Sarah explained to Harlan why she was eager not to wait.

"That's not a problem right now."

"Why?"

"Chief Gerard still thinks Jane is his most likely suspect in Alan's death, but he isn't going to do anything about it until the toxicology reports are back. Dr. Smith convinced him that those reports will either confirm his conclusion or force him to look in a different direction. Sarah, the problem is that the other direction definitely might take him back to Southwind."

"I don't understand."

"Dr. Smith performed the autopsy on Alan this afternoon. When he opened the body, he noted an odor in handling the lungs that he associated, from another case he had, with nicotine poisoning. Because that isn't routinely tested for, he's made a request for expedited tests for nicotine to be performed on the samples he provided. You know we've discussed how conservative in making decisions Dr. Smith is. He figures medical examiners or coroners often have guesses that are wrong, but they are heroes when they're right. Dr. Smith doesn't care about being a hero, but he does care about his findings being correct. I'm inclined to think his hunch is probably right. Because he's not going to make it formal until he has the proof, we have a little time."

"And that proof will include how he ingested it, including whether it was in Alan's drink or the food he ate?

But, if it's nicotine poisoning, couldn't it have been in the cigars?"

"All of those are possibilities. The thing is, nicotine poisoning doesn't have to be fatal if treated promptly and if the ingestion level is low. For death, it usually takes buildup in the system or a high ingestion level. One cigar isn't going to be enough nicotine to kill anyone. From how Alan knocked over the vase, showed signs of vomiting, paleness, and blue lips, Dr. Smith thinks he may have had some early symptoms he ignored and then been in the later stages when he was in the entry hall. In that stage, one can have seizures or become dizzy, which may explain him bumping into the vase stand. Because Chef Bernardi's symptoms weren't as pronounced as Alan's, Dr. Smith isn't ready to suggest the same means for him to have died. He could have died naturally."

"And ended up hanging upside down out of the dishwasher conveyor belt?"

"Someone might have found him and become frightened and thought that would be a cover-up. Remember, his clothes were wet, as if someone tried to wash off any DNA evidence. Who knows, we might have more than one killer."

"Although in Chief Gerard's mind, Jane is it because she was the one on the spot both times."

"Right, but for tonight he's not going to do anything about Jane."

Or, for that matter, Southwind, Sarah thought.

"Sarah, I'm going home to bed. I suggest you get some sleep too. See you at the office in a few hours."

Sarah's mind was racing too fast to consider going to bed. She wished she could have brainstormed with Harlan to get beyond Jane and Southwind, but she realized neither of them were high priority. His mind was on the trial coming up on Thursday.

She glanced at her watch. She hadn't realized how long they had been talking. Much as she wanted to, having seen how tired her sister was, there was no way Sarah was going to wake up her twin to brainstorm. That left her with her one other sounding board that always listened, but never responded—the two sitting at her feet.

She figured her chaperoning duties were done. There was no way the network could finish the competition with two deaths, only one cake vendor left to compete, and the eerie way Chef Bernardi was integral to the floral arranging segment. She made an executive decision. "RahRah and Fluffy, let's talk in my bedroom. I'm staying here for the rest of the night."

By the time Sarah changed into a nightgown and brushed her teeth, Fluffy was already in her doggie bed, sound asleep. The little fur ball didn't budge when Sarah walked across the room, got into bed, or turned off the light. As Sarah made room on the bed for RahRah, she chuckled at the way Fluffy slept half in and half out of the bed, her mouth flopped partially open.

Sarah pulled the covers up to her neck and smiled as RahRah snuggled to her. Gently, Sarah stroked her cat. There were many times RahRah's warm body pressed against Sarah's, either in bed or simply clutched in her arms, had comforted Sarah during the rough transition after her divorce. Tonight, it wasn't comfort but an objective opinion Sarah sought.

"RahRah, if there was a person talking about her daughter, it had to have been either Heather or Barbie, but which one do you think? What could it have been that Chef Bernardi promised wouldn't happen? Losing? Based upon today's floral arranging, that was almost a given for Barbie and Starr unless Chef Bernardi threw his vote. And even if he did, with the averaging system Flynn talked about, would it be enough to keep them in the competition?"

RahRah stirred, burrowing deeper into the comforter.

"Everyone said Barbie lost out in the past. Was she trying to live her life through Starr? Was there something in it for her if Starr won? Participating in beauty pageants was expensive, even if Starr won college scholarship money. Why was she adamant about winning scholarship money instead of having either or both of her parents pay for college? Did Jake pay for any of fulfilling Barbie's dream for Starr while Starr was on the pageantry circuit? Was the perfect wedding for Starr anything that neither her parents or Lance and she paid for?"

RahRah was paying more attention to his paw than to what Sarah said, so she tried a different tactic. "What about Heather? She hasn't seemed as gung-ho about Veronica winning as much as she'd like Trey and Veronica to get their own reality show. Why? And speaking of why, is there any significance that Trey wore a different shirt tonight than the one he had on at dinner? Was there a reason Veronica was singled out to play the bridezilla on camera during the Mudbowl competition? Wouldn't Natalie, who was the one going to be eliminated, if the line was correct, been a better choice to make a scene rather than chancing some of the Alabama fans being turned off by Veronica's behavior?"

RahRah turned over and rolled into a ball. Sarah concluded that he wasn't any more interested in the possibility Heather was the woman Jane overheard with Chef Bernardi than he'd been weighing the possibility of the speaker being Barbie. If it wasn't one of them, who could it have been? There was a female cameraperson, but she wasn't around all the time. It seemed doubtful that she was a suspect. Besides, Jane specifically heard a daughter mentioned.

"RahRah, I don't disagree with Jane's assessment of how Chief Gerard will react once he ties her to Chef Bernardi's gambling. He's old-school in following the blood or the money. The blood didn't pan out, but there's no doubt in my mind that Chief Gerard will consider Jane losing the bulk of her savings and Jane's Place as a solid motive. If there is nicotine in that drink she made for Alan, it's going to be all over in the chief's mind."

The soft rhythm of RahRah's breathing made Sarah realize he was asleep. He obviously hadn't been too impressed by any of Sarah's rambling thoughts. Or maybe, RahRah was indeed telling her something: Go to sleep.

Sarah texted her mother so she wouldn't be frightened to find Sarah's bed at Jane's Place unslept in and then happily pulled her comforter to her neck and followed RahRah's advice.

CHAPTER 28

To Sarah's surprise, she beat Harlan to the office. She knew she couldn't make up for keeping him up half the night, but at least she could have coffee brewed for when he arrived.

She was just putting two natural sugars into her own mug of coffee when she heard his key in the back door. Sipping her coffee, she walked into the hallway outside the break room to greet him. For a man who hadn't gotten much sleep, he looked dapper. In fact, she half expected him to jump into the air and click his heels together. "What's going on?"

He handed her a small brown bag. "I stopped at Betty's for a breakfast biscuit. It was so good, I brought you one."

"Thank you." Although Harlan liked his Betty's biscuit every now and again, he tended to eat healthy and never snack. Unlike other workplaces, he wasn't one to bring or have her bring doughnuts, cookies, or even birthday cakes or cupcakes into the office. In so many other ways he was a good boss, but he wasn't one to indulge Sarah's sweet tooth or, for that matter, to bring her breakfast unless he was being sweet after a night she'd worked late.

Maybe that was it, but on second thought Harlan was too happy for that to be the case. "Harlan, I give up. I appreciate the biscuit, but why are you in such a good mood this morning? I'd have thought you'd be exhausted."

"I am, but I just had the best breakfast."

Sarah scrunched her eyebrows and forehead together. "Betty makes a wonderful biscuit, but you've had them before and never been this exuberant."

"That's because in the past I didn't share a table with Thursday morning's opposing counsel."

"He was at Betty's?"

"Yup."

It had to be happenstance. Unlike some of the businessmen in town, Harlan wasn't a regular morning Betty's customer. Consequently, the other lawyer wouldn't have known or expected to run into Harlan there. Besides, being an attorney with one of the large Birmingham firms, the lawyer surely went to breakfast places on his own home turf as opposed to fifteen minutes down the road. "What was he doing in town this morning?"

"Well, it seems he had a before-breakfast meeting with his client."

His being in town made sense then. But that still didn't explain why Harlan was so elated.

She followed Harlan to his office. He dropped his briefcase on his conference table and then walked around his desk. Seated, he looked up at Sarah and smiled. "We settled."

"What?" Now, Sarah shared his excitement. She knew Harlan felt he had a good case, but they'd been so far apart he was sure it was going to go to trial. "How?"

"Apparently, when we didn't accept their ridiculous offer, the other firm got serious about preparing its case for trial and realized it had a few major holes in it. When they reviewed my earlier counteroffer and balanced it against the facts of the case, the legal team not only felt the offer was fair, but offering a sweetened version of it might close off a floodgate of similar nuisance litigation. Consequently, the lead counsel came into town this morning for the meeting with his client. He was going to call me when he got back to his office, but when we ran into each other, we ironed out the details in person. Through a joint call, we advised the judge's clerk of our settlement and that I'd be drafting the final paperwork for the court. I'll have it to you to type later today."

"Wonderful. Without that hanging over you, maybe we can find a time to brainstorm more about what Jane told us."

"Sure." Harlan pulled a file from those stacked on his credenza and placed it next to the clean legal pad he'd left in the middle of his desk. He picked up his pen.

Happy herself, Sarah shut his door and went back to her desk. Rounding the partition to her reception area, she heard the ringtone for her mother coming from the drawer where her purse was stashed. She wasn't fast enough to catch the call, but she hit the number to call back. Her mother answered immediately.

"Sarah, they're not canceling the competition!"

"Whoa, Mom, calm down." Sarah knew her mother

was upset—she hadn't told her to call her Maybelle. "Tell me exactly what happened this morning."

"I woke up and found a new call sheet stuck under my door. You have one too. I picked it up for you."

"That's good. I'll get it from you later. What's on it?"

Sarah heard paper rustling.

"I'm so discombobulated that I folded the call sheet up. Here, I've got it now. It only has one thing on it: a bold black box highlighting a statement in italics."

"Read me what it says, please."

"Oh, yes. Here goes: '*Considering the tragedy of last night, after much discussion, there will be no Wednesday activities. The Southern Belle competition will be concluded—*'"

"Then, they're canceling it?"

"You didn't let me finish reading."

"Sorry," Sarah muttered.

Her mother picked up where she had left off. "*. . . concluded by having one more competition on Thursday between the three remaining contestants. More details will follow during a mandatory cast, crew, and chaperone dinner tonight at six at Southwind. For the remainder of the competition, the craft table and all planned meals will be at Southwind.*"

Sarah tried to get her head around the message. Not only was the competition not canceled, but she was required to be at a dinner tonight almost as if nothing had happened. "I'm stunned. Does the call sheet clarify anything else?"

"No, that's it. You'll be at dinner, won't you?"

"I wouldn't miss it."

CHAPTER 29

With the settlement papers prepared and the trial taken off the docket, Harlan was in a relaxed mood. Although their brainstorming got no further than her session with RahRah had, Sarah suggested Harlan crash the Southern Belle dinner. "Maybe you'll notice something I'm missing. If you hang with my mother and me, I'm sure neither Sam nor Flynn will make a scene to throw you out. And, if they won't pay for your dinner, I think I can get it comped. I know two of the owners well and the other one intimately."

Harlan laughed. "Look, it's four o'clock. I know it's not Christmas or New Year's Eve, but today's been such a good day, why don't we knock off early. I'll meet you at Southwind at six." Still smiling, he added, "This will give you time to check on RahRah and Fluffy before dinner. You get going while I empty the coffeepot." Without waiting for her to continue their conversation, Harlan strolled toward the break room, whistling.

Sarah knew Harlan wouldn't change his mind, but she still quickly powered down her computer, grabbed her purse and jacket, and left. She was looking forward to an hour or so of downtime with RahRah and Fluffy.

To Sarah's surprise, her mother's car was parked in front of the carriage house. Worried, Sarah hurried into the house. Neither RahRah nor Fluffy greeted her. She threw her keys into the bowl by the door and walked through the house. She found everyone in the kitchen.

RahRah was stretched out on the linoleum in his favorite spot, the sunshine bathing him. Fluffy lay partially under the kitchen table, near George's feet, munching on a dog treat. Her mother was stirring something on Sarah's stove.

"I didn't expect you this early," Maybelle said.

Sarah bent and kissed her shorter mother. "What are you doing here?" She peeked into the pot, but Sarah didn't recognize what her mother was making.

"With no activities today, George and I went to the political lecture at his place this morning and then out to a nice, long lunch at Little Italy. Afterwards, we were at loose ends. Neither of us particularly wants to go back to Jane's Place except to collect my clothes, especially with all the TV vans parked in front of it today. The last thing we want is to be interviewed about Chef Bernardi and Alan's deaths. Honestly, neither of us can believe they didn't end the competition."

"I can't either."

"Anyway, I suggested to George that we go visit Fluffy. You can guess his reaction to my offer."

Considering her mother usually complained she was

allergic to animals, her offering George the opportunity to visit Fluffy was a big deal. Sarah glanced toward where George sat at the kitchen table and saw he was petting Fluffy. "I can see his reaction. That was nice of you." This time she added "Maybelle" without any prompting. "What are you making?"

"Well, we've both been on edge since yesterday morning."

"I can imagine. You both knew Chef Bernardi." After Sarah spoke, her brain processed her mother's comment. "Since yesterday morning?"

"Yes. We both had a funny feeling after the flower arranging competition. It bothered us that Chef Bernardi was so involved with it, but Wanda wasn't featured. It was like he'd already been anointed as the winning pastry chef or they were giving him extra exposure to garner more votes."

"I never thought about that."

"Anyway, to avoid Jane's Place, we came here to kill time until dinner. I hope that's all right."

One part of Sarah wanted to suggest that it would have been nice if her mother asked first, but under the circumstances, she pressed her lips together, avoided taking a deep breath, and simply said, "No problem. What are you making?"

"Turmeric latte. I thought its natural healing powers would be calming for George and me. Would you like some?"

"Who am I to turn down something calming?" Sarah didn't think she should tell her mother about Dr. Smith's tentative finding that Alan died from nicotine poisoning, but she was curious if her mother or George had any thoughts about Chef Bernardi's death. Sarah figured part of their long lunch had to include some brainstorming of their own. "Have you given any more thought to who might have killed Chef Bernardi?"

Maybelle took an extra cup out of Sarah's cupboard. She poured the latte mixture evenly between the three. No one got a full cup, but there was enough. Maybelle took her time rinsing out the pot and turning it over on Sarah's drainboard.

"You can put the pot in the dishwasher."

"It's always better to wash them by hand. Where do you keep your dish towels?"

"I don't really use any. Would a paper towel work?" Sarah handed her mother the roll that sat next to the sink.

Wordlessly, her mother tore off two sheets and dried the pot. She used a third one to dry her hands. Only after she wiped the sink and threw the paper towels into Sarah's trash can did she return to the subject Sarah was concerned with. "Over lunch, George and I compared notes as to how we saw the competition from our respective would-be bride and groom sides. In some ways, we've been participating in two different competitions."

Sarah leaned against the sink. "What do you mean?"

"Well, for the most part, other than the tug-of-war, the activities were all slanted to the women or—"

"Even the car wash?"

Maybelle joined George at the table. "George and I, as the show's designated fragile old fogies, were put on the side there and for the tug-of-war, but the car wash physically involved everyone equally. Some washed, some sprayed, but that part wasn't dominated by one sex. It was enticing people into the car wash that relied on female wiles."

"I thought George and you were the ones holding signs."

"We were, but the show called Starr and Veronica's beauty pageant and cheerleading talents into play by having them wave to passing cars in short shorts and wet T-shirts. For the tug-of-war, our costumes and Veronica's act were tied to Southern tradition, but the competition itself needed the men's strength. It was slanted toward which of the guys could hold on longest. If Lance hadn't lost his footing, his team, having Ralph on it, should have won."

"I hadn't thought about that."

George took off his pince-nez glasses and put them on the table. Knowing his penchant for elaborate explanations, Sarah braced herself, but he kept his observation short.

"Every other event, except sticking the men out on the porch for cigars and brandy or whatever, played to skills traditionally related to Southern women or were set up so that there could be a bless-your-heart bridezilla or mamazilla moment. Even the gifts they gave us after we taped the introductory segment tied into the concept the show wanted to promote."

"You must have gotten your gifts after I left. I know the men received cigar cases and cigars, but I thought those were for use during your porch get-togethers. I think someone mentioned there were gifts for the women, but I don't know what they were."

"They were token gifts. The grooms-to-be received the pocket-sized plastic cigar cases with three cigars marked with the network logo. The women were given folding fans small enough to fit into their pockets or purses. I guess the network thought we might need them to keep from becoming overcome by our Southern heat."

Finishing her drink, Sarah rinsed out her cup and put it in the dishwasher. "Considering who the network cast, I don't think that was ever going to be the case. I still can't believe rather than canceling the competition, the network blessed another scheduled dinner and event."

Just before six, George took Fluffy for a quick walk. Sarah put out fresh water and food for her pets. She glanced at RahRah and grinned. "Okay, you win. The way you're looking at me makes me feel guilty for having to leave again."

Sarah went to the cabinet where she kept her pet supplies. As she took out the bag of cat treats, RahRah immediately strutted to his bowl. He positioned himself in front of it, paws ready to pounce.

When George, Maybelle, and Sarah left for Southwind, RahRah and Fluffy were too busy with the treats at the top of their bowls to acknowledge the click of the door, let alone their departure.

Chapter 30

As Sarah walked into Southwind's porch dining room with George and her mother, she felt a chill. Emily and Marcus had again set the room up for its maximum dining capacity. With everyone, including the entire crew, having to attend tonight's dinner, the packed room reminded her of the first night of the competition.

"Look, over there." Maybelle pointed to a table in the middle of the room. "Cliff and Harlan saved us seats." She led the way to where Cliff was waving to them.

"Hi," Sarah said. "I'm surprised to see you here tonight."

"Everyone, including outside contractors or vendors still in the competition, received word we needed to be here tonight."

"I keep forgetting to count you in that group. I couldn't

believe when my mother called me and told me they weren't canceling the competition."

"Neither could I. It just doesn't feel right."

Their discussion was cut short by the xylophone tones. Sarah wasn't sure why she'd thought them melodic the other night. Tonight, the tinny sound of the mallet hitting the metal grated on her nerves. She had the feeling she wasn't the only one on edge.

Once again, Sam welcomed everyone. He expressed Flynn, his, and the network's sorrow over Chef Bernardi's death. But as soon as he began talking about how the competition would proceed, he was interrupted by questions and comments from the diners.

A woman seated at the table with the invitation and floral vendors stood up. She gestured toward the people around her. "We all agree that as much as we'd like our products featured, we believe continuing with this competition is disrespectful to the dead. Plus, the two deaths during the Southern Belle competition are all over the media."

"I'll take that one," Flynn said. He spoke into a hand-held microphone. "We're going to start tomorrow's show with a clip in memory of Alan and Chef Bernardi, saying that they would want the show they loved to go on. Although we never wanted this to happen, the reality is that, with all the media hype, people are going to tune in tomorrow and stick around for the remaining segments. Our ratings and your exposure will be higher than we ever anticipated. I know the situation is not to any of our liking, but in the end, it will be good for everyone."

"Except Alan and Chef Bernardi," Sarah almost whispered to her mother.

"I'm still not sure I want that kind of PR," the woman said.

Flynn smiled at her. "I understand. But while everyone involved with the show never wanted any of this to happen, the network has made it clear that they will hold everyone to their contracts. If anyone tries to quit now, leaving the show in the lurch so close to the end, litigation could commence."

A murmur of disbelief went through the room.

Sam stepped forward and grabbed the microphone from Flynn. "Let me explain that a little bit. Although we deeply regret Chef Bernardi's death, we are sensitive to our viewers and to your concerns."

"Sure, you are," someone from the crew tables muttered loudly enough to be heard. Sam ignored the comment.

"We already taped the vendor competitions except for the dress and cake making. This afternoon, we ran the winners for everything except those two things. Tomorrow, rather than run another segment with Chef Bernardi, we're scrapping the floral arranging competition. Instead, we'll show a minute montage of the table with the voters' present choices and end on a shot of Wanda's *Bambi*-themed groom's cake. While the montage plays, Flynn will do a voice-over announcing the winning dress and cake vendors and reminding viewers that the only way to see the final wedding cake and dress will be to watch Friday's wedding."

Maybelle stood up. "I'm not happy with proceeding with the competition, and I'm very uncomfortable having us do anything at Jane's Place."

"Maybelle and everyone," Sam said, "we appreciate your discomfort with spending any more time at Jane's Place. We've worked out a way to minimize it. On the table near where Flynn is standing is a stack of new call sheets for tomorrow. Please pick one up when you finish dinner. You'll see we rearranged things so that tonight is the last night any of you will need to stay at Jane's Place. By taping the last competition early tomorrow morning, there will still be time to show it on the national network tomorrow afternoon."

Sarah could tell her mother was concerned about Sam's reference to "early," but before her mother could inquire what that meant, Barbie shouted out that question from the other side of the room. Sam's response of six was met with groans from both the contestants and the crew.

"I know it's early, but the time difference and transmitting the film backed us into that time. The good thing, except for the winning couple, is that you're free after that taping unless you want to be a wedding guest. We're going to film the winning couple's wedding tomorrow afternoon. The audience won't see the wedding until Friday afternoon."

Trey raised the next question. "Sam, how are you going to go from three couples to one? I thought the plan was to eliminate one per day."

"It was, but as I said earlier, we feel it would be inappropriate to air the flower arranging footage with Chef Bernardi, so we are not sending anyone home for that challenge. Because we rearranged the schedule to let everyone leave a day early, we've decided against having another time-consuming physical challenge."

Maybelle whispered to Sarah. "That's a cop-out. They obviously couldn't come up with another physical challenge that they thought George and I could compete in safely. They didn't want to chance another death or two on film."

Sarah giggled. Cliff shot her a questioning look. "Mother," she mouthed. He gave her a thumbs-up.

"In order to fairly eliminate from three couples to a winner, we decided to model the last competition after an old game show, *The Newlywed Game*. I'm going to let Flynn explain how it will work to you." He handed the microphone back to Flynn.

"The three finalist couples will come to the set where we taped your introductions. I will introduce each couple and then, for round one, send the men from the room. Once they're gone, I'll pose a series of questions to the Belles, asking them to respond the way they think their prospective grooms will. After three questions, we'll bring the grooms back and award ten points per answer that matches. Round two will be played the same way, but with the men predicting how their better halves will respond. In the final round, each contestant will be given a card on which to write their own answer to one question. If the couple's answers match, they'll receive twenty-five points. The couple with the highest number of points after the bonus round will be declared the winner."

Heather raised her hand.

"Yes, Heather."

"That sounds like a fair way to resolve the competition, but I'd like to go back to Maybelle's question. If we're uncomfortable staying at Jane's Place tonight, can we get a room somewhere else, even if we have to pay for it?"

Flynn glanced at Sam, who didn't bother with the microphone to answer. "We thought about moving all of the Belles and chaperones for the night, but there are two big conferences in town, plus people making a long weekend out of Saturday's game. We couldn't find enough hotel rooms at the same place, even in Birmingham. Because Wheaton is on Central Standard Time, but we're broadcasting on Eastern Standard Time, we didn't want to chance not having everyone in place on time. That's why we're asking you to please put up with one more night at Jane's Place. Are there any more questions?"

Hearing none, Sam signaled for Marcus and Emily. They came into the dining room and, while the waiters served everyone, explained what was being served for dinner. They finished their explanation and Marcus wished everyone "bon appétit." Someone at a table clapped. It was picked up by the rest of the room, which also applauded. Marcus and Emily graciously accepted the accolades and hightailed it out of the dining room.

After dinner, everyone except the chaperones and contestants left quickly. As Sarah and her group lingered over freshly poured cups of coffee, Heather and Veronica approached their table.

"Maybelle, Veronica and I just want to tell you that we completely agree with you. This competition should have been canceled or they should have let us drop out."

"Did you try to drop out?" Harlan put down his coffee cup.

Heather nodded. "We did, but Sam said we'd be in breach of contract if we didn't stick it out one more day."

"I don't think under the circumstances that would hold up. I'm sure there's a clause in the contract that would give you an out."

"That's what our entertainment lawyer said, but he reminded us that fighting the contract or walking out before the competition finished could get us labeled as 'difficult.' If Veronica and Trey are going to have a shot at an A-ranked newlywed or other reality show, they can't be labeled as trouble. That kind of notoriety in this business only gets you on B-level dancing or survival skills shows."

Sarah stifled the comment welling in her throat. Considering two people were dead, she couldn't believe the selfishness of Heather's analysis. She glanced at Veronica, who was intently staring at a fingernail. Veronica raised her head, meeting Sarah's gaze for an instant. Pushing her hands into her pockets, Veronica looked away. This Veronica wasn't the same woman who stood up to Sam at the Mudbowl. She was, Sarah realized, more like the Veronica in the greenroom the night Alan died, tentatively waiting for her mother's response.

"I understand." Maybelle patted Heather's arm. "You and Veronica are between a rock and a hard place. Once I get back to Jane's Place, I'm going straight to my room, locking the door, and going to bed. No one will see me again until we have to be on the set."

"Veronica and I will be doing the same thing across the hall from you. It was bad enough staying at Jane's Place after we found Alan, but now . . ." Heather rolled her eyes upward. "We can't wait for this competition to end."

"Harlan, what do you make of Sam's insistence that they stay on the show?" Cliff asked.

Harlan rubbed his hand across the back of his neck. "It sounds to me like the one threatening the notoriety may be the one afraid of it."

"Or the one threatened may also be afraid." Sarah stood, bumping the table hard enough that the coffee in her cup sloshed onto the table. She ignored it as she faced Veronica. "Your mother and you came in, saw Alan, and went back outside, didn't you?"

Veronica's face paled. "I—"

"I don't know what you're saying, Sarah," Heather said. "You were there when we came into Jane's Place. You saw us and pointed out Alan lying there with Jane standing over him, with blood on her hands."

Veronica glanced from her mother to Sarah. This time she met Sarah's fixed gaze. "You're right."

"Veronica!" Heather grabbed her daughter's arm as Sarah simultaneously asked, "Did you see Jane the first time?"

Twisting free of her mother's grasp, Veronica faced Sarah and Harlan. "No." She turned toward her mother. "A TV show isn't worth lying about. Trey and I decided last night if Chief Gerard arrested Jane, I'd tell him the truth."

"And what is that?" Harlan asked.

Heather whimpered but didn't do anything to stop Veronica from speaking. "That Mother, Trey, and I left Southwind way ahead of the rest of you. We got to Jane's

Place first. Trey walked up the driveway and around the house to get his car while Mother and I used the front door. Like you, we saw Alan lying in the entryway. Mother pushed me back and checked his pulse, but even from where I was standing, it was obvious he was gone. We didn't want to go back out through the front door in case you were behind us, so we sidled around the room to the dining room being used as the greenroom."

"There wasn't any sign of Jane during all of this entering and sidling?"

"No. We heard someone in the kitchen, which may have been her, but we were scared of getting involved after we saw Alan, and we went out the dining room door. Trey was across the parking lot. Sam was stopped mid-lane, blocking Trey's truck. It didn't look like it mattered because he was talking to Sam and Flynn through Sam's open car window. We joined them."

Heather found her voice, but it was a mere croak. "It was wrong, but I couldn't let Veronica get involved. Not this close to our goal."

Harlan slid his chair back. "For Jane's sake, you're going to have to tell Chief Gerard. If you like, I'll call him and try to keep this low-key."

When they nodded their acquiescence, he stepped away from the table to the far side of the porch where no one was standing. Sarah followed him. She noticed that he scrolled down on whatever screen he opened, but only hit the face of the phone once. Apparently, Chief Gerard was in his favorites list. He finished his call and turned back toward where everyone now stood, stopping in front of Sarah. "Chief Gerard is going to meet Heather, Trey,

Veronica and me at the station. By the way, that was a good deduction. What clued you in?"

"Veronica's behavior tonight lacked the swagger of the Mudbowl. Like the night Alan died, it was only after Heather set up their story that Veronica jumped in and followed along. Harlan, throughout this competition, I've thought Barbie was the overbearing mother bear and Heather the calming influence, but when I talked to Heather, she emphasized her chaperoning was tied to her mother's instinct to protect her daughter. Seeing how uncomfortable Veronica was until she told the truth, it strikes me that maybe we've been wrong about which mother Jane overheard in the kitchen with Chef Bernardi."

"Good catch. I'll make sure Chief Gerard follows up while we're at the station, but even if it was Heather arguing in the kitchen with him, it doesn't prove she killed Chef Bernardi."

"Maybe not. But it gives Chief Gerard another suspect to consider. I'm only glad I found a way to get Jane off the top of his list."

"You didn't. The night Alan died, Heather and Veronica heard someone in the kitchen that they rightfully feared might be the killer. Even though Jane said she came out of the kitchen after hearing a thud, Chief Gerard can still presume that she heard the thud of Alan or the vase hitting the floor before she went into the kitchen and didn't pretend to help him until she already knew he was dead. Remember, with poisoning, one doesn't have to be next to the person when death occurs."

"But the five can't alibi each other now. There are gaps in their timelines of seeing each other. Plus, the chief should probably consider Alan's old roommate, Jake, too. We know he was in town at least the night before Alan died." Sarah paused to reflect for a moment. "Depending upon how Alan was poisoned. the killer could have been far gone from the crime scene."

"True, but until Chief Gerard or another member of the force closes the poisoning timeline, Jane still is front and center for the chief."

CHAPTER 31

After they left, Maybelle asked Sarah to get her a copy of the new call sheet. Before Sarah could, Cliff offered to do it. He returned in a moment with copies for all of them.

"Thank you," Sarah said. "I would have walked out of here without one." Sarah stuck hers in her pocket.

Maybelle dropped hers into her pocketbook that carried everything. "I'm sure most people did." She looked at George. "I'm ready to go."

"If you wait a moment so I can say hello to Emily, I'll walk back with you," Sarah said.

"That's okay, honey. I'm going to drive George back to his place and visit for a while. I'll come back to Jane's Place in plenty of time to be on the set. Lock your door and don't wait up for me. I'll be late."

Sarah stared at her mother, who simply smiled sweetly

before leaving the dining room. A grinning George scampered behind her. Apparently, her mother's need to be chaperoned for the show was no longer a priority.

"I'll be." Cliff guffawed. "I don't think they were worried about us talking to each other this time."

Sarah angled her head in the direction Maybelle and George had gone. "Neither do I. I guess they think we've reconnected, so their job is done."

Cliff's laughter stopped. "As friends?" When she didn't answer, he added, "That's enough for now," before changing the subject. "May I walk you back to Jane's Place?"

"If you don't mind waiting for me to say a quick hello to my sister, that would be nice."

There was still at least one media van parked in front of Jane's Place as they walked out of Southwind. Cliff made a face. "Wonder when they'll get tired of waiting for a story? Are you game to walk down beyond the veterinarian clinic and then cut through the back parking lot to go in the back way?"

"Definitely."

They walked down Main Street, staying on the Southwind side, both lost in their own thoughts. Sarah had no idea what Cliff was thinking about, but she couldn't get it out of her mind that Harlan still felt Jane was Chief Gerard's top suspect. Just as she had put two and two together by remembering how uncomfortable Veronica was on the night Alan's body was found, she tried to pull whatever was eluding her from the recesses of her mind by mentally reviewing the times she'd seen everyone together, the events she'd observed or participated in, or what she'd seen on a monitor. Nothing popped up on her mental screen.

She was glad that tonight, even though the monitors were still hooked up in the Southwind dining room, Sam and Flynn hadn't chosen to show any more filmed moments. Because the segments they had aired were edited, she made a mental note to suggest to Harlan that it might be worth watching some of the outtakes.

Beyond the veterinarian clinic, Cliff and Sarah crossed the street, walked around the clinic, and cut through the parking lot that Jane's Place and the clinic shared. As they reached the back of Jane's Place, Cliff didn't stop at the kitchen door. Instead, he put his hand on her elbow and guided her around the corner of the kitchen to the chimeless smaller dining room's door.

Sarah didn't pull away. Instead, she followed the gentle pressure he exerted until Cliff opened the door and stepped aside to let her enter. Rather than saying good night, he followed her over the threshold. Sarah didn't object, especially when he said, "I'll be more comfortable leaving you here tonight if I look around a bit first. Is that okay?"

He took her silence as approval and immediately peeked into the kitchen. Satisfied, he moved on to the front hall and the big dining room, while she waited in the greenroom. Secretly, she was a little relieved at his gallantry. She wasn't happy to be spending the night here, but his actions and concern made her feel a little safer.

Being honest, one part of her wanted to run back to the carriage house, but even though her mother had made suggestive noises, she knew when her mother, a prude at heart, said she'd be home late, Maybelle would be coming back to Jane's Place tonight. Sarah felt obligated to be in the building as her mother's protector.

One more night of being under Jane's roof didn't thrill

her, but it eased the prickle of worry Sarah felt at the back of her neck for her mother. She knew part of her feeling stemmed from what might have happened to her mother while Sarah stayed at the carriage house. Maybelle said she'd heard a door close. Who had been on the floor? Was it Trey visiting with Veronica? Or was it the killer coming or going? Had her mother heard something that might have put her in danger while Sarah was indulging her desire to spend the night in her own bed?

Cliff returned from his scouting mission. "From what I can see, the coast is clear. Do you want me to walk you up to your room or stay down here and you can call me and let me know you got upstairs safely?"

"I think both of those options are a bit of overkill."

"Maybe, but I'm a little jumpy tonight." He walked over to the main staircase and ran his hand over the polished banister. "This is a grand old house. I loved visiting it when I was a child and my aunt and uncle lived here. I was told never to slide down this, but of course I did."

"If you want to do it now, I won't tell."

Cliff pointed to the back of his head. "Once was enough, thank you. I never realized how slick a polished rail can be."

"You got hurt?"

He fingered the finial at the bottom of the banister. "Two stitches. I didn't consider the stairwell's final twist. I went flying off to the side and knocked my head hard on that oak stair." He pointed at the second step and then rubbed the back of his head. "It hurts even talking about it."

"At least it's a memory of what the house once was."

Cliff agreed. "After Uncle George sold it to Jane, renovating it while keeping its hardwood and innate beauty was one of my favorite projects. I had to convince her to keep this stairwell intact, but she finally agreed."

Stroking the oak with his hand, he faced Sarah square on. "Having a murder in the parking lot earlier this year was bad enough, but two deaths in the house, both probably murder too? I don't know if that stigma is beatable." He pushed his fist against his mouth.

Feeling his pain, but knowing the future of Jane's ownership of the house was in serious question, Sarah still felt the need to reassure him for the moment. "If Jane must sell, someone will buy this house just for your renovations. If they don't use it for a bed-and-breakfast or for a hospitality purpose, I bet you could remodel it back into a one- or two-family home. It seems to me you could have a family on every floor."

"That's sort of what we did when we visited. My brother and I took the third floor your room is on as our special area. My aunt and uncle didn't have live-in help staying up there, unlike when my aunt grew up in the house. That gave Tom and me the entire floor to ourselves. And since the master bedroom was on the second floor, near the main staircase, Tom and I learned early that the backstairs were the way to come and go as we wanted."

Sarah stared at Cliff. "You used the one from the kitchen?"

"Yeah. That way we never got caught breaking curfew." Cliff peered at Sarah. "Is something wrong?"

"No, I think you're a genius."

"You told me that the other night. It's nice to know, but why now?"

Instead of answering his question, she posed one of her own. "Cliff, when you get home from work, what do you do?"

"It depends. I'm usually tired and filthy, so I strip and shower rather than getting the house dirty."

"Putting on clean clothes or your pajamas?"

"Are you kidding? I'm not going to put my pj's on at seven o'clock. I usually pull on a pair of jeans or shorts and a T-shirt."

"And if you don't shower right away, what do you do?"

Cliff thought for a minute. "Well, if I want to take a quick spin on the boat or sit outside watching the sunset with a beer or a glass of wine, I take off my work boots and crash in one of the wooden chairs on the porch or on the lower deck. Why?"

"I think you just solved the clicking door my mother heard and why Trey was wearing a different shirt than the one he had on at dinner when Officer Robinson brought everyone downstairs after Chef Bernardi was killed."

From Cliff's blank face, Sarah realized he wasn't making the connection she was. "Heather didn't want any tinge of impropriety, and considering everything, Veronica wasn't going to flout the overnight guest and chaperone rules either. They'd have made sure Trey went back to his hotel when he should have."

"Okay, they were going to be Goody-Two-shoes."

"But Cliff, do you remember when Veronica said she was upset, and that Trey and she decided last night to tell all? What if their discussion wasn't on the telephone?"

She paused for him to react, but when he didn't, she continued her explanation. "We know Trey went back to his hotel with Lance. If Trey thought he was in for the evening, Trey, like you, would have gotten comfortable. If Veronica called emotionally distraught, I think, from what we know of Trey, he would have immediately hurried back to Jane's Place to calm her down, but not to break the rules by spending the night."

"Wearing whatever he had on?"

"Right. But, when he got here, with the chaperone rule, he didn't dare come in through the front door. He likely parked in the small area behind the house near the dining room door. That way, like we just did, he could use that entrance without it setting off a chime. Once inside, he went through the kitchen to the backstairs because they came out closer to Veronica's room. I'm sure the door clicking Mother heard was Veronica closing the door after she let Trey in."

"That's a great supposition of the facts, but what does it mean and how do you prove it?"

"What it means is that if when he went through the kitchen to the stairs, Chef Bernardi either wasn't in the kitchen or Trey found him on the floor and being afraid that was why Veronica was upset, put the chef headfirst into the conveyor belt to confuse things."

"I can buy your first theory, Sarah, but not the second. Trey is a decent guy. If he upended Chef Bernardi, Trey wouldn't have been able to focus on calming Veronica and he would have given off more telltale signs when he gave his statement. It seems more likely that he came running because Veronica was upset about everything going on in general and the fact that her mother and she lied to create their alibi."

"I'm inclined to agree with you. I'm betting Trey was in the kitchen at Jane's Place during the time when Chef Bernardi was outside smoking after dissing Jane."

"But shouldn't they have seen each other when Trey was in the parking lot?"

"Trey would have parked beyond where he could see the kitchen entrance. Chef Bernardi may have observed him drive by and go around to that parking pad, but in the dark Trey probably never noticed Chef Bernardi outside."

"You might be on to something, but how are you going to prove what you think happened?"

"I'm not." She pulled out her cell phone and typed in a text. "I'm going to let Harlan and Chief Gerard figure this one out with Veronica and Trey." She grinned. "You always tell me to leave it to the professionals. In this case, with them already at the police station, I am."

"Somehow I feel like your decisions to leave it to the professionals has an ulterior motive."

She laughed. "Well, it might add some credibility to Jane's story if Harlan guides Chief Gerard in a way that the chief stumbles on the truth himself."

Sarah glanced at her phone, willing Harlan to respond to her text. The message showed as delivered. She hoped Harlan would let her know he received it. Otherwise, to make sure he had the information while Chief Gerard had Trey and Veronica at the station, she'd have to call Harlan. Sarah wanted to avoid that so Chief Gerard didn't think she was meddling.

A beep let Sarah know she had a message. She read it and turned the phone so Cliff could see Harlan's response. **K. Will get right on it.**

"Cliff, I'm sure what we figured out about Trey and Veronica is right, but I feel we're missing something obvious. Something that I'm seeing, but not seeing. Sort of like the screens that were set up on the Southwind dining porch for the first dinner the cast, chaperones, and crew were required to be at. I knew everything about that room from its inception to when you built it, but that night I didn't notice those screens until Alan had them roll the introduction segment."

"That's because you knew the room so well. You weren't looking for anything extra, so you skimmed over it."

"But for Jane's sake, I've got to focus in on whatever it is that I'm missing."

"Well, don't stay up too late fretting. It's an early call tomorrow morning for the game show part to be televised on time." He leaned over, lightly kissed the top of her head, and left.

CHAPTER 32

Sarah stared at the closed front door. Without thinking, Sarah put her hand to her forehead. It was just a friendly peck. After all, Cliff and she had been friends for a long time. Still?

No, this was not something she was going to add to her list to fret about. As Sarah put her hand on the banister and her foot on the front staircase's first step, she heard the back door chime. Sarah froze. She knew she should hurry up the stairs and be out of sight if the person came out of the kitchen, but her curiosity as to who it was won out. Rather than going up the stairs, Sarah bent over the shoe already on a step and pretended to examine it. Footsteps coming through the greenroom rewarded her dawdling.

"Oh!" Flynn said. A smile spread across his face. "Hi,

Sarah. With tomorrow's shoot schedule, I didn't expect to run into anyone still downstairs."

"I was just on my way up to bed so I can be up and ready at that ungodly hour. Shouldn't you be counting sheep at your hotel instead of being here?"

He laughed. "Believe me, I won't need to count sheep tonight. When my head hits the pillow, I'll be out cold. With Alan not here to attend to the details, there are a few final things Sam wanted me to check to make sure there are no problems tomorrow."

"Do you expect any?"

"No, but the way things have gone this week, I'm holding my breath to get through tomorrow without any more unforeseen disasters." He comically struck a pose. "Under this handsome, cool, and collected shell is jiggling Jell-O. Until we finish the wedding tomorrow my insides will be churning."

"That's how my mother feels. If you want to talk, I'm glad to listen." Sarah sat on the step, leaving room for Flynn to join her. He did.

"Thanks. I appreciate the offer, but I won't burden you with my problems. Tell me, though—is Maybelle okay? I've really come to enjoy her wit."

"She's stressed. Two seemingly senseless murders in less than a week has her on edge—it's bad enough having to tape tomorrow morning's show at Jane's Place, but spending another night here has her spooked."

"Maybelle isn't the only one. I wish we could have worked out other housing for everyone for tonight, but like everything else this week, Sam and I hit a dead end. It would have been better if we ended everything when Alan died."

"But I thought the two of you were eager after his passing to continue the show?"

"We were, but we never expected the complications we've run into."

"You mean Chef Bernardi's death?"

"That's the worst one, but there have been so many other problems I can't even count them on one hand."

"Like what?"

"You name it. Logistics, ratings, constant bickering between Barbie and Heather, the suits telling us what we can do, and, if all that wasn't enough—" he tapped the plastic souvenir cigar case protruding from his shirt pocket—"I lost my personal cigar case."

"Whoa. I've been around this show just long enough to know that when you say *suits*, you mean the network executives, but I'm not sure how the other things you've mentioned are problems. Are the ratings bad?"

"No, but they aren't going through the roof as I would have expected with the media coverage we've been getting."

"What about the bickering between Barbie and Heather? I thought that was part of the gimmick you were using to grab the audience. And what's the problem you're having with logistics?"

"Okay. Logistically, this show originally was to be filmed at Jane's Place and a few other locations. Sam and Alan decided bringing in Southwind for more filming would be a good idea. That immediately created a problem for us with Jane and Chef Bernardi. Now, with the murders, there's effectively a taint on Jane's Place. We're taping the morning segment here because we have the set built, but none of the contestants are happy being here tonight or tomorrow. You can't tell anyone, but to minimize potential bad press about the wedding venue, we've all agreed we'll name Southwind the venue winner."

"Without the viewers voting?"

"We'll flimflam that a bit if we have to. Sam made the decision. He said that we don't have any other choice but to do it this way because of the mess we're in. The only way he could have everything set up for filming the wedding tomorrow afternoon required him to go with this scenario. Once Jane reads the call sheet we gave out at dinner, she's not going to be a happy camper. It will be worse when we play up Marcus and Emily at Southwind."

Sarah felt sorry for Jane, but she was glad for the national plugs Southwind and her sister and Marcus would receive. There might be some benefit from this reality show after all. Lying through her teeth, she indicated that was a shame about Jane and Jane's Place.

"Don't worry. She'll be happy when she calms down long enough for Sam to tell her how much the show is paying her as a kill fee. I doubt she even hears him tell her that we'll also incorporate kind words about Jane's Place into the final shows."

"Kill fee?"

"Money not to use something. We suggested and the network agreed to pay her what she thought she should have made in meals, plus a premium on that. I'm betting that will make her happy. For those of us attending the wedding, we'll be guaranteed better food than if the venue was Jane's Place."

Flynn was right about the food. As for the money Jane was being paid, it might not be enough money for her to hold on to Jane's Place, but it sounded like it would be enough to get her out of her immediate financial hole.

Now, if Sarah could only figure out how to get Jane out of Chief Gerard's gunsight. "What other problems are you having?"

"Because of compressing our schedule, we also have a logistical problem with the dress. The designer should have had a day after we announced the bride to deliver the dress in the right size and do any necessary alterations. Instead, Sam's gone to the hotel where the designer is to fetch the dress so we can do a rush job on it."

"Can't you simply use a big clip and pins like they do in a bridal store?" Although Sarah's marriage was impetuous, she had gone to one store and tried on a dress she loved. The dress was too big, so the salesperson used a giant clip to pull the fabric together so she could see what it would look like from the front. She'd loved the look, but in the end, when she discovered it would take several months to obtain the dress, she'd ended up wearing a simple dress she bought off the rack.

"That's pretty much what we are going to do, except the clips will be hidden. Pins, clips, and a few strategic stitches will let us shoot the bride from the front and the back." He held up his hands, shaping them into a heart-shaped frame. "Viewers love one good image of the back of the bride and groom."

"I never would have thought of that."

"Alan was a master of knowing what shots please viewers and how to publicize them between segments. He'd get our shows talked about by other television media outlets or by viewers themselves, automatically resulting in an increase in viewers and ratings."

And that translated into advertising dollars and won brownie points for those involved, Sarah knew. "It sounds like Alan, Sam, and you were a good team."

"We were. Alan was a visionary and Sam makes things happen. Both were mentors to me."

"It seems like you added to the team too. A good announcer is hard to come by."

Flynn fingered a baluster next to him. Sarah waited as he ran his hand up and down the wood spindle. "It seems that way, but there are always handsome guys willing to be an announcer. Only a few land a gig that goes on indefinitely."

"You mean like the Alex Trebeks or Pat Sajaks of TV land?"

"Exactly. They were the most recent in our lifetime, since they came on their shows in the 1980s. Looking back, there was Bob Barker, who had two long-running shows. Wink Martindale made a career from hosting several game shows, but for him it was hit-and-miss. He never found one that lasted like the other three hosts I mentioned. My goal is to be more like Alan. He tried his hand at announcing but found a more sustained career behind the scenes."

"What about Sam?"

"He's always been behind the scenes, so he jumped at the chance to step up and show he can fill Alan's shoes. Sam is good at what he does, but the next move up in the business for him are the jobs at Alan's level. Alan's death was horrible, but it's given Sam and me a chance to shine. I've still got some wiggle room, but for Sam, who bet everything to keep this shoot going, there's nothing else that can go wrong. The wrong label on him could be the kiss of death to his career."

This was the second time labels had come up during this show. Sam feared the wrong label would end his career mobility and Heather essentially made the same point about how being considered difficult would keep Veronica and Trey from getting started in show business. Although Sarah knew Michelin stars or being a James Beard Foundation Award nominee or winner was a big deal in the restaurant business, she hadn't really thought about the impact labeling had in the entertainment world. She guessed, after this show, Southwind and Wanda, gaining national recognition for winning venue and pastry chef titles, would have new labels associated with them.

When it came to the culinary world, Sarah didn't want to think what label people could associate with her. For that matter, she wasn't sure what words anyone would pick to describe her. Perhaps, nice?

Flynn looked at his watch. "It's almost ten. If I'm going to get any sleep before I need to be back here, I guess I better go check the set and vendor table for Sam." He stood and sighed. "Would you believe someone sent Sam an email saying they thought they saw the wrong napkins on the table?"

"You're kidding."

"I only wish. As if we didn't have enough balls in the air. I keep reminding myself that it's only one more day. That's all we have to get through."

"Not even a full day anymore," Sarah said.

"Right. And you know what, I bet you that a week from now we all will have more pleasant rather than unpleasant memories of the Southern Belle competition."

CHAPTER 33

Hoping Flynn's prediction would come true, Sarah went upstairs to her room. Opening the connecting bathroom doors, she checked to see if her mother was in her room. Not yet. Sarah put on a long T-shirt and crawled into bed, but she couldn't sleep. She wondered if this was how her mother had been when she and Emily had been out on dates—restless, worried, and wide awake?

Lying in bed, Sarah again went over her mental list of suspects and motives. Considering everything, she didn't think Flynn would win his bet that in a week she'd have more pleasant than unpleasant memories of the Southern Belle competition.

Sarah bolted upright. If Flynn and Sam already knew Southwind was going to be the venue, did Emily know? She grabbed her cell phone from the nightstand and called her twin, hoping that if the night was winding down at Southwind, Emily was somewhere near her cell phone and would see Sarah's name flash up on the screen.

Emily answered on the second ring. "What's up, Sarah?"

"A little bird just told me you're going to have a busy afternoon tomorrow. Why didn't you mention it when I was at Southwind?"

"Just a minute. Let me go outside." From the sounds she could hear, Sarah assumed Emily was in the kitchen and was walking out to the back porch. "Are you still there, Sarah?"

"Yes."

"I had to go outside to talk."

"Why, is this a secret? And why would you keep it from me? I'm an owner of Southwind too."

"I know, but you're also Mom's chaperone. When he came and told us this morning that we were going to be the venue winner, we had to promise to keep it a secret until they announced it to everyone. Marcus and I specifically had to assure him we wouldn't tell you because of your involvement with the show. We were only getting a heads-up because we'd have to order appropriate food for the reception and be available to work with the other vendors tomorrow morning."

"Who came and told you?"

"Flynn Quinn, but he said he was speaking on behalf of Sam and the network."

It seemed strange to Sarah that Flynn was the emissary. Then again, if Sam was busy with other details of rearranging the shooting schedule to finish everything tomorrow, perhaps it made sense that Flynn took on this responsibility. "Em, did any of the vendors contact you before dinner tonight?"

"No, the only one I've talked to is Suzy from Suzy's

Flowers. She left Southwind after dinner but turned around and came back to discuss when she could get in to Southwind to set up. We took about a half hour talking everything through. She diagrammed where we'll set up the ceremony and how we will arrange the seating and centerpieces."

"I know she was the agreed-to florist after the flower arrangement segment was scratched, but did she tell you who told her Southwind was going to be the venue of choice?"

"She didn't mention it, but I assumed it was announced during dinner."

"It wasn't. Tell me, what about Wanda and the cake? What is she doing to prep a cake for the winner in time for the wedding?"

"She made most of the cake today."

"How? She doesn't know who the winner is going to be."

"We're assuming it will be Veronica and Trey or Starr and Lance, but the cake she made will work for any of the couples. Once the winner is declared, she only needs about an hour to add the last touches she's already pre-pared."

"You seem to think Mom and George are out of it. Why? Did someone say something to you or Wanda?"

"Not directly, but Wanda noticed that the groom's cakes she and Chef Bernardi were charged with making were close to the introductions of the two younger cou-ples. For the actual wedding cake, Wanda spent today making a couple of sheet cakes and different-sized circu-lar cakes layers that she stacked and already covered with a fondant icing. As soon as she knows the winner, she'll add a few extra touches. Other than the toppers she uses, her basic cake is finished. She'll have no problem having it ready for the reception."

"Thanks, Em. I won't keep you. Good night."

"Good night."

After hanging up, Sarah thought about how Suzy could have known Southwind was the venue of choice. It was not announced at dinner, but Suzy had known almost immediately after leaving Southwind. How? Suddenly, it hit Sarah. She rose and reached for the pants she'd worn earlier in the evening. Pulling out the call sheet she'd stuck into her pocket, she remembered her mother's admonishment when Sarah skimmed the first call sheet. This time, she read each line carefully.

Sarah smiled. The obvious answer she'd felt she was missing was hidden right in front of her.

CHAPTER 34

Mid-page, the wedding heading was printed in a large-point font. Underneath it, in almost the same-sized font, were the names of the vendor participants who'd already been announced. Sarah's eye went to the one line that was so small it was almost impossible to read. Like Suzy, though, she read it: *Location: Southwind Cast: S&L.*

Now she knew who Sam was bringing the dress to tonight. Sarah pulled on the pants she wore earlier and stuffed her T-shirt into them. Until Sarah saw Starr face-to-face, Sarah wasn't sure if her mission was one of warning Starr about what was going on or investigating why Starr was going along with the fix.

As Sarah started down the stairs to Starr's room, Sarah heard someone coming up the steps. She stopped and peeked over the curve of the banister. It was Sam carrying

a dress over his shoulder. Sarah waited until he reached
the second-floor landing and left the staircase before she
quietly made her way down. At the second floor, she peered
around the wall and saw Sam enter a doorway, the dress
flouncing behind him until Barbie's ring-covered hand
pulled its excess material into the room.

Slowly, Sarah moved down the hall toward Starr and
Barbie's rooms. She wasn't sure how she was going to
explain her presence if Sam or Barbie came out of Barbie's room, but Sarah needed to see Starr face-to-face to
know if she was involved in rigging the competition.

As Sarah reached Starr's door, she saw that the one beyond, Barbie's, hadn't been fully closed. Able to hear
Barbie and Sam talking, she inched forward, pressed
against the wall between Starr and Barbie's rooms, and
listened.

"How are you going to get Starr into that dress tonight
in order for you to pin it for the designer to do the alterations in the morning?" Sam asked.

"I'll remind Starr that this is dress is going to be available for order in all sizes by the designer as soon as the
show airs. Then, I'll tell her that because of the differences in size between the three finalists and the time
crunch, the designer and you brought the same dress to
each finalist tonight for pinning. While the designer is
pinning the other dresses, she jumped at it when I volunteered to do Starr's because of how many times I've
pinned, clipped, or sewed for pageants, beginning with
my own."

"That won't work."

"Why not?"

Sarah couldn't see Barbie, but she could imagine her
stubborn stance.

"Starr's not stupid. If you also give her the answers tonight, she'll realize we're setting her up to win and question whether anyone else actually is having a dress pinned."

"I've got that figured out. I just need you to give me the bonus question. Then, like I do before pageants, while I'm pinning her dress, I'll brainstorm with her what kind of topics a show like this might ask. Of course, one I'll suggest will be the bonus question."

Sam responded, but Sarah couldn't hear that part of his answer. What she did hear was Barbie's reply invoking the name of her ex-husband, Jake, as a saint in making it possible for Starr to have this prime-time exposure.

"More of a snake," Sam said. "Jake the Snake fits him to the T. Tonight, I expect you to let him know I upheld my part of our bargain, so we're even."

"Of course."

Sarah was so busy eavesdropping that for a moment, she forgot where she was. Seeing Sam's fingers grasping the door as he said something else to Barbie, she realized she needed to move. But, as the door swung open, there was no time for her to retreat to the stairs. Instead, she backed up to just beyond Starr's door and raised her hand to rap on it.

"What are you doing here?"

Seeing Sam's clenched fists, Sarah froze her hand in midair. "I just stopped by to see Starr. She asked me about an eye makeup remover my sister raved about, but I couldn't remember the name. When I talked to Emily tonight, she told me its name. I came downstairs to tell Starr. With you cramming so much in tomorrow, I was sure I'd forget to bring it up during the craziness." She raised her fist again to knock on the door.

As Sarah rambled, Barbie came into the hall. "Don't knock," she ordered. "Starr already went to bed."

"Oh, I'm sorry." She glanced at her watch, taking a step back toward the stairwell. "Emily and I were gabbing away, and I didn't realize how late it was. I'll make sure I see her tomorrow." Before Barbie or Sam could say anything else, Sarah fled to the stairs.

Once Sarah reached the safety of her room, she slammed the door and locked it behind her. She was shaking. Sarah leaned against the locked door, wishing her mother was back.

Between the call sheet and what she'd just heard, there was no question the show was rigged, but what should she do? If she took her information to Chief Gerard, he would discount it as coming from a hysterical female. If he even deigned to follow up, he wouldn't do much except ask a question or two. He'd accept whatever answer Sam gave him.

Even with the initials in black-and-white on the sheet, Sam could say it was a typo. In her head, Sarah could hear him saying, "That's why we used initials, so we could get all of the contestants in that slot, but someone must have left them off." He'd probably blame Flynn for not proofreading the call sheet.

Then again, the two of them were running the show together. She wondered if Flynn was equally involved. From the sound of it, though, Sam only talked about himself being even with Jake the Snake. What was it that he owed him? The chance to run the show? A gambling debt? Something else? Could Barbie have wanted this exposure so badly for Starr that she was the mastermind behind knocking off anyone who stood in her daughter's way?

Obviously, if they took their plan to Alan or he found out about it and he refused to allow the competition to be thrown, he would have been an obstacle to Barbie getting what she wanted and Sam extricating himself from whatever he owed Jake. In a way, that made sense as to why Barbie, despite having her hair rolled and being in her nightgown, didn't throw more of a fit and absolutely refuse to come downstairs when Officer Robinson brought everyone down for questioning. Her costume gave her a perfect alibi for when Alan died. By the same token, Sam and Flynn also had alibis, as they were at their hotel. And Jake had supposedly left Wheaton.

The key was when and how Alan ingested the nicotine poison. If Sarah could tie the ingestion point back to Sam and Barbie, she might have enough ammunition to get Chief Gerard to look beyond Jane. Sarah grabbed her phone and punched *nicotine poisoning* into the search engine. She skimmed the articles that came up.

The timing didn't quite seem to fit. Alan might have had some nausea within fifteen to sixty minutes of ingestion and then, if the level was enough, his body would have wound down to death without intervention. During dinner, Sam and Alan were half a table apart and Barbie was at a completely different table. Sarah didn't recall seeing either of them anywhere near anything Alan ate. No, if the nicotine was ingested at dinner, it was either in the tea or the vegetable plate, which couldn't be, because then Jane or Southwind would be implicated.

Sarah kept reading. Nicotine overdoses required a good amount of exposure, but the combination of e-cigarettes with a smoke cessation product could be problematic, as it could increase levels of nicotine usage. Could it have been an overdose from his own sucking on cigars all day, wearing the nicotine patch, and either one cigar or e-cigarette too many? It was possible, but not probable, since unlike someone who didn't use tobacco products, Alan did. He would have been mindful of his nicotine consumption. In Sarah's mind, there had to be an outside source of excess ingestion for Alan's poisoning.

Although she didn't know how Chef Bernardi died, his symptoms were so like Alan's—no wound, spittle, and blue lips—that she bet Chef Bernardi had also been poisoned. But how? Except for knowing he went outside to smoke one cigar, she hadn't known of him being a regular smoker like Flynn, Sam, or Alan.

Tying Sam and Barbie to his death was easier than Alan's. Barbie was in the house when he died, plus she had opportunity. It also made sense to believe Barbie was the one who had words about her daughter with Chef Bernardi. As the flower arrangement judge, he could have voted to keep Starr in the competition, but if he refused, based upon the actual arrangements, not only could she claim he was at fault, but she might think he was going to benefit from the change in the line on the bets that had been placed. Whether she had money bet with him, or she believed he was going to use his flower arranging vote to make her daughter one of the final two couples in the competition and then gone back on his word, she had motive.

Sam also could have had the opportunity to kill Chef Bernardi, since he was in and out of the house all the time. But even if he didn't do it, Barbie might have been able to force him to help her move or stage the body because of whatever Jake the Snake had on Sam. Because there was no blood, they could easily have dumped a dead Chef Bernardi headfirst into the dishwasher conveyor belt and pulled the chain for the scalding water to wash away any trace of them. They could have heard Jane coming back and decided her being found with the body was a great diversion from anyone thinking they had a motive to kill Chef Bernardi.

It was a good theory, but Sarah was stumped how to proceed with it. Once again, she felt she was missing the obvious. Her racing thoughts and what she'd heard couldn't wait until morning. There was only one thing to do. She hated waking him again, but she needed Harlan's counsel. At least, she thought, as she punched in his number, it wasn't quite midnight yet.

CHAPTER 35

Skittish, Sarah asked who it was before she opened her bedroom door for Harlan. As he walked in, he pointed over his shoulder with the hand that wasn't carrying his ever-present briefcase. "Guess who I found?"

"What are you still doing up?" her mother asked. "And what is Harlan doing here?"

"Sit down and I'll explain." Sarah told them everything that had transpired and her theories. Her mother propped herself up on the pillows on the bed, while Harlan sat on the room's only chair, making notes on the yellow legal pad he'd pulled from his briefcase. "Rigging the contest isn't right, but I don't see how we go to Chief Gerard with my ideas."

Harlan flipped the top page of his pad over the page he'd made his notes on. "I agree with you. At this point, there's no local crime for Chief Gerard to investigate tied to rigging the game. Most of the time, these things are handled through civil lawsuits." He capped his pen. "None of what you suggested has any evidentiary tie-in with Alan or Chef Bernardi's deaths."

"I know Chief Gerard hesitated to arrest Jane until the toxicology reports are back, but from what you said, Dr. Smith is certain Alan's death was somehow tied to nicotine poisoning. Has he pinpointed anything as the cause of Chef Bernardi's death that might tie Jane to that one too?"

"Chef Bernardi's autopsy showed similar indications of nicotine poisoning, which is too much coincidence, but again, they want the toxicology reports back before they proceed. Dr. Smith is thorough. He even sent samples of the cake Chef Bernardi was working on to be tested."

"That seems like overkill."

"He has the body tied to Jane's Place, but narrowing down the chef's source of nicotine poisoning isn't that easy. Consequently, Dr. Smith looked for things in the kitchen that might have given Chef Bernardi a lot of contact exposure. The only thing Dr. Smith saw that he had a lot of contact with was the cake. The chef had his hands in the dough, the fondant, and every other aspect of putting together the cake."

Sarah weighed what Harlan was saying. "I guess it could have been an ingredient or on one of the things he handled quite a bit while preparing the cake, like a rolling pin or even a spatula. But, if the killer's target was Chef Bernardi through the cake he was making, wouldn't there be a danger of poisoning the crew and cast who might eat the cake or lick the icing while setting it up for vendor shots?"

"Probably not if we circle back to where we began this discussion."

"Barbie and Sam?"

"Chef Bernardi was assigned to make a groom's cake that tied to Veronica and Trey's interests."

"Alabama?"

"Right, Sarah. With Wanda the winning pastry chef, his Alabama cake would be tossed."

Maybelle disagreed. "Not around here. Anything extra would be devoured by the crew or some of our male cast members. Trey and Lance, plus some of the cameramen, nibble all day."

"Plus," Sarah said, "I think someone said the show was going to donate the cakes somewhere as its last charitable contribution."

"None of them will touch this cake after it became part of a crime scene. The cake has been poked and prodded until it's a mess. Even if someone got a lick or a taste, there wouldn't be enough nicotine exposure ingested to poison them. By the time the cake is cleared based upon the toxicology reports, it will be too stale and handled for anyone to eat."

"That takes us back to Barbie and Sam because the groom's cake displayed on the vendor table was Wanda's, which just happens to be the one that fulfills what Lance and Starr want."

"But again, we don't have enough to convince Chief Gerard that they've done something wrong."

"Why not?" Maybelle demanded. "Isn't it obvious that Barbie was the one who threatened Chef Bernardi? I could easily see her on sheer adrenaline flipping Chef Bernardi onto the dishwasher belt or at least getting Sam to help her."

"Maybelle, envisioning isn't the same as proving." Harlan tapped his pen on his pad. "Courts may consider circumstantial evidence, but we need a better tie-in and clarification of motive before Chief Gerard will pursue anything."

Sarah sighed. "Like he thinks he has with Jane?"

"Exactly."

"We know better, though." Maybelle crossed her arms and scowled. "At least, is there something the chief could get them on for not playing fair with the show? Technically, the way Sam and Flynn kicked off Natalie and Ralph wasn't fair, nor is the way they're declaring Southwind as the venue winner."

"Mother! Don't take that away from Southwind. It's a great advertising boost. Plus, unlike Jane, just by being themselves, the viewers have come to love Marcus and Emily as a couple. Flynn said they could be an extra set of contestants."

"Fine." Maybelle put her lips together in a pout.

Harlan put his legal pad and pen into his briefcase and snapped the locks. "We really don't have enough to dispute the decisions Sam and Flynn made, especially since many of them, like eliminating Natalie and Ralph, they can blame on the network. Remember, they said that was tied to a polling determination."

"Very convenient," Maybelle said. "Just like getting away with murder will be."

"Now, Maybelle. In terms of how the show ends, Sam bringing Barbie the dress and their discussion about throwing the contest in Starr's favor doesn't make it so. Sam and Barbie may have conspired to rig the ending, but Sarah didn't hear either of them confess. All we can do, now that Chef Bernardi and Alan are out of the way, is see if they proceed with their plan."

Maybelle swung her feet off the bed and leaned toward Harlan. "If I'm understanding you correctly, you're telling me George and I have to participate in a farce that will be shown nationally, and we can't do anything to protest the outcome."

"You could always sue Sam, Flynn, and the network on the grounds that they acted in a manner to your detriment," Harlan said, "but lawsuits are expensive and take a lot of time to conclude."

"It just doesn't seem fair."

"Mom, you may not be able to protest the outcome, but you might be able to influence it."

"I don't follow you."

"Neither do I, Sarah."

"You remember the old saying that you can lead a horse to water, but you can't make him drink?"

Harlan nodded.

"I like Starr. She's a straight shooter. Even if her mother plants some of the questions in Starr's mind or discusses them with Lance and her, what do you think Starr would do if a little bird let her know no one else had a dress delivered or had any information to speculate what kind of questions might be asked?"

"I don't see how that can be done," Harlan said.

"Oh, I do." Maybelle flapped her arms like wings.

Chapter 36

Considering the early hour of the morning, the dining rooms being used as the stage area and the green-room were overflowing with people. Sarah stepped into the front hall to avoid the zoo atmosphere. She glanced into the big dining room. The three would-be grooms stood apart from the confusion of people making sure cords were taped down and the curtains drawn, so the lighting when the sun came up would be controlled by the crew. Repeated numbers being said aloud indicated someone was doing a sound check. The one person who seemed to be missing was Jane. Maybe that was a good thing, considering Jane might cause a scene.

Heather had her back to Sarah, but she appeared to be adjusting the collar of Veronica's blouse. The two had their heads close to each other, laughing about something. As Sarah watched the pre-competition show play itself out, the front door opened and a well-dressed man about her mother's age walked in.

He paused and checked his watch, which Sarah easily recognized as being a Rolex.

He glanced between the two rooms, as if trying to decide which one to enter.

"May I help you?" Sarah asked.

"Yes, thank you." He brushed a strand of his combed-over hair back into place. "I'm looking for my daughter and her mother."

"Are you looking for Starr?"

"That's right."

She pointed into the large dining room. "Starr's in there. I'm not sure where Barbie is."

"Starr is really the one I want to see. Thank you."

Sarah watched him walk into the dining room. Starr raised her hand to her mouth before shouting "Daddy" and reaching to embrace him. It was clear Starr hadn't been expecting him. From Starr's reaction, as Heather had indicated, it was obvious Starr had not seen her father on Saturday. In that case, what had he been doing at Jane's Place before going to dinner with Alan, Sam, and Flynn? Heather also said he'd been in Wheaton on business, but if he hadn't taken the time to see his daughter earlier, was it some kind of monkey business? She felt certain, from the information she'd found about him when she Googled, that his presence on Saturday and probably today, tied in with rigging or betting on the show and the call sheet Alan was holding when he died.

As father and daughter walked to the side of the room, engaged in a serious conversation, Sarah caught Maybelle's eye. Sarah raised her hands in a *what's up* fashion. Her mother shot her an *okay* symbol.

Before Sarah could go into the dining room and find out exactly what her mother meant, Sam clapped his hands for everyone's attention. "Except for the contestants, clear the set, please. The screen is on in the greenroom for those who want to watch. Remember, we're taping this to edit and show nationally this afternoon."

Sarah went into the greenroom and positioned herself where she could see the screen but could also peek across the front hall to where the couples were settling behind the hearts that had their names on them. She saw Flynn take his place near a small podium positioned to the side of the three couples.

As Heather turned away from Veronica, she bumped into Starr's father. For a moment they stared at each other, frozen, but Sam's repeat prodding pushed them into motion. They walked out of the dining room and stood next to Sarah, watching what was going on in person, but also able to see the screen. Sarah couldn't help but listen to their conversation.

"Jake, I'm surprised to see you back here. I thought the other night you said your business was done and you were going back to Atlanta."

"That's a nice way to say hello, Heather. You're looking well. And for your information and curiosity, Barbie called and thought if I could swing it, Starr would appreciate having me here for the end of the competition."

"So, you just hopped in the car and came over to Alabama. I would have thought you were too busy to spare the driving time."

"I am. I flew."

From the way Heather's body stiffened, Sarah figured she was holding herself back from a doozy of a sarcastic comeback. Jake the Snake was as relaxed as Heather was tight.

He pointed toward the three couples. "I see Veronica's all grown up. She's beautiful. I know you're proud of her."

Heather relaxed and answered with simple words of agreement, plus a compliment about Starr. At that moment, Jane and Barbie came down the central steps. A crew person waved them away from the big dining room. Both came into the greenroom. When Barbie spotted Jake, she left Jane's side. Barging between Heather and him, Barbie planted a big kiss on the side of his face.

"Hello, Barbie." He pulled a handkerchief from his pocket and wiped his face.

Glancing at Heather as if to rub in what she was saying, Barbie told Jake, "I'm so glad you're here to support Starr. This is going to be another launching ground for her."

"I thought the goal was to win the perfect wedding, not to take off into the air," Heather said.

"Heather—" Barbie began, but Sam's call for "action" hushed everyone in the greenroom.

Sarah joined the three of them as they moved closer to watch and hear through the monitor. Flynn did a basic introduction of the three finalist couples and the game that was about to be played. He asked the women to leave and posed three easy questions to the men. Flynn commented on some of their answers and at least once, Trey and Lance, outside of their answers, exchanged light taunts about Alabama and Auburn that provoked those on the stage and in the greenroom to laugh.

When the women returned, Flynn repeated the questions. Veronica and Maybelle quickly earned five points responding to the first question: "What is your groom-to-be's favorite color?"

When he turned to Starr and repeated the question, Sarah heard Barbie, who stood next to her, whisper "blue." But "orange"—Auburn's other color—is what came out of Starr's mouth. Barbie jerked her head up as Lance turned over his card that read *blue*.

Flynn began the next series of questions with Starr and Lance. This time their answers matched, but so did those of the other contestants. When Flynn posed the final question, whether the couple's preference was to live in the city or the country, Sarah knew it was a no-brainer for Starr. Sarah could still remember she and Lance expressing their desire to be city dwellers when Jed and Lucy professed their preference for country living.

Starr's "country" response was loud and firm.

Staring at Starr wide-eyed, Lance barely got his *city* card flipped up, when Barbie shouted, "What's going on?" She brushed past Sarah and burst into the big dining room.

Sam yelled, "Cut. Barbie, get out of here."

She ignored him. Instead, she squared off in front of her daughter's heart and demanded to know what was going on. Starr stood. Lance joined her. As Starr met her mother's gaze, her hand was in Lance's.

Quietly, Jake cut in front of Sarah as he made his way to the doorway of the big dining room, but he didn't intrude on whatever was happening.

"When I compete, Mother, I compete fairly. It was one thing to do pageants for scholarship money, but I already told you, I'm done with that. Lance and I would have liked to have won the perfect wedding without paying for it, but whatever wedding we have will be on our terms.

And you know what? It will be perfect. We're done here."
Starr, with Lance still holding her hand, followed her
from behind their heart and together they walked out of
the dining room.

For the first time, Barbie didn't follow her daughter
out of the room. She stood alone, her mouth agape, staring at the heart with Starr and Lance's name on it. Instead
of yelling or ranting, Barbie was still, except for the tears
that began to run down her face.

Jake met the couple in the archway to the front hall.
Lance let go of Starr's hand as she fell into her father's
embrace. If the glare Jake shot into the main dining room
at Barbie and Sam could kill, Sarah thought there would
be two additional bodies added to the Southern Belle
death count.

Sam turned on Barbie. "You've ruined everything."
Before the moment escalated, Flynn came out from behind his podium and walked over to Sam. He put his hand
on Sam's arm. "Sam, she isn't worth it. We can fix this."

"How? It's a disaster. Everything was set."

Sarah didn't think they were talking about the same
thing. Flynn's focus was the show, but whatever Sam was
worried about was personal. The way he was sweating
and fretting reminded Sarah of how Jane lost control on
the porch when pleading with Chef Bernardi to cancel the
bets.

Based upon what she'd read about Jake, Sarah was
convinced Sam and Jake's involvement was tied to gambling. Jake's presence on Saturday, without having seen
Starr, indicated his business in Wheaton had to have been
tied to more than a dinner with his old roommate and his
daughter being on the show. From Sam's visceral reac-

tion, she was convinced that probably, over dinner, a discussion of the odds on the show was raised and Sam booked a larger bet with Jake.

It wasn't solid evidence, but if what Jake said led to Alan investigating to make sure his show was in compliance, and what Alan turned up was Chef Bernardi's two-bit bookie operation, Alan would have been furious. Furious enough to bring the information to the show's compliance officer. That might explain why he'd jotted down Chef Bernardi's line on the back of a call sheet. It could also explain why Sam or Chef Bernardi might have feared being exposed by Alan. There was no question Sarah now had more solid motivations for Chief Gerard and Harlan to follow up, but what she'd learned still didn't pinpoint the final how and why of the two murders.

Watching Starr and her father interact as they left Jane's Place, as well as the flash of anger he'd shown toward Barbie, Sarah thought his feelings for his daughter were genuine. She didn't believe he was involved in rigging the show, but rather in handling larger bets than Chef Bernardi—if he even knew Chef Bernardi was running a line. One thing she was sure of was that Jake's controlled rage at his daughter being wronged was enough for her to fear for Sam's well-being. Sarah doubted Jake the Snake let gambling debts slide.

Flynn was talking a mile a minute and gesturing to where the remaining four contestants sat. "Look, Sam, it's simple. I can redub my opening to say that the couple with the lowest score at the end of the first round will be leaving us. You edit the tape to where Starr answered 'country,' and then have me announce Starr and Lance were great competitors and that we're sorry to see them go. You either go to the second round at that point or, if you caught footage of them leaving the room, you splice that in. It's a simple solution and one the public will buy."

Sam rubbed his hand over his scruffy beard. "That actually might work." He instructed his digital person what he needed done. During all of this, Maybelle and George and Veronica and Trey hadn't moved. Sam walked over to where they sat. "We're going to film the next round with just you two couples. Are you ready?"

Trey rubbed the back of his neck and stared at Veronica. Instead of returning his gaze, her head was turned as she beckoned for her mother. From the room's doorway, Heather glanced at Flynn and Sam. Flynn nodded his head and Heather went to her daughter. After they exchanged a few words, Heather returned to where Sarah and Jane stood at the edge of the greenroom.

Heather rested her hands on her stomach and let out a little groan.

"Are you all right?"

"No." She ran out of the room and up the stairs. Veronica, seeing her mother's reaction, jumped up and started to follow her.

Sam stopped her with a sharp, "Veronica, sit down. We're on a schedule."

"But my mother."

"Will be fine. Stop whimpering like a baby."

"Don't you talk to my wife that way!" Trey shouted. He clapped his hand over his mouth and whispered "I'm sorry" in Veronica's direction.

Sam jerked his head in Trey's direction. "What did you say?"

Trey moved closer to Veronica. He put his arm around her and she raised her face toward his. "It's okay," she said.

Turning back toward Sam, Trey spoke in a normal but firm tone. "I said don't talk to my wife that way."

"Your wife?" Sam stood silent, his mouth gaping open.

Trey put his arm around Veronica. "My wife, my lovely bride."

Sam sputtered out something about them being married. "When? We vetted everyone carefully."

"We got married in Tuscaloosa on Saturday evening by a minister friend of mine. Lance and Starr stood up for us. It was a late night, but the four us thought it would be a win-win all around."

"How did you figure that?" Sam's tone was icy.

"Because Lance and Starr really wanted the perfect wedding without having to pay for it, while just being together is what matters to us. Whether we get Veronica's mom's dream of a reality show or I get my dream job as the first one after graduation, we're happy knowing we're together." Trey stared down at Veronica and smiled. "Guess we're done here, wife."

She grinned up at him. "I think we are, hubby." Together, they slid out from behind their heart.

Unlike them, Sam didn't move. He simply stared at Maybelle and George.

The silence was broken by Maybelle gasping for air. "George."

"I know." He patted her hand, then rested his hand on her back, trying to calm her sudden hysterical crying. "Maybelle, take a deep breath. It's going to be okay." As he tended to her, raising his voice to ask if someone could get her some water, Sarah hurried to her mother.

She knelt in front of Maybelle's heart. "Mom, what is it? What's wrong?"

Her mother sobbed harder.

A hand thrust a glass of water at Sarah. She took the glass, barely noticing that it was Jane who had brought it to her. Sarah handed the water to her mother, who stared at it but didn't drink it. "Are you okay?"

"I think she's having a panic attack," George said.

"My mother doesn't have panic attacks. She gives them to other people."

Maybelle nodded.

"This time I think she is. We can't win."

Maybelle nodded again.

Sam and Flynn crowded into the narrow space next to Sarah. "What do you mean, you can't win?" Sam asked.

Having taken a few sips of water, Maybelle said, "We can't afford to get married."

"Mom, what do you mean?"

Maybelle glanced at George. "You explain."

It was his turn to nod. He took a deep breath. "Once we were named as finalists, we did the math. The impact on our Social Security benefits if we marry hurts us economically. We're financially better off staying the way we are. We can't win."

Sam groaned. He backed away from them. "Once you figured that out, why did you stay in the contest?"

"For the fun of it. We were sure we wouldn't win, and at our ages, how many reality shows do you think we'll ever be on again? We've had a blast. You can't believe what a following we've been building where I live."

Sarah chuckled at the idea of the residents of the retirement home crowded into the TV room to watch her mother and George compete. It was probably a highlight of their day.

From the way Sam was ranting, it wasn't going down as a highlight of his. "You can't do this to me. We've got to finish this competition with a wedding. Why don't you get married and then divorced?"

"Nope. Can't do that." George's professorial side took over as he started to explain that once they did that, it would change their benefits and Maybelle's status.

Sam talked over George's recitation. "I appreciate what you're saying, but we've got a major problem here. We've got to do something. The public and the network aren't going to be happy without the perfect wedding they've been expecting. Not at this point."

Jane laughed in Sam's face. "What goes around comes around. So much for your perfect wedding."

"A perfect wedding," Sarah repeated. "I have an idea. I think I know a couple who would love the opportunity for a perfect wedding." She shared her idea with the others. "Of course, you might need to tape the wedding tomorrow in order to let them get a license."

"You can't do that," Jane said.

Flynn raised his hand, cutting off any further discussion. "It's not a problem. We can make this work. If they agree, we tape the wedding as planned in a couple of hours and then they can go to the courthouse afterwards to make it legal at their convenience." Ignoring Jane's resumed protests, he pulled a small ring box out of his pocket and opened it so Sarah could see what was in the box. "This is the ring we had designed especially for this wedding. I was supposed to give it to the winner to formally propose. Shall we?"

"Yes."

Sarah and Flynn walked across the street toward the carriage house. The sun was up, which Sarah took as a good sign because she firmly believed light triumphed over darkness.

Excitement at her idea built up in her, but Sarah held back to let Flynn walk slightly ahead of her so that neither of them had to step in the grass, still wet with dew. Halfway to the carriage house, she saw Marcus outside walking Fluffy. Sarah shouted to get his attention. He waited for them, Fluffy pulling on her leash, straining to say hello to Sarah.

"I thought you guys were taping. Done already?"

"Not exactly," Sarah said. "We've got a proposition for you. Flynn?"

Flynn opened the box and flashed the ring at Marcus. "We ran into a little problem. We have the perfect wedding, but we're lacking the perfect couple. Sarah tells me Emily and you have talked plans, but with the pains of opening Southwind still on your plate, you didn't feel you could financially pull off the wedding the two of you want. How about if you take this ring and the Southern Belle competition underwrites the perfect wedding for you?"

Marcus didn't have to think twice. He handed Fluffy's leash to Sarah and took the ring box. Flynn, and the ever-present cameraman who had suddenly caught up to them, followed Marcus as he quickly strode back to the carriage house. "Emily," he shouted. "Em."

She came out of the house, wiping her hands on a paper towel. She wore an *Eat at Your Own Risk* apron Sarah had forgotten she owned. "What's the matter?"

Instead of answering, Marcus got down on one knee

on the damp grass and opened the box. "Emily Johnson, you are the love of my life. Will you marry me?"

"Are you being silly?"

"No. Will you marry me?" He glanced at Sarah, but it was Flynn who explained the situation.

"The perfect Southern Belle wedding is available for the two of you in two hours. Of course, you'll have to stop by the courthouse to make it legal afterwards."

Emily shook her head. "My answer to marrying you is 'yes,' but not this way. I don't want someone else to pick out my dress, flowers, or any of the other things that will make it perfect. No matter how small or large, I want to marry you in front of the people we love."

Marcus rose and hugged her. "I understand." He closed the ring box and held it out to Flynn. "Thank you, anyway."

Flynn didn't take the ring. He ran his hand through his hair and down his face. "Emily, what if you took this ring—which, by the way, is beautiful—and went through with the wedding today?"

When she shook her head, he put up his hand. "Let me finish. If you go through with today's wedding, the network will agree to assume the entire cost of what you deem to be a perfect wedding."

"I don't think they'll do that simply on your word," Sarah observed.

"Sam and I have the authority to enter into contracts for the competition. I think this will qualify."

Emily glanced at Sarah. "If you can get it in writing with the exact terms you just laid out, I think Marcus and Emily will agree. Right?"

When Emily and Marcus nodded affirmatively, Flynn smiled. "Consider it a done deal."

The cameraman waited, his camera posed and running.

Opening the box and getting down on his knee again, Marcus repeated his question.

"Yes. Of course, yes."

Marcus slid the ring on her finger, stood, and hugged Emily.

Sarah whispered to Flynn, "I think we should leave them alone for a few minutes and go calm things down back at Jane's Place. Plus, there needs to be a contract executed before any wedding, even a mock one, is filmed."

He glanced at Marcus and Emily still embracing. "Sounds like a plan to me."

CHAPTER 37

As Sarah and Flynn left the carriage house, he reached into his breast pocket and pulled out a leather cigar case. He opened it, but before he could take a cigar out, Sarah held up her hand. "Please, don't light up. I'm as bad as my mother when it comes to the smell of cigars."

"I wasn't planning on lighting a cigar." He turned the case so she could see what was in it. "Alan and Sam are the cigar smokers. I'm more into this newer thing, a cig-a-like. When we were in Europe on a shoot last year, I was introduced to these electronic cigarettes. They've been around in some form for a long time, but a Chinese inventor really figured them out four or five years ago. Here in the States, they're catching on."

Sarah stared at the case and the cig-a-like. "How do they work?"

"They heat e-liquid and create a vapor."

"Is the liquid refillable?"

"Yes. You get a bottle or a vial of it and you use a little at a time."

"Did you say Alan and Sam smoke them too?"

"Alan was a big tobacco cigarette smoker. When he got on his natural kick, he started using a nicotine patch and cut out the cigarettes, but took up cigars as his vice. He could chomp on one all day without lighting it, but his after-dinner smoke was sacred. I gave him a few of these to try during this shoot."

Thinking back to their first dinner, Sarah remembered Alan telling her about his love for Cuban cigars and that Flynn and Sam had brought back the last batch of them from a Canada trip. As they neared the railings of Southwind's back porch, Sarah started putting things together.

"Flynn, what would have happened if there was no wedding today?"

"There would have been a lot of unhappy people. Like we talked about before, the network put up money to have a crew down here and Sam and I have a lot riding on this, especially after we convinced them to go on with the competition after Alan's death."

She didn't want to reveal what she'd heard in the hallway last night, but maybe she could come at it from a different way. "The night Jane broke up the cigars and beers you were having on Southwind's back porch for the male contestants, she and others seemed upset because Chef Bernardi wasn't willing to restart the gambling pool. What happened with that when he died? Did it go away? Did people get their money back?"

He stopped walking. "You ask a lot of questions, don't you?"

"My mother always said I was curious." Sarah strained to force out a giggle. "You've met Maybelle, so you know I come by it naturally. I don't know much about gambling. That's why I'm asking."

Flynn narrowed his eyes, but he answered. "Chef Bernardi wasn't the only one making book on the show. For those who bet only with Chef Bernardi, his death took care of things, but Jake the Snake had a line too. I didn't bet with him, but Sam did on this and some other things."

The smile on Flynn's face made Sarah nervous. "It's a shame, but Sam owes him big," he added.

Sarah opened her eyes wide. "Oh, my. What will happen to him now that Starr isn't in the competition?"

Flynn's smile turned to a scowl. "You've already figured that one out, haven't you? Sam told me about you being in the hall last night. He wasn't sure if you heard anything, but you're smarter than he is. You put it together, haven't you?" Flynn moved closer to Sarah.

Frightened, Sarah looked for a way to get away from him. She was too far from the carriage house to outrun him in that direction. With her eye, Sarah measured the distance between where they were and the top of Southwind's back porch. Then she realized the kitchen door was locked at this hour, especially if Marcus and Emily were at the carriage house. Her only hope, as Flynn edged closer to her, was to get to the public area on Main Street. She started walking again, trying to get them as close to Main Street as possible before she made a run for it.

"I don't know what you mean," she said.

"Yes, you do." He reached for her arm.

She was quick enough to twist so he missed. "I guess

I'm understanding part of it. Sam is on the hook to Jake the Snake, but you're not. That was smart of you, like you've been in a lot of things tied to this competition."

"My goal, like I told you before, was opening up my career promotional opportunities."

This time, he successfully grabbed Sarah's arm.

Rather than fighting, she took a few more steps closer to Main Street. "I gather when Alan wouldn't help by throwing the show, you saw your chance. How did you make sure Alan took in enough nicotine to kill him? Did you spike the tea Jane made?"

"That would have been too easy and obvious. Between his patch and my soaking the tips of the e-cigs and the cigars he sucked on all day in e-juice, it was only a matter of time. I let Alan do himself in."

Sarah involuntarily recoiled. Flynn tightened his grasp on her arm. "But why Chef Bernardi? Did he figure out what you'd done?"

"Don't flatter the chef. He was a gambler first and foremost. After he worked out behind-the-scenes deals with Alan and Sam for the show to be in Wheaton, he made book on it."

"But you were the one who bet on it." From the pressure of his fingers digging into her arm, she realized this was another time she should have kept her observation to herself.

"I bet on what we all knew was going to be a sure thing for the first two days of the show. If Chef Bernardi had given us a push when the mess-up with Jed and Lucy happened, he'd probably be making your sister's cake for tomorrow."

"You didn't have money to cover what you lost any

more than Jane did? That's why you were upset on the porch."

Sarah thought back to the porch and the sequence of events: of Flynn putting his cigar out on the porch, Chef Bernardi throwing his beer can into the bushes, the cigar falling off the porch, and Chef Bernardi palming the thin object from the railing before he walked into Southwind. She glanced at the cigar case hanging out of his pocket.

"Jane said Chef Bernardi pulled out a leather cigar case before he went out to smoke. That was your missing case, wasn't it? The one with the good Cuban cigars. He took it the night you all were on the porch. When we talked, you showed me one of the souvenir cases, but now you've got your original one. Did you take it back when you upended him into the dishwasher?"

"I'd heard you were good at putting things together. Well, I hope you're happy that you've solved the case of the missing Cuban cigars and their case. But now, I think you're going to have to try an e-cigarette and have a bit of a reaction."

"You're not going to get away with that. Everyone knows I don't smoke."

"But you drink beverages."

"Is that how you got rid of Chef Bernardi? You wouldn't have tampered with your own cigars. Did you put it in a drink?" She kept thinking aloud, stalling for time. "No, not his drink. You put it in something with the cake. Something he handled?"

He didn't answer her. She tried to wrest her arm from him, but his grasp was like iron.

"That's why you threw him in the dishwasher. To wash it off his hands. You're not going to get away with that. They're testing the cake too."

"I doubt that, but even if they do, I'll be gone by then and they won't know if it was the cigar he smoked or whether he accidentally spilled some vapor juice into his cake mix or on his hands. Those little vials look a lot like some of the flavorings used in baking."

Flynn yanked her arm, forcing Sarah to move forward. Apparently, rather than kill her in the driveway, he was going to do it at Jane's Place. She tried to wrap her head around why he would do it in a public place when it would be just as easy to have done it on Southwind's back porch or near the tree where she'd hidden to eavesdrop. As he pulled on her arm again, it dawned on her that he must not have any of the liquid on him.

To avoid the pain in her arm, she kept walking and talking. "With Alan and Chef Bernardi out of the way, why didn't you kill Sam too?"

"Why bother? He created his own demise through his gambling with Jake the Snake. By now, one of the network executives and the show's compliance person has received my texts saying I think there's something fishy going on with Sam, but I've come up with a way to tie everything together with a wedding. After Emily and Marcus are married, I'm going to smell like a rose. Sam is simply going to smell."

"But if something happens to me, Emily isn't going to go through with a wedding."

"Nothing is going to happen to you until after the wedding. You see, nicotine poisoning takes a bit of time." He looked at his watch. "You may feel a little sick during the wedding, but by the time the symptoms really kick in, the film will be shot and even if I help rush you to the hospital, it will be too late."

"I'm not going to cooperate."

"Do you want something to happen to your mother too? She's a tea drinker, isn't she?"

"I won't drink it."

"You will or I'll lace your mother's drink instead."

"As soon as you let me go after I drink it, I'll tell everyone what you did. And if I didn't drink it, I'd still tell, so you wouldn't have the chance to poison my mother's tea. Your only option now is to let me go and run."

"Running is not an option. Thanks for pointing out the flaw in my plan. If killing you slow won't work, then I can do it fast. There are ways."

"You're crazy."

"That's a matter of opinion. Come on." He pulled her arm roughly, forcing her to the sidewalk in front of Southwind. As they reached the curb, she saw Cliff walking up the walkway to Jane's Place. With a jerk, Sarah stepped off the curb and, praying he'd hear her, yelled as loudly as she could for Cliff's help. Cliff turned his head in the direction of her voice. As she shouted again, Flynn put his free hand over her mouth to muffle the sound.

Sarah bit him as hard as she could. For the instance, he eased his hand off her mouth and released his grasp on her arm. She screamed again and tried to get away from him. He grabbed her again. Flynn only let her go when he was tackled by Cliff. As the two wrestled on the ground, Sarah ran up the walkway and called for help.

Crew members and Jane came running out, as did George and Maybelle.

"Grab him," Flynn yelled. "He's gone crazy." One of the cameramen went to do what Flynn asked, but Sarah threw herself in front of him.

"No, it's Flynn. He's the one who killed Alan. Hold him!"

In the confusion, crew members pulled Flynn and Cliff apart. Sarah screamed for them to hold on to Flynn, while Flynn yelled that Cliff was the one they should hold. The crew held both.

Sarah pulled her phone out of her pocket and called the police. Officer Robinson answered. "We've got Alan and Chef Bernardi's real killer outside Jane's Place."

She wasn't sure what Officer Robinson responded, but it was only a matter of minutes until Chief Gerard and he pulled up and took in the melee in front of Jane's Place. Although Jane kept trying to explain things over Flynn's protests, this time Chief Gerard zeroed in on what Sarah was saying. After hearing her out, he asked Cliff what had happened and then had Officer Robinson take Flynn in.

Holding Cliff's hand as naturally as she had in the past, Sarah realized that sometimes living in a town five miles square, where everyone knows everyone, had its advantages. Or, in Jane's case, as Jane walked back into the house without even thanking Cliff or Sarah, its disadvantages.

Sarah was positive Flynn wouldn't be able to use his smooth voice to talk his way out of this one. She only hoped the notoriety tied to the competition and maybe a good word from Starr to her dad would make things go a little easier for Sam. In the meantime, there was one more segment for Sam to direct.

CHAPTER 38

Sarah sipped her champagne as she glanced across the makeshift dance floor set up at the far end of Southwind's main dining room. Almost everyone involved with the Southern Belle show had attended Marcus and Emily's wedding, but none were smiling and dancing like Maybelle and George.

She was sorry to see Sam hadn't stayed for the festivities. Sarah wasn't sure if the network would ever employ him again because of his gambling on the outcome of the Southern Belle competition, but no one could fault his direction of the ceremony. It had gone off without a hitch.

Somehow, despite everyone's differences, during the short amount of time between Marcus and Emily's substitution as the bride and groom and Sam filming the wedding segment, the various competitors, chaperones, vendors, friends, and family pulled together to make the ceremony and reception more than simply an add-on ending to the competition. Of course, Sarah knew, most of the credit for the wedding being personalized belonged to her mother.

Once Maybelle recovered from the shock of almost winning and learning Flynn tried killing Sarah, her natural take-charge self emerged. Figuring the network wouldn't mind a few modifications *if* a wedding took place as announced, Maybelle, without asking permission, called Suzy at Suzy's Flowers, Wanda and Grace at Southwind, and many of her friends in Birmingham and Wheaton. The result was a bouquet more to Emily's liking, additions to the cake and food reflecting the bride and groom, and a room overflowing with people Emily and Marcus cherished.

A touch to her arm made Sarah jump, almost spilling her champagne. She turned to see Heather and Veronica beside her.

Heather lifted her own champagne glass toward where Emily and Marcus danced. "Emily looks beautiful."

"She was absolutely radiant coming down the aisle," Veronica added. "I can't imagine how the group winning dress could have looked as good on anyone else."

"Emily owes that to Barbie. Knowing how her mother worked magic on her pageant dresses over the years, Starr, when she learned that Emily was going to be the bride, made peace with her mother. She convinced Barbie to help the show's costumer nip and tuck the dress to fit Em like a glove."

"They did an excellent job and I'm glad to hear Starr and Barbie made up. There's nothing worse than being on the outs with your mother." Veronica put her arm around Heather.

"No, there's not." Heather leaned into the hug her daughter gave her while drinking the last of her champagne. "Speaking of looking good, Cliff and you certainly made a picture-perfect maid of honor and best man."

Sarah squirmed at Heather's compliment. "That was all Sam's doing. He positioned us just so in case the makeup didn't perfectly cover the black eye Flynn gave Cliff while they were fighting."

"Sam did well. I didn't even notice." Heather laughed as she moved away from her daughter. "Tell me, in all the commotion, I never did find out how you figured out Flynn killed Alan and Chef Bernardi?"

"It was sort of an accident."

"What do you mean?"

"Well, I knew Chef Bernardi and Alan died of nicotine poisoning, but I couldn't think of another link between their deaths until, as we walked back to Jane's Place, Flynn pulled his leather cigar case out of his pocket. You see, last night he complained about having to use one of the plastic cases because he'd lost his leather one."

"Apparently he found it after the two of you talked," Heather said.

Sarah waited as Heather, stopping a waiter passing by with a tray of full champagne glasses, exchanged her empty glass for one two-thirds full of golden liquid.

"That was my first thought, but as Flynn and I neared Southwind's back porch, seeing the porch railings triggered everything together in my mind."

"How?"

"I had a flashback of Chef Bernardi palming something thin from the railing before he went into South-wind. Coupling that with Jane saying Chef Bernardi, who wasn't known for being a smoker, had a leather cigar case when he went outside for a smoke, made me realize Flynn's case was what Chef Bernardi probably picked up off the railing. I surmised that the case fell from Chef Bernardi's hand or pocket and Flynn retrieved it when he upended Chef Bernardi into the dishwasher."

"Instead of wrestling him into the dishwasher, it seems like it would have been simpler to leave Chef Bernardi on the floor."

"It would have been, Heather, but Flynn thought the scalding water would wash away any traces of nicotine from Chef Bernardi's hands and clothing."

"I get it," Veronica said. "He must have hoped a soaking from a commercial dishwasher would keep people from realizing how much direct contact with nicotine Chef Bernardi had when he made the cake."

"That's right. Of course, think-aloud person that I am, I shared my thoughts as they came to me with Flynn. I'm just lucky he didn't have a vial of nicotine in his pocket, or I might not have been the maid of honor this afternoon."

"Oh, look," Veronica interrupted, "Emily is getting ready to throw the bouquet. I'm taken, but the two of you should try to catch it."

Dutifully, Heather and Sarah obeyed just as Emily released the bouquet. Arms were raised upward, ready to catch the bouquet, but Sarah, considering her newly developed Cliff-Glenn quandary, stepped away from the melee, her hands to her side. Hearing Maybelle shout her name, Sarah looked up—and instinctively caught the falling bouquet.

Chef Bernardi's Breakfast Biscuits

Depending upon how big you cut them, this recipe makes 1–3 dozen biscuits

2 cups all-purpose flour
1 tablespoon baking powder
1 teaspoon sugar
1 teaspoon salt
8 tablespoons cubed butter
¾ cup milk (this can be adjusted as needed)

1 large bowl; 1 small biscuit cutter; skillet

Preheat the oven to 425 degrees.

In the large bowl, combine the flour, baking powder, sugar, and salt.

Cut the butter into the mixture—keep at it until it begins to look like cornmeal.

With your fingers, make a well in the middle of your combined ingredients.

Slowly add milk into the middle, while kneading the dough with your fingers. Add more milk as necessary.

On a lightly floured surface, roll out the dough to your desired thickness.

Cut out biscuits to the size you want. Note: The number of biscuits you will get out of the recipe reflects your cutting size (very small—more like pull-a-parts, equals 3 dozen, but larger-sized ones may only produce a dozen).

Butter the bottom of the skillet.

Place the biscuits in it.

Bake 12 minutes or until golden.

Chef Wanda's Honey Baked Apples

6 servings

6 green apples
1½ cup of cranberries (works best with fresh ones)
2¼ cups of water
¾ cup of packed brown sugar
3 tablespoons of honey

Preheat the oven to 350 degrees.

Core the apples, removing the peel from the top third of each apple.

Place the apples in a baking dish.

Fill the core holes with cranberries.

In a small saucepan, mix the water, brown sugar, and honey.

Bring to a boil. Note: Stir occasionally, making sure, if necessary, the sugar and honey dissolves.

Once boiled, pour the hot mixture over the apples.

Bake one hour at 350 degrees. Every fifteen to twenty minutes, baste with the juices.

Serve with vanilla ice cream.

Wanda's Baked Pears

4 servings

4 Bartlett pears (use ripe pears)
¾ cup of brown sugar
¾ cup oats
½ teaspoon nutmeg
1 teaspoon cinnamon
6 tablespoons butter
1½ cups apple juice (you can use two six-ounce cans inside)

Preheat oven to 350 degrees.

Core the Bartlett pears, but do not peel them.

Place pears in a greased 9" square pan.

Combine the sugar, oats, spices, and butter until crumbly.

Stuff pears with the combined mixture. Any excess may be allowed to fall into the pan.

Pour ¾ cup apple juice into the pan.

Bake for one hour at 350 degrees, basting after thirty minutes. If necessary, add more juice.

Cool for thirty minutes, then serve.

Visit us online at
KensingtonBooks.com
to read more from your favorite authors,
see books by series, view reading
group guides, and more!

BOOK **CLUB**
BETWEEN THE CHAPTERS

Visit us online for sneak peeks, exclusive
giveaways, special discounts, author content,
and engaging discussions with your fellow readers.

Betweenthechapters.net

Sign up for our newsletters and be the first
to get exciting news and announcements about
your favorite authors!
Kensingtonbooks.com/newsletter